FIRE
on the
FIRTH

Daniel Miller

FIRE
on the
FIRTH

A Church Street Kirk Mystery

Daniel K. Miller

LEVEL
BEST BOOKS

First published by Level Best Books 2021

This novel is entirely a work of fiction. The names, characters and incidents portrayed in it are the work of the author's imagination. Any resemblance to actual persons, living or dead, events or localities is entirely coincidental.

Daniel K. Miller asserts the moral right to be identified as the author of this work.

Author Photo Credit: Chera Hammons

First edition

ISBN: 978-1-68512-013-9

Cover art by Michael Tompsett (artist)/Level Best Designs

This book was professionally typeset on Reedsy.
Find out more at reedsy.com

To Chera

Praise for FIRE ON THE FIRTH

"*Fire on the Firth* is a superbly crafted amateur sleuth mystery that entertains from beginning to end. But it's much more than that. Author Daniel Miller has taken his story — about American minister Daniel Darrow's quest to solve an arson and murder in the Scottish Highlands — and infused it with lessons on punishment, the environment, and a much-needed look at history and how we must avoid repeating it. But none of those weighty topics take away from the humor woven throughout the narrative, along with a sweet romance any reader is sure to enjoy. A wonderful debut from an author I want to read more of. And soon."—Rick Treon, author of *Let the Guilty Pay*, finalist for the 2021 Silver Falchion Award for Best Suspense Novel.

"In *Fire on the Firth*, Daniel K. Miller delivers a delightful romp through the Scottish Highlands. Grab a good scotch and settle in for a heart-warming visit to Inverness with Daniel Darrow, the new reverend of Church Street Kirk, as he muddles his way through his new duties and attempts to win over his eccentric parishioners. Rev. Darrow hails from North Carolina in this charming fish out of water story with heart, humor and a side of arson. Daniel can't ignore his calling, as an amateur sleuth, that is. With a burned-out castle at the heart of the mystery, layers of intrigue, and underpinnings of corruption, *Fire on the Firth* is sheer pleasure. But don't be fooled, there is something nefarious beneath those ashes." —Tina deBellegarde, Agatha-nominated author of *Winter Witness, a Batavia-on-Hudson Mystery*.

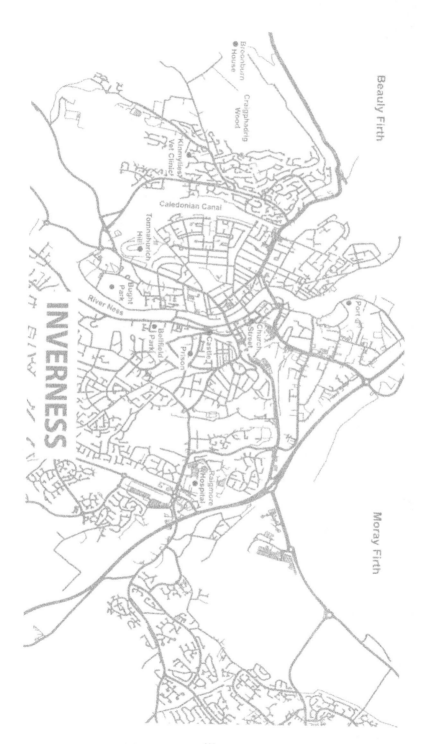

INVERNESS

Beauly Firth

Moray Firth

Broonburn House

Craigphadrig Wood

Kinmylies Vet Clinic

Caledonian Canal

Tomnahurich Hill

Bught Park

River Ness

Bellfield Park

Castle

Church Street

Prison

Port a...

Raigmore Hospital

Chapter One

Smoke filled the air around the great house and rose in hot, billowy columns. It mingled with low clouds to obscure the evening moon. What muted moonlight succeeded in penetrating the gray clouds and black smoke mixed with the fiery red and orange glow from the ground to produce an eerie veil over the scene. On the opposite bank, from the Black Isle peninsula roughly a mile away, the ancient house's several burning chimneys and turrets coalesced into a single, bright matchstick head floating on the cold waters of the Beauly Firth. From further afield, in the Scottish Highlands city of Inverness, the flames were not yet visible, but when an easterly breeze picked up, they could be smelled – sharp, ashy, and acrid.

Possessing a history older than many modern nation-states, this was not the house's first fire. The fault for the first fire lay with an absent-minded farmer named Angus and his even more absent-minded cow. In 1522, when the house was a mere two-bedroom hovel shared by the farmer's family and his animals, Angus left an oil lamp burning after his early morning breakfast. With his wife away visiting her mother at an adjacent farm croft, no one was home to turn off the lamp before Angus became preoccupied outside with the construction of a small dovecot.

Restless and ready to be let out for her morning's grazing, Angus's black cow paced about her section of the house. She huffed at the wide wooden doors that remained inexplicably closed to her, letting out heavy, impatient breaths. The room's stone walls bore the blows of her stamping hoof. Exhausting all other potential exits, she finally came to the partition separating her space from that of her human masters. In two butts of her stubby horns, she had it open.

The cow happily trotted through the human quarters, hoping to find grass with the sweet, wet taste of morning dew. Instead, she rummaged clumsily around the tightly packed human furniture and settled for a breakfast of musky smelling hay that lined the human bed. In the process, her hindquarters knocked the still burning lamp off its stand. When Angus's wife returned home later the next day, she found a frantic husband, four partially collapsed, charred walls, and a singed though no longer hungry cow.

An abundance of sheep and whiskey precipitated the house's second fire. This incident occurred around 1780. By then the original blackened walls had long ago been incorporated into a much larger construction. The house had become a fine country estate with the aspirations of a castle. It had several exclusively human rooms, manicured lawns, and a narrow moat on three sides. It even possessed a name, Broonburn House – for the muddy stream that once flowed nearby and was now redirected to create the moat. The house's second fire occurred while its lord and owner was in the middle of upgrading the exterior walls with a slotted parapet. The ease with which the second fire transpired proved this addition to be more decorative than defensive.

The spark began in the most unlikely of circumstances. Wanting to postpone going home to their wives and children, a crew of men from the Inverness shipyard headed to their favorite pub after work. Having been raised in the country, these men found city life too confining for harmonious relationships with their spouses. When the barkeep suggested the men continue their rowdy delay elsewhere, they decided to take a ride out to the country. Letting their horses take the lead, they soon discovered themselves on the road to Broonburn House. Passing the great house only served to remind the men of their cramped lives in the city.

Despite their disagreeable urban predicament, these men were considered the lucky ones. They had found work. Many of their friends and family from the glen south of Broonburn House had simply fled their Highland homes for the prospect of better lives in foreign countries. Rising rents forced families off the small crofts they had farmed for generations. In their place, the lord of Broonburn moved in sheep – an investment that required less human capital and turned a higher profit than traditional farm rents. The sight of Broonburn House, its green open spaces and extravagant renovations, reminded the men passing by of their resentment toward the estate's lord and anger at their own impotence to change their fates.

They had enjoyed several consoling rounds at the pub and now, after a few more emptied bottles of whiskey and a loud discussion, the men from the shipyard discovered the courage to make their resentment known. One of the gang unpocketed a flint and steel while his friends gathered a pile of damp heather and grass. The first man stuffed the mixture into an empty whiskey bottle, lit it, and hurled it at the house. Instead of exploding into a ball of fire on impact, the weak flame smoldered out mid flight. The bottle did not even break upon hitting the stone wall. The disappointed arsonist cursed and ordered more fuel. His companions brought more damp grass – not because of their inebriated state, but simply because no other kind of kindling existed that evening along the eastern coast of the Scottish Highlands.

With no more empty bottles, the men formed the grass into balls, lit the balls in their cupped hands, and hastily tossed them. Most of the balls smoked out before clumping against the house's exterior. One, however, eventually carried its flame intact to a patch of dry sawdust left over from construction. If not for the wooden scaffolding left behind for the decorative parapet, it would have likely sputtered out like the rest. Instead, the weak flame quickly took hold and employed the scaffolding to scale the house's otherwise impenetrable stone walls. Soon the parapet itself was ablaze and in quick succession the house's thatched roof.

Roused by the noise outside and the sudden rise in temperature, all domestic servants fled the house. Frightened by the hasty flames and fleeing servants, the men from the shipyard agreed they had sufficiently delayed their homecoming. They mounted their horses, shouted a few last insults at the house and its lord, and flew back to Inverness. When the men finally arrived at their respective homes, their wives had the curious job of mending several mysteriously burned hands.

The cause of the house's third great fire, the night when its flames could be seen from the Black Isle and when clouds hung low and blotted out the moon's glow, was still under investigation. Once again flames consumed unfinished renovations. This time Broonburn House was being transformed from a neglected castle into a modern, luxury guesthouse – Broonburn House Hotel. Construction kept the house's newest owner away that evening, though he had never planned on spending much time in the Scottish Highlands anyway. He had other lavish residences to the south in the more bustling city centers of Edinburgh and London. He had purchased Broonburn for the prestige he thought it might add to his name. In truth, the estate's land, or more specifically what lay under its land, was of more value to him than Broonburn House itself. The mysterious identity of this new owner caused a great local stir, when an Inverness paper first leaked the sale. Before long, however, the promise of tourist money and jobs soon distracted the people's curiosity.

When emergency services first arrived at the scene, they were shocked by the severity of the fire. The Scottish Fire and Rescue Service scrambled to contain the flames and prevent them from crossing into the nearby Craigphadrig Wood. If the fire reached the tree line, it would have plenty of fuel to grow and continue on westward into Inverness. The Caledonian Canal would likely prevent it from entering the center of the city, but the thousands of souls in its western suburbs, sandwiched between the woods and the canal, would be lost. The Scottish Police set up roadblocks along the A862 highway for the dual purposes of questioning motorists and preventing accidents caused by reduced visibility from the smoke. So far, they had only one witness. They were desperate to not let any additional clues escape.

Broonburn House sat off from the highway at the end of a narrow private drive, Auld Angus Rd. On a typical cloudy night, the lamps that marked the front gate twinkled, but the house itself remained mostly hidden behind a stone fence and row of short evergreen trees. But on this night, an unfamiliar orange glow shone, visible from the end of the road out to the highway. It was this extra light that first attracted the witness. At approximately 9:40 p.m., she had been driving along the A862 when she noticed the strange light.

She pulled off the highway to get a better look. She could smell the smoke.

Unfortunately for the police, their sole witness could provide little information about the cause of the fire. She had noticed and phoned it in after most of its damage was done. Like a cancer, the fire had already devastated the interior of the house before any outward symptoms manifested. Flames metastasized from room to room. By the time the windows shattered from the extreme heat and red sparks burst out through the wooden roof, the inside of the house had been completely consumed. Fortunately for the firefighters, no one had to be rescued from the inferno. The construction work that was supposed to transform the house into a luxury hotel had ensured that no one was living in it at the time. Unfortunately for the home's absentee owner, this also meant the fire had had free reign to consume nearly everything but the ancient stone walls before anyone noticed.

Broonburn House's roof gave way while most of the firefighters were busy making their stand at the edge of the woods. The weight of the wooden roof caused the top floor, already weakened and partially collapsed itself in places, to completely fail. This multiplied the pressure on each lower floor until the entire structure shattered. Decade after decade came crashing down; centuries of history, of lives lived and lost, collapsed in on themselves in one final throe. When the last floor met ground level, cinders and sparks erupted out of the blackening outer walls like a volcano. The few firefighters that were not battling the perimeter, raced to extinguish the new flames that fell down and seared the already black, crispy lawn.

Once the Craigphadrig Wood was deemed secure and the suburban population of western Inverness safe, firefighters were able to focus on the house fire proper. The intensity of the fire inside the house prevented them from getting too close. The safest option seemed to be spraying water from a distance and waiting for it to burn itself out. Eventually fresh faces relieved tired, soot covered ones as reinforcements from the smaller village of Beauly arrived. Wiping the ash from her eyes with a dirty rag, one firefighter snubbed out an eager spark with her heavy boot. She sat beside an ambulance waiting for a drink. When it arrived, she downed it greedily, hoping the cool water would sooth her smoke parched throat and lungs. Between coughs she thanked the EMT and returned the empty cup indicating that it needed refilling.

After her second cup, the EMT asked her, "Any idea how this started?"

"No. We've been too busy trying to stop it," she responded.

"Aye, but such a fire? Something big had to happen."

"You'd be surprised," she said. "We responded to a house fire last month – nothing like this of course, just a wee two bedroom over in Westhill. A mouse got into the walls and chewed through some wiring. The resident started his laundry machine and next thing you know, the damaged wire overloaded and the whole house went up. Poor chap didn't even know he had a mouse problem."

"Whoa. So you think something like that happened here?"

"All I do is put 'em out. An investigative team will come along later to sort it all. Construction crew could've forgotten to turn off a lamp or the old wiring just couldn't handle all the equipment. Could be arson. Thank God this didn't happen with guests – place was unoccupied."

"Who would want to burn down Broonburn House?" the EMT asked.

The firefighter shrugged and sent him off for another cup of water.

The next day, when police investigators eventually had a chance to examine the scene, they would discover a charred human body hidden away between two interior basement walls. For now, however, the house revealed only flame and heat and ash.

Chapter Two

Daniel Darrow's plane arrived at the Inverness airport in the late morning. After he disembarked he was instructed to "queue up," or join an appropriate line, among three discriminating groups: UK citizens, European passport holders, and Others. Daniel was an Other.

While his own queue inched forward, he watched with envy as the British and European travelers streamed steadily past immigration. Once, his eyes happened to meet those of a slim man in a tweed jacket. The man nodded and waved his folded newspaper in a short, anonymous acknowledgement before passing through the UK immigration.

The woman behind him nudged his back. "Go on. You're holding up the line." He looked around and was surprised to find that the angry voice had come from such a small woman. In front he saw the immigration officer waving him forward. The officer's bald head reflected and highlighted the irritation on his face. Daniel pulled his carry-on suitcase to the protective glass encased immigration kiosk. He placed his US passport and completed landing card on the desk. The officer scanned the passport into a computer, eyed Daniel suspiciously, and handed back the passport. *Note to self,* Daniel thought, *Don't get a new haircut the day before you travel.*

"This is you first time to Scotland, is it?" the officer said.

Daniel wasn't sure if this was a question or an allegation. "Yes," he answered. "It's my first time anywhere really. Well, I've lived in both North and South Carolina, but nothing like this. Do you travel much?" Words spewed out of Daniel's mouth, quick and nervous. The officer's curt manner and black eyes unnerved him. Daniel unconsciously put a hand through his hair to make it look more like his passport photo.

"I ask the questions, mate."

"Of course. Sorry."

"You've no return ticket. Planning on staying a while, are you?"

"Um, yes. I'm a minister and I've taken a position at a parish here in Inverness. This is my first real charge. All scary and exciting at the same time. New position, new country – it's a lot," Daniel rambled.

"Documentation?"

"Oh, um, here." Daniel offered his credentials and work visa. The officer scanned them.

"A priest you say? How did you end up way out here?"

"Well, *minister*," Daniel corrected. He detected a hint of genuine interest in the officer's question, so he did not press the distinction between these pastoral offices. The distinction involved a lengthy theological argument, of which the technicalities exhausted even his own interest at times. When he was in seminary he simply told his lay friends back home that the difference mostly came down to a greater preference for decorative robes in the one than the other.

"One of my professors at seminary was Scottish," Daniel answered the officer. "He's friends with the minister at a church here and knew they were looking for a new assistant. So, he recommended me."

"My mum's Catholic," the officer said and smiled, as if that settled the matter. He stamped Daniel's passport and visa. Daniel thought about informing the man he was headed for a Church of Scotland rather than Catholic parish, but changed his mind. He had obtained his stamp and the officer seemed happy enough. Why muddle things with denominational particulars? "Everything seems in order," the officer said and returned Daniel's papers. "Welcome to Scotland."

After he had collected his luggage, Daniel passed an airport gift shop on his search for the exit. The recorded bagpipe music and garish display of trinkets, lighters, mugs, and stuffed animals, all in bright tartan plaids, gave him pause. It drew him like an open wound or a car crash; he could not help himself a look. Eventually his eye settled on a newspaper stand in the corner. The front page pictured what appeared to be a castle enveloped in flames. *Inverness Arson?* was printed boldly above the image. Curiosity got the better of him and he purchased a copy.

Daniel was surprised at how easy the paper was to read. He didn't know why this should surprise him. He had moved to a foreign country, but one that still spoke English – had invented it actually. The full headline read: *Inverness Arson? Flames light up night sky while historic house burns.* He had a weakness for sensationalist headlines. Daniel wheeled his luggage to a nearby wall so he could continue reading out of the way of more hurried travelers.

A historic landmark, Broonburn House has survived two major fires in its centuries long history. This latest one, though, may have finally sounded the old bird's death knell. The fire is thought to have started close to 9pm and its flames could be seen from as far off as North Kessock.

Though authorities have yet to comment on the fire's cause, they have not ruled out arson ...

Daniel heard a final boarding announcement over the airport intercom. He didn't catch the flight number, but he did hear the time. He put the paper down. Arson would have to wait. He had more pressing matters. He still had to find a bus into town, meet his supervisor, the Rev. Sarah Calder, and discover what she had meant by, "No need to worry about accommodation." On top of that were the myriad mental preparations he must make in what remained of the Saturday before his first Sunday at a new parish. So, he folded the newspaper, placed it halfway into a recycling bin. Hesitating, unable to let go, he quickly tucked it back in his pocket. *I don't want to be completely ignorant about the goings on in my new city,* he told himself. He wheeled his luggage away from the wall.

Mystery had always captivated Daniel Darrow. He suspected this was one of the reasons he had pursued an ecclesial career – to better understand the big questions in life, the sacred mysteries. His parents were faithful churchgoers and made sure that his young body filled the space in the pew next to them each Sunday. He grew up hearing Bible stories - Jesus' teachings, his Sermon on the Mount and parables of love and forgiveness. These of course contributed to Daniel's ministerial aspirations, but he could not deny the appeal of mystery.

He liked to imagine that had he not become a minister he would have made a good private detective. He had majored in psychology for two semesters as an undergrad followed by a brief stint in comparative literature before finally settling on religious studies. During his literary days he theorized that people, when faced with mystery, came in one of three kinds. Upon seeing a white rabbit wearing a waistcoat and fretting about the time, the first kind of person will ignore the rabbit. The second will rationalize it away. The third, will jump down the rabbit hole after it. Daniel Darrow realized at an early age that he was the kind of person that jumped.

* * *

Spotting a sign with a vague cartoonish bus icon, Daniel made his way out of the airport. The Inverness airport could not boast such a density of travelers as larger airports like Dublin or Heathrow; however, its steady crowds, together with the heft of Daniel's luggage, made his journey slow and clumsy. He felt like a pixelated frog navigating through an unending maze of traffic. He tried to keep close to the walls where the stream of people flowed at a calmer pace.

This path provided him a postered introduction to his new home. Commercial advertisements greeted him with bold colors and slogans: a smoky bottle of single malt whiskey, a brightly colored dolphin sightseeing tour, and a bland advertisement for an energy company, Philarguria Energy, whose only remarkable feature was that its bottom half had been ripped away. Then came images of dramatic Highlands scenery: rugged stony crags and deep green glens. Daniel passed by larger-than-life sized prints of kilted men and dancing women. He mentally noted the names of iconic buildings and castles as he lumbered by – Urquhart Castle on Loch Ness, Inverness Castle as seen from a pedestrian bridge crossing the River Ness, and historic Broonburn House. "Fàilte gu Alba" the final poster read: Welcome to Scotland.

Chapter Three

The airport shuttlebus opened its door to a rush of crisp, sea air. It dropped off its passengers and waited to be filled again before retracing its journey. Once the other travelers dispersed, Daniel Darrow found himself alone on the platform. He pulled his luggage close for company and took a deep breath. He wanted to savor the first salty scent of his new city. Instead, he inhaled a thick cloud of diesel exhaust and buckled over with coughing. When he recovered, he wiped his teary eyes and tried to take in his surroundings. Buses and taxies moved steadily around him in the large asphalt and brick square of the Inverness bus station. Two and three story buildings formed a tight perimeter. Daniel scanned the sidewalks for an individual he knew only by telephone.

"Reverend Darrow!"

The shouted words did not immediately register in his consciousness. Though the voice sounded familiar, Daniel was still unaccustomed to hearing his name in a Scottish brogue rather than a Southern drawl. The ministerial prefix which he had so recently acquired only added to his disorientation.

"Daniel Darrow!"

He turned in the direction of the call and saw a smallish woman in a thick brown coat and plaid scarf waving at him. The woman stood under the stone columns of a public library building – just where Rev. Sarah Calder said she would be waiting. The height of the columns contrasted with that of the woman such that Daniel could not judge her true stature. He returned her wave and, upon reaching her, found her to be nearly two heads shorter than himself. Her scarf hid her hair, but up-close Daniel could estimate her age by the lines on her face. The creases on her forehead and at the corners of her eyes were deep set, but not so much that she would qualify for a senior discount meal at most restaurants. She seemed only slightly older than the professor who had recommended him for this job.

"Reverend Calder?" Daniel asked.

"Call me Sarah," she replied with a smile that squinted her eyes and crowded her plump, rosy cheeks. "It's nice to finally meet you in person. You're rather taller than you sounded over the phone."

Daniel nearly responded with, *You're shorter than you sounded*, but refrained, unsure of his new boss's sense of humor. He settled on, "It's nice to finally meet you too."

"You picked a breezy day to arrive," she said, pulling her coat more tightly around her short, wide body. "Well, what do you think of her?" she asked and gazed out at nothing in particular. Daniel glanced around and returned a puzzled look.

"Inverness, Capital of the Highlands."

"Nice bus station I guess," Daniel said.

"Just you wait," Rev. Calder said. Looking down at his luggage she added, "Is that all you brought?"

"I didn't have much." Daniel looked apologetically at his satchel, and two suitcases. "I stuffed 'em full though."

"Well, my car's just there. Let me help you with those." She reached for one of his suitcases. She strained over its weight, lifting it off the ground an inch and moving it only twice that. "On second thought, I'll let you carry your own things," she laughed and gave up her brief possession of the suitcase. "What did you pack in there? Bricks?"

"Books," Daniel replied as he lugged his bags along behind her to the car. Daniel put his luggage in the back and opened the door. Yet, before he entered, he hesitated outside the car for several disoriented seconds. Rev. Calder scooted through the door he held open and took her seat behind the steering wheel.

"Ta, such a gentleman," she said and shut the door.

This is going to take some getting used to, Daniel thought as he walked around to the left side of the car, which should not have been the passenger's side. In the large airport bus, he had not paid much attention as to what side of the road he was traveling, but now he winced at the unfamiliar passing of on-coming traffic. After a few blocks, however, the novelty began to fade and Daniel was able to more easily engage in the obligatory small talk of work colleagues who have just met. He confirmed that his flight had been long, but pleasant. Rev. Calder reminded him of what to expect from the chilly, damp Highlands weather in autumn, though Daniel had already read this in guidebooks. Before long, she parked her car in front of a church building.

"Here we are – Church Street Kirk," Rev. Calder announced proudly. "Or the Holy Redundancy, as we like to say."

Daniel smiled at her quip. In Scots, the word for church is *kirk*. He peered out the car's small windshield at the building. Its skin was light gray stone. It had an ancient look, but compared to the United States most of the buildings he had seen so far in Scotland had an ancient look. The building possessed a simplicity of design, common to churches in the Reformed tradition, with touches of gothic flair. The tall, pointed, wooden doors opened to the street and were encased in decorative but modest stonework. A square tower stood grandly above the rest of the building, pointing toward the heavens with a wooden shingled spire that matched the lower roof. Not as easily visible from the street, sat the church's semi-circular nave with its several stained glass, lancet windows – tall and narrow with pointed arches at the tops. From the outside the stained glass appeared dull and opaque, but Daniel knew that inside they told stories of faith, bright and colorful.

"No need to get out, I just wanted to give you a wee look. Tomorrow we'll do the grand tour," Rev. Calder said.

"It's a beautiful building."

"Aye," she admitted with admiration. "Now you'll want to rest and get settled after your flight."

"Yes, I was wondering about that," Daniel said. "You mentioned that I should not worry about accommodation?"

"I think you'll like your new crib."

"Huh? My what?"

"Crib," Rev. Calder answered. "It's American for house or flat. I heard it on telly once. Is that not what you say?"

"No," Daniel laughed. "At least that's not what I've ever said."

"Em," she muttered with slight disappointment, "I think you'll like it nonetheless."

Rev. Calder put the car in gear and drove away from Church Street to Bank Street, which runs along the River Ness through the heart of Inverness. She took pleasure in the wide-eyed awe that overcame Daniel's face as he looked upon her city for the first time. She knew that this part of Inverness would impress him. It impressed everyone who had never before seen its deep blue river lined gracefully with greenery and handsome stone buildings. Having grown up in the city, its beauty came natural to her and she envied newcomers their first impressions, like a groom on his wedding day. Yet, on early autumn afternoons such as this, when the sun shone in the pale blue sky and glinted off the water, even a native of the city could not help but pause and admire it. The trees hinted at the bare cold to come, but had not yet given up summer's green warmth. The ancient river moved along, unhurried but determined, into the Beauly Firth. From there it opened into the larger Moray Firth before finally escaping to the North Sea.

They passed Inverness Castle, the red sandstone goliath sitting quiet watch over its city. For centuries a stronghold of some sort had stood guard on the bank of the river, playing host to Scottish legend. Shakespeare's King Duncan breathed his last on that hill before going on to haunt poor Macbeth. Centuries later the castle shut its doors and then had them opened by force to Mary, Queen of Scots. In another hundred years, the castle exploded into a pile of rubble under the gunpowder and fire of the Jacobite army. Later, in the mid-nineteenth century, the castle was rebuilt into the dominating complex that Daniel now saw through Rev. Calder's car window.

Past the castle, they exited Bank Street onto a residential road. After several minutes, the car turned onto a narrow street lined on one side with high trees and a leafy hedge and on the other with two story, duplex style houses. Rev. Calder parked in front of one of the houses. Its gray stone façade yellowed slightly toward the center. The house consisted of two halves identical in every way save one – their twin entry doors. These too were identical except for their differing colors. The doors, one red and one blue, were separated by a short stone wall, not quite waist high, that branched out near the road to enclose twin patches of garden.

"Welcome to Bellfield Park. Yours is on the right, the blue one," Rev. Calder said and stepped out of the car.

Daniel opened his door and stretched. He had been sitting for most of the day. A breeze passed by, ruffling tree leaves and encouraging birds to flit and sing among the branches. He heard people shouting and laughing and another sound he could not place – a twangy thump, thump. Rev. Calder answered his unspoken question. "There are tennis courts beyond the hedge there."

Daniel pulled his luggage out of the car and they walked through the short gate to the red door on the left. Rev. Calder rang the bell. "Right, this is Hugh and Marjory Macpherson. They've been parishioners of Church Street since before my time," she said. "They live here and rent out the other side. For this location, they could charge much more than what they do, but since it's for the kirk they consider it charity. I never asked if they try to count it on their taxes," she laughed. "Oh, better give them these." Several envelopes lay on the doormat. One hung halfway out the door's brass mail slot. "This one looks like a bill – Philarguria Energy Co. Wouldn't want the lights getting shut off, would we."

Rev. Calder rang the bell again. "Sometimes they take two rings. You'll want to speak loudly. Marjory will tell you it's only Hugh that's hard of hearing, but really she's just as bad." After a few more minutes the door opened to reveal two people whose matching wrinkles, white hair, and clothing mirrored the twin appearance of their home. Mrs. Macpherson wore a dark blue blouse with a light green knit shawl draped around her shoulders. Mr. Macpherson's dark slacks and button-down shirt matched hers for color and loose fitting.

"You're late," Hugh Macpherson said.

"Do come in," invited Marjory. After thanking Rev. Calder for her mail she sent her husband into the kitchen for tea. She directed her visitors to a sitting room with a small fireplace on one wall and a large bookcase on the other. Family photos, ancient and modern, adorned a third wall. She took her place in one of two high backed chairs upholstered in a red-purple fabric that Daniel could tell had once held an elegant sheen. He and Rev. Calder sat down opposite Marjory on a couch that offered more comfort to the eye than to the seat. The room was typical amongst those of the older generation in Britain for whom afternoon tea constituted a civic duty as much as a way of life. When Hugh Macpherson returned, Rev. Calder made introductions.

"We've been so looking forward to having Reverend Darrow stay with us. The young side has been empty for too long," Marjory said, indicating the residence attached to their own.

"I appreciate your hospitality. You have a lovely home," Daniel said.

"Eh, you'll have to speak up son, Mr. Macpherson does not hear well," she said, leaning in closer.

"Sorry." Daniel spoke loudly, "I said I appreciate your hospitality. You have a lovely home. And, please, call me Daniel."

"Oh, I don't know about that," she blushed and sipped her tea, "Reverend Darrow will do fine." Her insistence on formality did not surprise him. During his field training at seminary, he had experienced differing levels of pastoral familiarity with which people seemed comfortable. Somewhere around the age of forty marked the cutting off point for which parishioners preferred first names compared to those who preferred his full title.

"Darrow, that's a Scottish name isn't it," Hugh Macpherson said.

"Um, yes, I think so. I remember my father saying something about how his side of the family immigrated from Scotland some time in," Daniel thought for a moment, "in the 1800s I think? We've never really looked into it much. Maybe now I should."

"Oh you must," Marjory Macpherson said. "And Reverend Calder has a marvelous collection of family records at the kirk. Perhaps she'll let you have a peek."

"Perhaps. Now earlier you said the *young side* has been empty?" Daniel asked.

"Oh, that's just what we call Young Hugh's side. Hugh here is actually Hugh II," she said looking at her husband, "and his father was just plain Hugh, I suppose. Our son is Hugh III."

"We bought this place before Young Hugh went off to university. We thought it would be nice for him to have a place to come back to when he graduated," Hugh II chimed in.

"But then he got a job in London," Marjory continued. "He still comes back home, but not as often as we would like. And never for very long. He's working in Leeds now."

"No love, he's in Liverpool now," Hugh corrected her.

"I thought it was Leeds?" she said again. Hugh shook his head. "But he *was* in Leeds? After that stint in Paris?"

"Yes, but that was a year ago. He's got a job in Liverpool now. Something in shipping."

"Oh, and all this time I've been telling people he's still in Leeds," Marjory Macpherson sat back in her chair and placed her tea cup on the side table. "If you couldn't tell, our Young Hugh has a bit of what you might call a free spirit. He's never in one place for too long."

"You'll be staying in Young Hugh's side," Mr. Macpherson informed Daniel. "Until he decides to settle down, we rent it. But when he visits it is still his home. That's the catch for such low rent."

"There's no catch," Marjory rolled her eyes. "He always says that." Turning to Daniel she continued, "You'll like Young Hugh. Everyone does. He's very sociable. And he's used to having other people living there. There's two rooms, so you shouldn't be too inconvenienced when he visits."

"If he visits," Hugh added grimly.

Daniel tried to absorb this barrage of family history and the uncertain implications it had on his new housing situation, all while keeping a smile on his face. His seminary training had taught him that skill as well. People had a way of divulging great quantities of information to ministers, not all of it immediately relevant or encouraging.

"I'm sure we'll get along like old pals," Daniel reassured them with a yawn. "I lived in the dorms at college, so having an occasional roommate is not a big deal." What else could he say? He had just arrived in a new city and had no other prospects. And he was tired. Though it was only afternoon in Inverness, it felt like much later, or earlier, Daniel's body was not sure from the time change. The plane ride had not been conducive to sleep and he was now simply thankful for the promise of a bed that was not 30,000 feet above the ocean and surrounded by shuffling children and glowing chair-back video screens.

He must not have been as persuasive with his cheerful smile as he had thought, because his hosts sensed his exhaustion. Though, if he were honest, he had not given much effort to concealing it. "Poor thing," Marjory said, "you must be tired from your trip and here we are prattling on about Young Hugh." She turned to her husband, "Be a dear and get the key for Reverend Darrow." Her husband stood and opened a small wooden box on the bookshelf with an obedience that seemed an implicit fact of their relationship. "We can continue our little talk later, after you get some rest," she said to Daniel.

"That's probably a good idea," Rev. Calder said. "Sunday service is at eight in the morning. First day on the job!" She stood and gave Daniel a firm pat on the back. Daniel rose as well and felt queasy as the full realization of his new position settled in with his already present travel fatigue. Hugh Macpherson handed him a key and directed him, in an elongated U course, down the path from the Macpherson's front door to the stone wall by the street and, a few feet over, back up an identical path to the door of the *young side*.

Once inside and alone, Daniel dragged his luggage into the nearer of the two bedrooms. He left the bags by the door. A proper exploration of his accommodation could wait until later. Gravity pulled his willing body to the duvet-covered bed and his mind replayed in starts and stops the events of the day. Before long, he woke with a jerk and was surprised to find the sun had gone down and taken the room's light with it.

Chapter Four

On Sunday morning Daniel woke early, though later than he had intended. Before arriving in Inverness, he had plans of unpacking and settling in before he met his new congregation. He would have a pleasant local dinner, iron his shirt the night before, and read a little from the Psalms to help him relax – perhaps from the 121st Psalm, the traveler's Psalm. "The LORD shall preserve thy going out and thy coming in." None of that had happened of course. He had failed to anticipate the exhaustion of so many traveling hours without sleep or the severe markup of airport food. He hadn't eaten a real meal since before the taxi dropped him off at Raleigh-Durham airport.

Now he rushed frantically about his Inverness flat carrying a wrinkled shirt, searching every kitchen cupboard for leftover food. He breakfasted that morning on a stale package of thin, slightly sweet crackers. He would later discover these were properly meant as an accompaniment to tea and were called *biscuits* – a nomenclature to which his Carolina ears would balk, used as they were to fluffy dough smothered in gravy. Perhaps he should have read from the 94th Psalm instead: "The LORD knoweth the plans of man, that they are vanity."

Just as he had begun to iron his shirt, the doorbell rang. "Coming!" he shouted and unplugged the hot iron. He slipped on the wrinkled shirt hoping that, if he were able to keep his jacket buttoned all morning, no one would notice. With his tie in one hand and shoes in the other he opened the front door to a tidily dressed Hugh Macpherson. "Please tell me you brought coffee," Daniel said.

"Em," Mr. Macpherson was caught off guard by such a disheveled greeting. "I don't know if we have time."

"That's ok. I wasn't really serious," Daniel replied.

Hugh looked Daniel up and down with a wary eye, unamused. He then proceeded to say what he had originally intended. "Marjory, eh, Mrs. Macpherson, thought you might like a lift to the kirk this morning."

"Yes, that was thoughtful. Thank you," Daniel said as he slipped on his shoes. "I haven't quite adjusted to Scotland time. Its only 2 am or thereabouts as far as my internal clock is concerned," Daniel joked as he followed his new landlord to the car. Marjory Macpherson was already in the passenger seat. Daniel took his place in the back and finished dressing as they drove to Church Street. Though they arrived half an hour before the start of the service, cars had already begun to line the curb in front of the church. Once inside, Hugh Macpherson sat down in the pew nearest the door while Marjory continued walking down one of the side aisles toward the pulpit. Daniel took a few steps then stopped, unsure whom to follow.

"I usually wait here while she goes to work," Hugh informed him. "It's her month to make up the flowers." From somewhere inside his coat, Mr. Macpherson produced a neatly folded newspaper. He gave it a sharp flick to loosen the crease before settling in on the front page. The headline reminded Daniel of the paper he had bought at the airport. *Fire on the Firth: Historic Broonburn House burns. Police still investigating.* Daniel tried to remember where he had stowed his own paper and was shocked to realize that hardly one day had passed since he had bought it.

Before his imagination could toy with the headline too long, Daniel heard a familiar cry. "Reverend Darrow!" Rev. Sarah Calder called to him from behind the pulpit. When Daniel approached her, she handed him a bible with a marker in one of the pages. "I thought you might like to do the New Testament reading," she said.

Daniel opened to the marked page. "Which verses?" he asked. Instead of an answer Rev. Calder motioned for him to follow her. She led him to a group of people in a state of incomplete dress. They all had shirts and trousers or dresses on, but on top of these formal underclothes, the members of the group wrestled with a bulk of choir robes. Rev. Calder introduced Daniel to their part-time choir director, Mr. Fisher, "or just Fisher," as she said. He stood slightly apart from the group, a tall man with blond, thinning hair. When Fisher was not leading the choir on Sundays, she informed Daniel, he directed one of the local school's music programs. The protruding belly on Fisher's otherwise thin frame told Daniel that when he was not at either of these two occupations, he could likely be found directing a sing-along at his local pub. Fisher shook Daniel's hand and introduced him to the choir. Welcoming hugs and handshakes from robed hands and partially covered arms and heads commenced.

"If you've a singing voice, you're welcome to join!" Fisher told Daniel. "I'm sure we can uncover a robe somewhere for you."

"I appreciate the offer, but I think Reverend Calder has other plans for me this morning," Daniel responded in an attempt to politely decline. He did not want to offend a significant portion of his new parish on his first day, but he also had no intention of joining them. The only audience he felt comfortable singing in front of consisted of a bar of soap, a shampoo bottle, and a shower curtain. "Besides," Daniel added, "I don't know the songs."

"Neither do we!" a voice shouted from somewhere inside the slowly untangling mess of robes. Fisher grimaced at the remark and the many giggles and Aye's it produced. He put on a look of frantic determination and attempted to reclaim his motley choir from chaos in order to practice a few choruses before the service started. The two reverends took this as their chance for escape. They fled to a pew near the pulpit where Rev. Calder gave Daniel a quick overview of the order of the service.

Before long, parishioners began trickling through the front door. The choir finished their last-minute practicing. With Fisher's composure calmed, they settled into their seats. At five past eight, Rev. Calder took her post behind the pulpit and opened the morning's worship with a greeting and a prayer. The service was not unlike those Daniel had experienced back home. Scripture readings were in their usual places; the hymns had a familiar cadence and Daniel recognized the words to one; Rev. Calder delivered a sermon both clever and heartfelt, though shorter than most Daniel had grown up hearing from preachers in the American South. What Southern churches lacked in grand ancient church buildings, they made up for in verbosity – a kind of ecclesiastic younger sibling syndrome.

When the service concluded, Daniel stood beside Rev. Calder at the main door to greet parishioners as they exited. Though this tradition was common to churches of nearly every creed, he nevertheless felt it a bit backward – not in the outdated sense, but in that it was ordered wrongly. He felt as if he were thanking people for leaving.

Tea and biscuits followed the service. Rather than return to their cars or city buses, most members of the congregation made their way to the kirk hall, a large open room attached to the side of the sanctuary. The hall had a more modern look than the main building, though its renovation appeared to have ended in the early 1990s. A large water stain in a corner of the ceiling closest the sanctuary gave further evidence that the kirk's maintenance budget had been in decline for some time.

After the last hands had been shaken, Daniel helped Rev. Calder tidy the Eucharistic materials and then followed her to this post-liturgical reception area. Though separate from the service, the kirk hall had a kind of ritual of its own. People queued up around a long table offering mugs and kettles of hot tea or coffee. They then dispersed to various round tables scattered about the room or simply stood in the in-between spaces. Three of four pairs of children buzzed around the adults with trays of symmetrical, store bought tea biscuits and lumpy, slightly burned homemade cookies.

While the spiritual life of the church centered on the pulpit and alter, its social life occurred in the kirk hall. Family groups intermingled, children ran off and were recalled, teenagers self-segregated to a lonesome corner. Adults compared workplace stories and lamented about the government and economy. Pensioners reminisced about the same. Yet, on this Sunday morning, most every conversation converged on a single topic – the burning, two nights prior, of Broonburn House.

"I heard arson. Some hoodie gang or such."

"No, no, who'd do such a thing?"

"Aye, it's true. The police brought along a fire dog to sniff out traces of petrol and lighter fluid."

Daniel could not help but eavesdrop on their conversations. He thought about trying to locate Hugh Macpherson's newspaper so he could join in on the speculation. Instead, he settled on observer status. A great deal could be learned from simply sitting back and letting people talk. One of his seminary professors had told him that listening was the key to pastoral counseling. People often had a way of talking themselves through their own problems. Speaking up too soon could lead to a false impression of the facts and well-meaning, though ultimately harmful, advice.

"Maybe they did it for the insurance money?"

"They? Does anyone even know who owns Broonburn House? I heard some rich Londoner bought it a couple years ago."

"I heard it was corporate revenge. A local group of investors had wanted to turn the estate into a new golf course, but got outbid."

"That's the truth, it is. Our own George Fraser was one one 'em. You know a man doesn't come into money like he's got by always playing by the rules."

Daniel meandered from conversation to conversation introducing himself. Each group kindly welcomed him, not minding the interruption. They made small talk and then he moved on to the next group. This was the expected protocol for new ministers and their congregations. Along the way he picked up and stored away pieces of information about the fire. Should he feel bad that he tried harder to remember these bits than the names of the individuals who offered them?

"No, I have a cousin in the police. Said it was old wiring."

"Typical. All that money and too miserly to keep up with basic maintenance."

Eventually Daniel stumbled into a conversation with one particular church member whose name he could not help but remember. Eliza MacGillivray sat talking with another woman in a far away corner of the room. She wore a long, slim-fitting, dark dress with lace around the cuffs and high collar. Around her neck, hung a flat, smooth stone strung through a hole in its center with a delicate golden chain. Partially concealed by the back of her chair, a large drooping bow tied around her waist and the bottom of her dress opened into several frilly layers nearly touching the floor. She had the look of a black and white photograph.

In her lap, Eliza MacGillivray carried a large handbag. Every few minutes she broke a tea biscuit into small pieces and slipped them one at a time into the bag. Daniel attempted to recreate the obligatory small talk he had engaged in with others, but found himself distracted by her strange habit. She noticed his eye following the pieces of biscuit into her bag. She held up a wrinkled, skeletal finger to her lips.

"Have a look," she said softly and opened the bag.

Daniel glanced at the other woman, who shrugged and gave him a look that said, "Humour her." Inside the bag a gray rabbit huddled down with its long ears pressed flat against its back. Eliza stroked its head reassuringly and let it nibble a piece of biscuit from her hand.

"She likes them because of the sugar," Eliza said. Daniel had no words to respond.

"One thing you will quickly learn about our Eliza, Reverend, is that she will not be parted from her wee furry friend," the other woman said.

"I can see that," Daniel said, recovering his composure. "Are those cookies good for it, uh, her?"

"Are they good for any of us?" Eliza replied.

"Well, you might want to be more discreet," the other woman said. "If Sir Walter sees her, all hell will break loose."

"That wouldn't be very proper for a church social," Daniel quipped. Confused eyes stared back at him. "Hell…church," he tried to explain. "I'm funny, really," he assured them.

Eliza returned her attention to the rabbit. "Sir Walter knows better than to cross me. I'll put a curse on him."

"Eliza! Come now, you'll scare off our new reverend," her friend said.

"Don't look so surprised, Mr. Darrow. I could if I really wanted to."

Daniel once again found himself without words. All he could think to do was smile and look around the room for an excuse to extricate himself from this increasingly strange conversation.

"Don't leave just yet," she said to him. "I've messages for you." She grabbed his arm with a surprisingly strong grip and pulled him closer. He could hear the rabbit munching and grinding its teeth. With one hand, Eliza MacGillivray held Daniel's arm and between the fingers of her other hand, she rubbed the smooth stone of her necklace.

"From across the sea shall a shepherd come

Professing grace divine,

Not to lead but to be led

By fur and feet toward love terrestrial."

Her grip tightened on the final word and then released.

"Ok, thanks, I think. Um, oh, I just remembered I promised Reverend Calder I'd help clean up. I'd better head on over before the work's all done," Daniel stammered out an excuse.

"Oh, Eliza, you've done it now. Just look at the poor thing. He cannot wait to get away," Eliza's companion said. Then to Daniel she added, "Our Eliza has a gift you see – a kind of second sight. We're all quite used to it, but she can be off putting to outsiders."

"And is she always so cryptic?" Daniel asked.

"What is seen must be said," Eliza said as she fed another crumb to her rabbit.

Daniel shook both their hands in turn. "It's been a pleasure meeting you both. Certainly one I will not forget. But I really did promise to help clean up." He took his leave and walked briskly toward Rev. Calder who was enjoying a cup of tea with a group of young couples. *What was that?* He asked himself as he walked away. *What have I gotten myself into?*

When he reached Rev. Calder he began collecting discarded napkins and coffee mugs. "Daniel, that's kind of you. You don't have to tidy up – at least not on your first day!" she joked.

"Yes, I do," he said. "I've just had a very, uh, interesting conversation with a Ms. Eliza MacGillivray."

"Say no more," she said knowingly. "Here," she handed him her mug, "the sink is just behind that counter."

As Daniel washed dishes the church crowd gradually dispersed until only a few lingering families remained. By the time he had laid the last wet mug on the drying rack, the room was empty. Daniel wiped his hands and headed for the exit. With the Macphersons and their car already gone, he was not entirely sure how he would get home. He was attempting to recreate a reverse mental map of their drive that morning when a strong, familiar force gripped his arm.

"Ms. MacGillivray, we must be the last two here," Daniel said with more unease in his voice than he could hide. He felt a scratching at his left shoe. Eliza MacGillivray's rabbit crouched on the floor with its neck outstretched and sniffed him. It took a nibble out of the heel of his shoe. Eliza pulled on a leash attached to the rabbit's harness. "You're taking it on a walk?" Daniel asked.

"Exercise. Those biscuits have a lot of calories," she answered.

"That makes sense," Daniel said. *Did it?* "You wouldn't happen to know what bus goes to Bellfield Park? I think my ride left without me."

"Em," Her hand loosened around his arm as she thought. "The 6 or 7 should do you."

"Thank you." Daniel took a step toward the door, but her grip quickly tightened again and held him.

"You left so quickly earlier."

"Yes, I'm sorry, I, uh . . ."

"You didn't let me finish," Eliza interrupted. "I told you I had messages for you."

"No, I heard you. Across the sea, shepherd, love. I got it."

"Messages – plural. That was the second. You missed the first."

"The first?" Daniel asked.

"You've heard of Broonburn House, yes?"

"Hard not to – even for a newcomer like myself. It's all over the newspapers. Everyone was talking about it earlier. Some say arson; some say the owner had faulty wiring or just wanted the insurance money."

"Some say teenagers. Some say murder. Some say the owner deserved it," Eliza said.

Daniel's eyes widened. He had gathered from previous conversations that most locals were either ignorant or indifferent about the House's owner.

He hadn't expected such open hostility on the subject. It was especially surprising coming from such a frail looking woman as Eliza MacGillivray. Now he was really curious.

"Who would deserve that?" he asked.

"The burning of Broonburn House was just the beginning," she said ominously, pulling him closer. He could smell grassy tea on her breath. She hung the rabbit's leash around her elbow and rubbed the stone from her necklace between her fingers. She stared directly at him, but something in her eyes prevented him from seeing her. A glossy cloud had enveloped them, or perhaps it was just cataracts. Her lips moved without emitting any sound. Then she spoke:

"The day will come when
Fire and water shall run in streams
Through all the streets and lanes of Inverness."

Chapter Five

Daniel Darrow had thought that he would have a chance to rest after his first Sunday at Church Street. Settle in and finally read the paper he'd picked up at the airport. If he could figure out the public transportation system, he might even indulge his curiosity and try to find this storied old mansion that had become the talk of the town. When Rev. Calder called to ask if he would join her on her round of home visits, he knew that once again, the headlines would have to wait.

Not every member of Church Street Kirk was able to attended regularly, for one reason or another, and it was their job as ministers to ensure they still felt a part of the family. "A shepherd must care for all her flock," she told him. "Those in the barn and those out in the pasture." So, Daniel downed a second cup of coffee and headed out the door. Though he would have liked a day of rest, he was truly glad for the opportunity to get to know more of the church's members. He was gladder still for the buffer that Rev. Calder provided. She knew much of their histories and could advise him as to what to expect. She also owned a car, which beat getting lost on the city's buses.

Their second call of the day turned out to have had a fall and was recovering at a room in Raigmore Hospital. After visiting her there and then noticing the late hour, they decided to split up their last remaining house calls. With a smile that carried a hint of mischievousness, Rev. Calder told Daniel, "You can take this one, William MacCrivag. His place is closer to a bus line. He has a reputation as a bit of a hermit, but he stays surprisingly in the loop." *So much for a buffer.*

Two bus transfers and a short walk later, Daniel rang the bell of a modest house at the end of Telford Gardens. With its two storied, dark gray-shingled roof and off-white, almost gray stucco façade, William MacCrivag's home had a nearly identical appearance to every other house on the street. The house's small, cluttered front yard was its only distinguishing feature. His neighbors also had narrow yards encased by short wooden picket fences, offering some little space between their houses and the asphalt. Their yards, or gardens, were variously decorated, but all uniform in their tidiness – short-cut grass here, a few potted flowers there, a gravel path off to the side.

William MacCrivag's garden boasted similar features, though none of them in the orderly design of his neighbors. A row of pots sat underneath the front window. Some held flowers, others only dirt. Decorative stone pavers lay in a heap beside the front door. A breadcrumb trail of stones snaked off to the middle of the garden and formed an unfinished round flowerbed. On his way from the wooden pickets to the front door, Daniel nearly tripped over a half-buried garden spade. He sidestepped to avoid the spade and landed his shoe in a muddy patch of ground that simultaneously squished and cracked. Underfoot lay part of a plastic flowerpot – the kind used to hold flowers at the nursery before a customer brought them home to plant. William MacCrivag had not yet made it to the planting part. While the yard was markedly untidy compared to its neighbors, Daniel sensed that this came not so much from neglect as from distraction.

This observation prepared him for his meeting with the yard's owner as much as any backstory Rev. Calder could have provided. When Daniel rang the doorbell, a light above the door flickered on and off and the chime repeated the same two notes as if it were being played on a worn vinyl record. The chime wanted to continue on to a third note, but was unable to break from its stutter. After a few seconds, a pop from within the wall put it out of its misery. When no one appeared at the door, Daniel gingerly touched the ringer again. It gave no electrical shock so he pressed it, repeating the whole flickering, stammering doorbell routine.

After the third ring, William MacCrivag opened his door. He was a man of average height – "too short for the rugby back line and not tall enough for the front" as he described himself. He wore green checked trousers and a white t-shirt. The lack of hair on his head mirrored the smooth plainness of the shirt. His age did not appear so ancient as to have completely given up on producing hair; rather, based on the slight stubble encircling the back of his head, Daniel thought he must keep his hair shaved in anticipation of that bare inevitability.

"Hello, Mr. MacCrivag, my name is Daniel Darrow. I'm the new assistant reverend at Church Street," Daniel announced and offered his hand.

"Ah, so you are. I thought you might not show. Thought Reverend Calder was coming," William MacCrivag said, shaking Daniel's hand.

"We got held up on an earlier errand, and she apologizes for not being able to make it," Daniel said.

"Right, right. Well, at least one of you is here now. Might as well come in. I think a few flies have already beat you to it."

Daniel did not see any flies, but he was happy to get out of the doorway. Mr. MacCrivag directed him through the entryway and into the living room.

"Have a seat and tell me about yourself. You don't sound Scottish. Canadian?"

"Um, no. I don't think I've heard that one before. I'm from America," Daniel answered.

"Canada's in the Americas," Mr. MacCrivag said. He stood suddenly. "I'm sorry, would you like a cuppa? I don't entertain much."

"I'm fine."

"No, no, of course you do. I'll just put the kettle on," Mr. MacCrivag insisted and headed into the kitchen.

Before the water had begun to boil, he returned to the living area. "I'm actually glad you were able to pop in, because I need help searching," he said.

"Searching?" Daniel asked.

"Aye, I'm in dire straits here. Full emergency."

Daniel stood. "Sure, I'm happy to help." He padded the cushion of his chair searching for – he did not know what he was searching for. "What are we looking for exactly?"

"Eh? She's a wee thing and rare. You can't miss her, unless she's gone missing herself."

Daniel scanned the room. Much like the front yard, its appearance was one of constantly interrupted order. He could imagine any number of things going missing here. "Mr. MacCrivag, I'm sorry, but you never said what it is we're looking for."

"Well, she's not in here is she? Go check the kitchen, I'll see about the bedroom," Mr. MacCrivag said and exited the room.

Daniel remained standing, unsure of what to do. He did not want to offend Mr. MacCrivag by refusing to help, but he also felt uncomfortable looking through a stranger's home. Further, he still had no clue as to what they were looking for. He glanced around the room again.

"Have you found her yet?" Mr. MacCrivag called from the bedroom.

"No, um, I'm still searching. It'd really help if you could tell me what we're-"

"Keep your looking. She can't have gone far, unless they've taken her. They tend to do that from time to time – nasty faeries."

Daniel shrugged and walked to the kitchen. She? Was he looking for some kind of animal or pet? He did not see any food or water bowls. No litter box for a cat, or cage for a bird. The distance of two rooms muffled Mr. MacCrivag's voice, but Daniel thought he heard him mention a *faerie*? "What does she sound like?" Daniel shouted a guess. "Should I be listening for her?"

"What does she sound like?" Mr. MacCrivag shouted in response. "What a silly thing to ask! I haven't even opened her yet."

So, not a pet or mystical creature. The mystery object was something that could be opened. Daniel looked around the kitchen. He stood in a room full of objects with lids. This was impossible. He was about to give up when he noticed the long neck of a bottle sticking out from between the recycling bin and the cabinetry. Foil still encased the bottle's mouth, so he pulled it out for a closer look. A full bottle of Scotch. The bottle's name began with "Glen" followed by several letters in a configuration unfamiliar to Daniel's American eyes. "Well, this doesn't look like trash," he said to himself, placing the bottle on the nearby kitchen table.

Near the bottle, lay three envelopes. The folded paper contents of one had been stuffed back in. The other two remained unopened. The unread mail did not warrant a second glance except for one oddity – each was identical to the other. Three pieces of mail with identical white envelopes, identical second-class stamps from the Royal Mail, identical return addresses in identical fonts from a London based Philarguria Energy. Thinking they might be unpaid electricity or gas bills, Daniel called to Mr. MacCrivag, "I think I might have found something. Come see."

A few seconds later, Mr. MacCrivag appeared in the kitchen. "Aye, ye found her!" he exclaimed. Daniel held out one of the envelopes for him, but he walked right past to embrace the bottle. "You've spared me an abundance of distress, Reverend. Where did you find her hiding, sneaky lass?"

"Um, just behind the recycling," Daniel answered. "So, we were searching for that bottle this whole time?"

"Of course. I told you," Mr. MacCrivag said, holding the bottle out to examine it. "I've been meaning to move that bin. I've had more than one bottle go missing before I had a chance to enjoy it. And oh what a tragedy this would have been!"

"I'm glad I could help. And your mail?"

"Leave it. I've got plenty more," he said. "Just some permission request or notice or other. Loads of people have gotten them. They've been buying up land around here for years now: everything west of the Craigphadrig Wood, Broonburn, the whole lot. You'd think they'd have their fill by now. All I know is I'm with SSE and I always pay my bill on time."

"Wait. Broonburn? As in that castle that burned down?" Daniel asked. It seemed he could not get away from the subject.

"Aye."

Just then the kettle let out a conversation-deafening whistle. Both men jumped. Mr. MacCrivag replaced the bottle of Scotch carefully on the table and rushed to the stove. "Mugs are up there," he said, nodding toward the cupboard. Having completed a thorough search of the place, Daniel already knew this.

He placed two mugs on the table and Mr. MacCrivag poured in the steaming black tea. He then uncorked an already opened bottle of scotch from the cupboard by the recycling bin and poured a liberal amount into each mug. "I mean no offence, Reverend, but that one's too good for a totty," he said indicating the bottle Daniel had recovered.

"It's fine. I've never actually had whiskey with tea before," Daniel replied.

"I'm sorry, I just poured away and never even asked how you took it. My hosting skills are a bit rusty. Well, have a seat and tell me what you came to discuss." Mr. MacCrivag took his tea and a seat at the table. He placed the other whiskey infused mug at an empty chair.

"Nothing in particular," Daniel said, sitting. "I just wanted to introduce myself and see how you are doing. I didn't get a chance to meet you on Sunday."

"No, you wouldn't have. I was feeling poorly. To tell the truth, I slept late. You have to once in a while, haven't you? Like taking a sickie from work. It's only human. Did I miss anything exceptional?"

"It being my first Sunday here, I'm not sure what might constitute as exceptional," Daniel admitted. "Wait, I did have an interesting encounter with a Miss Eliza MacGillivray."

Mr. MacCrivag laughed. "She's a kook, eh?"

"I don't know if I could say kook, perhaps unsettling."

"No, you can say kook. A rose by any other name and all – St. Paul said that."

"Um, I don't think so," Daniel said. "But anyway Ms. MacGillivray did have some interesting things to say. She had on this necklace with a smooth stone on it that she rubbed-"

"She prophesied you didn't she?" Mr. MacCrivag said excitedly. "It's a real treat to get a prophecy out of her, isn't it! And on your first day. Now you must tell me."

"It was such an unusual experience I had to write it down," Daniel said. He pulled out a palm-size notebook from his pocket and read: "From across the sea shall a shepherd come professing grace divine, not to lead but to be led by fur and feet toward love terrestrial."

"Wonderfully enigmatic isn't she!" Mr. MacCrivag said. He clearly enjoyed the subject of Eliza MacGillivray, though Daniel could not tell if it were all in jest or if a small part of him took her prophecies seriously. His tone steadied as he considered her words. "From across the sea a shepherd professing grace divine," he repeated. "That bit's obviously geared toward you. Coming across the Atlantic from Canada to us to preach the good news."

"America," Daniel corrected.

"Eh? Ah, right, America. But the second bit, now that's the puzzle. 'Not to lead,' fair enough. That's Reverend Calder's job. What goes next? Love for fur and feet? Beats me, or," Mr. MacCrivag slapped his thigh and nearly spit up a swallow of tea before he continued. "Or *bleats* me! There have been tales of lonely Highlanders and their sheep!"

Daniel took a second before realizing the off-color joke. He was not sure how to take it, as he had just met Mr. MacCrivag. His field experience at a rural North Carolina church the summer after his second year of seminary had taught him that people usually react one of two ways around ministers. They either put on their manners, furtively closing off their true, flawed selves, or they become more truly themselves than usual. Mr. MacCrivag clearly fell into the latter category.

"Mr. MacCrivag, my young impressionable ears," Daniel deflected. Then, hoping he read the man correctly, he added, "But to be on the safe side, I'll steer clear of any sheep farms."

"Ha ha, see that you do!" Mr. MacCrivag laughed and took another sip of his tea. "A fair amount of Eliza's prophecies do tend to work out true. She fancies herself a descendant of the auld Brahan Seer – not in the biological sense of course. More a like a spiritual descendant, an inheritor."

"The who?"

"The Brahan Seer. He's our own wee Nostradamus. Coinneach Odhar, that's his name, was a farmer in the seventh century. Was born blind in one eye, up north on the Isle of Lewis. Most blokes, especially back then, would have had a difficult time with only one eye – thought themselves cursed even. But our Coinneach saw it rather as a blessing. For that blind eye was not truly blind, more like out of focus - in time I mean. It was blind to this present world. But when he put the oracle stone – this wee ring of a stone he always had with him– to his blind eye, he could glimpse the future.

"He made the most amazing predictions. He predicted the bloody defeat of the Jacobites at Culloden. He saw ships sailing through the Caledonian Canal two centuries before it was built. He saw airships during the Great War flying over Strathpeffer. When Aberdeen was only a fishing village, he foresaw oil rigging off its shores. What else? The five bridges. Now Inverness was just a fishing village back then, but his blind eye showed him a fine city with four bridges crossing the River Ness. 'Four bridges! Who would need that many?' That's what people of his time thought. But that's what he saw. Yet, if a fifth bridge were ever constructed, he warned, a great tragedy would befall the entire world. And coincidence? Less than a week after the fifth bridge was built, Hitler invades Poland.

"Unlike Nostradamus, Coinneach Odhar was not afraid to speak truth to those in power. This got him into trouble. One day when the Earl of Seaforth was late in returning from France, his wife sought the advice of the Brahan Seer. She had a reputation for jealousy and justifiably, for she was widely held as the most hideous looking woman in all of Scotland. Coinneach held the oracle stone to his blind eye and, being an honest Highlands farmer, he told her the truth. Her husband was late because he was having an affair with a beautiful French woman. Not only that, Coinneach predicted her family, the whole Seaforth line, would be just as ugly as her and come to an untimely end. He should have probably left that last bit out because the Lady Seaforth took offence, naturally enough, and had him arrested and executed by being dunked into a barrel of boiling tar."

Daniel had nearly finished his tea by the time Mr. MacCrivag concluded his history. He placed his mug on the table and asked, "Ms. MacGillivray is the descendant of this Coinne-, um, Brahan Seer?"

"Only spiritually," Mr. MacCrivag corrected. "Or so she believes. You see, before Coinneach Odhar was killed he threw his oracle stone into Loch Ussie. He predicted it would be uncovered from the belly of a fish at some future date. Eliza MacGillivray, she grew up in nearby Dingwall and often traveled to Loch Ussie for holiday. After one such holiday when she was still a young woman, I never knew her back then, but I hear she was a touch off even as a girl, Eliza returns with that stone she now wears around her neck claiming she's found the famous oracle stone. I don't think it's genuine.

She's a terrible fisher. Had a kirk retreat several years ago to the Black Isle. She never had a bite.

"It's hard to deny the relevance of her prophecies though. She told Reverend Calder her niece would have a daughter before Reverend Calder's niece had even announced she was pregnant. She predicted my head would not have a hair on it by my fiftieth birthday and well, look at me. Granted, I do shave a bit on the sides, but if I didn't shave it, I'd look like ol' Friar Tuck. Ask anyone at Church Street. We've all had one vision or other from Eliza. She knew *you* were coming."

"That's not the only thing she told me," Daniel said. "She said that was the second prophecy. The first was-" he opened his notebook again and read: "The day will come when fire and water shall run in streams through all the streets and lanes of Inverness." Daniel shut his notebook. "Kind of sinister sounding."

"Ah, now that one shouldn't count," Mr. MacCrivag said. "The old girl's getting lazy. That's one of the original Seer's prophecies she told you."

"Really?"

"Yes, you don't live in Inverness for long or know the legend of Coinneach Odhar without hearing that one. Fire and water running down the streets. Least she could have done was recite an unfulfilled prophecy."

"It's come true already?" Daniel asked.

"Sure. Electricity and indoor plumbing."

Chapter Six

On the Sunday morning of Daniel Darrow's first sermon at Church Street Kirk, vehicles spilled out of the church's small parking lot and lined both sides of Church Street for nearly three blocks. Daniel recognized many faces from the previous Sunday's tea as well as a few of the house calls he'd made that week. Many more faces, however, were new to him. Everyone wanted to see the new preacher from America in action. "Don't be nervous," Rev. Calder told him. "We probably won't see a crowd like this again until Christmas."

Fisher, the choir director, promised to help out the new preacher in his own way. The "favorite, classic" hymns he planned were sure to "warm up the audience," he said with a wink. This kindness was offered despite Daniel's reluctance to join their melodious gang – a generosity of which Fisher had no trouble reminding him. The effectiveness of Fisher's strategy left no doubt, however. The old hymns did their trick. When the time came for Daniel's sermon, the congregation was full of comfortable good will and expectation.

Still, when he stepped up to the pulpit, Daniel was a bundle of nervous energy. He was thankful for the dark, loose fitting clerical robe covering the shirt that he was quickly perspiring through. After the first few faltering sentences, Daniel's nerves began to quiet and he found his rhythm. He attempted to annunciate clearly and was relieved to see most people nod in agreement or laugh at the appropriate times; yet he could not shake the feeling that every member of the congregation was, at one time or another, distracted. A woman looked down, preoccupied with something in her lap.

Was she texting? An old man whispered to a friend and discreetly, or at least he attempted discretion, held out his hands to receive some object. A child squirmed upside down on the pew, stuck her head under it, and giggled.

Distraction was not unexpected. Modern attention spans were not what they once were. During the Reformation, when Protestant services granted the sermon a greater place of prominence and length than it had previously enjoyed, people were not yet conditioned to the brevity of modern sound bites and commercial breaks. What Daniel found unusual about the distractions he presently witnessed, however, was the way they tended to move from pew to pew around the room with an almost predictable pattern. Like a spontaneous arm-raising wave from fans at a baseball game, distraction began at one end and moved from person to person down the aisle in various incarnations of head turns, whispers, childish giggles, and posture adjustments. Eliza MacGillivray, dressed again in a Victorian inspired black dress, was the only person who appeared to dislike the distractive wave. When it made its way down the pew near her, she clutched her bag tightly and made a "shoo shoo" sound.

Daniel tried his best to ignore the strange behaviors of the congregation without becoming distracted by them himself. He wondered if this was a unique phenomenon or if Rev. Calder had also experienced it. Sitting on the front pew last Sunday had not offered him an opportunity to notice any peculiar goings on behind him. Eventually he came to the conclusion of his sermon, admittedly rushing the last few lines, and took a seat so that Rev. Calder could offer a final blessing. He was glad to be seated – out of the spotlight and intermittently attentive listeners. Before dismissing the congregation, Rev. Calder mentioned a few upcoming events on the church's social calendar and made a special remark about the day's offering, or monetary collection.

"We all know Sir Walter and we are happy he has chosen Church Street as his own kirk. Or at least most of us," Rev. Calder said with a playful eye toward Eliza MacGillivray. Eliza huffed and whispered something into the bag on her lap. "It is time again for his yearly check up," Rev. Calder continued.

A woman from the congregation shouted out, "I saw him limping the other day."

"I thought something was off with him," Rev. Calder agreed, "though I wasn't able to catch up with him and see. We'll mention that to the doctor. As his appointment is scheduled for this afternoon, the money we collect today will pay for Sir Walter's expenses. So, if you have not already had the chance, I encourage you to drop a few extra pounds in the collection box as you leave today."

Like the previous Sunday, Daniel stood with Rev. Calder at the exit to greet parishioners as they made their ways home or down to the meeting room for tea and coffee. While he shook hands, hugged necks, and repeated names that he knew he would immediately forget, he kept an eye out for an elderly man with a limp. He wanted to meet this Sir Walter that the church cared so much about. In a land of free, or at least state subsidized health care, he was surprised someone would need such assistance from the church. His heart warmed, though, at the thought of being a part of a community that cared about its members so. *What better way to tangibly show the love of God?*, he thought?

"Where is this Sir Walter we're taking a collection for?" he asked Rev. Calder in between handshakes.

"Oh, I forget, you haven't met Sir Walter yet, have you?" she said. "He's around somewhere. I spied him earlier."

Just then a man with a cane approached them. He was tall; his head vaulted three or four inches above Daniel's and on top of it he wore a wave of thick white hair and a mustache. An ash gray tweed suit with blue pinstripe checks covered the rest of his beanstalk frame. Daniel looked at Rev. Calder with raised eyebrows.

"No, no. This is Mr. George Fraser," she laughed.

George Fraser. Daniel had heard that name before, but where? He had shaken so many hands in the prior week, it was impossible to remember them all. But that wasn't it. Rev. Calder was introducing him, so clearly they hadn't met before. Then Daniel remembered. One week earlier, in the kirk hall. He had been eavesdropping on the Broonburn gossip and overheard that name – George Fraser. Was he an investor? Something about wanting revenge on whoever bought Broonburn House?

"What's that? Have I missed a joke?" the man asked, shaking Rev. Calder's hand.

"Sorry, George. I couldn't help myself," Rev. Calder said. "Reverend Darrow here asked if you might be Sir Walter. They have not yet met."

"Me, Sir Walter? I've been called a lot of things, but- You say he does not know who Walter is? Reverend Darrow, when you do have the pleasure of meeting that mangy fellow, I am sure you will discover the humor in your question," he said.

"I hope so Mr. Fraser," Daniel said. *More like Mr. Tweed*, he thought to himself. Daniel had known the odd college professor to wear tweed jackets, but never before had he seen a full suit like George Fraser's: matching tweed jacket, vest, and trousers. A flat cap and coat hung over Mr. Tweed's arm, darker, though both consisting of the same material. The man certainly didn't look like an arsonist. "In any case, I'm sure he cannot be better dressed. That is quite a suit," Daniel said. Rev. Calder and Mr. Tweed, or George Fraser, burst into another fit of laughter.

"Better dressed? I should hope not!" Mr. Tweed laughed.

A woman with hair as white as Mr. Tweed's came up and addressed him, "George, there you are. I should have guessed – trying to sneak away without me."

"I thought you were behind me, dear. I do not have time to chatter away at everyone that passes by."

"This is Mrs. Mary Fraser," Rev. Calder said. "So, you won't be joining us for tea?"

"I'm afraid not. I have to be at the club by one and must change first," Mr. Tweed said.

"Surely they wouldn't kick you out wearing that," Rev. Calder said.

"You know George," Mary said, "he has a tweed for every occasion." The two women shared a smile.

"I do not find the humor," Mr. Tweed objected. "This is not a practical suit for golf. It is the wrong cut." The women's smiles turned into giggles.

"Rev. Darrow will agree with me. He is from Carolina, top links there, for the States."

"I would probably have trouble swinging a club in that," Daniel said, trying to be inoffensive.

"Good man! For that you must join me some time. I'll ring you later, but now we really must go," Mr. Tweed said and moved closer to the door.

"I think he likes you. He's never asked me to join him," Mary said and patted Daniel on the back. "Good luck!"

* * *

Many more people filed by for a quick greeting and handshake with the new reverend. Others, like the Frasers, tarried for a brief conversation. Mr. William MacCrivag lamented the dreary weather. With a wink he thanked Daniel for his help in recovering his missing Scotch. Ms. Eliza MacGillivray, rabbit in tow, greeted both reverends warmly, but on second thought asked Rev. Calder why the church continued to fuss over Sir Walter so. She asked Daniel if he remembered what she had told him the previous Sunday. "I couldn't forget," he assured her. By the time the procession ended, after all the hands were shaken, necks hugged, and cheeks kissed, the elusive Sir Walter remained unseen.

"I think it is time you met our famous Walter," Rev. Calder said and led Daniel down one of the pew aisles to where a lone, late middle-aged woman still sat. She wore a dark blue mid-length dress with a small, coordinating purse to her side. White, silk gloved hands rested on her lap. "Elspeth," Rev. Calder addressed the woman, "have you had a chance to meet our new assistant reverend?" The woman shook her head. "Mrs. Elspeth Gray, let me introduce you to Reverend Daniel Darrow."

Daniel and Elspeth shook hands. It was odd, he thought, holding a gloved hand when his was not. She winced when he squeezed her hand. "I'm sorry, I hope that wasn't too hard," Daniel said. "That's just how we shake back home."

"No, you're fine. I'm happy to finally meet you," she said.

"Those are lovely gloves, Elspeth. I don't know that I've ever seen you in gloves – at least not before December. Are you on to a new fashion trend you haven't told me about?" Rev. Calder asked. She reached for Elspeth's hand to further inspect a glove, but Elspeth retracted her hands and rubbed them softly.

"Kind of you to say Reverend. They're just something new I'm trying," she said.

"Well, I think you pull them off magnificently," Rev. Calder said. "I came over to ask if you've seen Sir Walter? You usually know where he's run off to."

"Aye, he's just here under the pew," Elspeth answered. She put her hand under her seat and rubbed her fingers together. In a few seconds the furry, strawberry blond head of a cat with green-gold eyes peeked out from under the pew and rubbed its face against Elspeth Gray's hand.

"Sir Walter is a cat?" Daniel asked incredulously. Suddenly the phantom distractions during his sermon took flesh and made sense.

Rev. Calder smiled a toothy smile and nodded. "Reverend Daniel Darrow, Sir Walter Scott – named after the famous novelist and poet."

"So that conversation with Mr. Twe- uh, Mr. Fraser?" Daniel asked.

Rev. Calder burst into a laugh. "I'm sorry. I should've said something, but it was just so funny! George Fraser is not accustomed to being compared to a cat." She recounted the misunderstanding to Elspeth Gray, in whom it produced another laugh. "Are you all set to take our wee friend on his appointment this afternoon?" Rev. Calder asked Elspeth.

Elspeth, who was now gently scratching behind the cat's ears as he sat on her lap, shook her head. "I know I usually take care of that, but I am not feeling up to it today. I'm sure we could reschedule," she said in an elusive though apologetic tone.

"I'm so sorry to hear that. You're not getting sick, are you?" Rev. Calder asked, placing a hand on Elspeth's shoulder. "I hate to trouble the vet with rescheduling. They do so much already. We could- " she paused. "Or?" she looked at Daniel with eyebrows raised.

"You want me to take him, don't you?" Daniel said.

"It's just that my schedule is full today. And it would give you a chance to better get to know him."

"He's a cat."

"A cat that we have adopted, or he has adopted us," Rev. Calder explained. "He may walk on four feet and have a little more hair than the rest of us, but he's still one of God's creatures."

"And I'm the new guy," Daniel said.

"Aye, and you're the new guy."

* * *

The Kinmylies Veterinary Clinic was located on General Booth Rd. in Kinmylies – a westerly part of Inverness between the Craigphadrig Wood and the Caledonian Canal. First opened in the early 2000s it specialized in small animal care and enjoyed a loyal clientele of pet owners who, despite the clinic's smaller size and slightly higher prices, preferred the friendliness of its staff and the convenience of not having to travel across town to the larger clinic with a sick pet in tow. At 2:20 Sunday afternoon, after a forty-minute journey that began on the east side of the canal and required a change of buses on the other side, Daniel Darrow was in a position to fully appreciate that local convenience.

The trip from Church Street to Kinmylies, as Rev. Calder suggested, had given Daniel plenty time to better get to know Sir Walter. Daniel now knew, for example, that, as much as Sir Walter disliked being inside his plastic carrying crate, he disliked bus rides even more. Daniel learned that no amount of pleading or cat treats could convince Sir Walter that yowling the entire trip would not make it end any more quickly. He also discovered, in an attempt to pet the cat through the crate's finger-sized air holes, that all of Sir Walter's claws remained intact and sharp. By the time he signed in at the veterinary reception desk, Daniel was fully ready to hand the cat over and let someone else have a chance to better get to know Sir Walter.

Daniel passed the time as they waited for the doctor by attempting to shield his feline charge from the few dogs and other cats in the room. Sir

Walter clearly preferred distracted churchgoers to other animals. Once the cat calmed down, Daniel distracted himself by reading a wall decorated with plaques and certificates touting the credentials of the doctors and support staff. One notice in particular drew his attention: Elspeth Gray, Veterinary Assistant, University of Edinburgh. *So that's why we had to come all the way out here*, Daniel realized.

A few minutes later the receptionist announced gravely, "Sir Walter Scott, we're ready for you. Room 3."

Daniel carried Sir Walter in his crate to the indicated room. Familiar with the rituals of doctors' offices, Daniel knew that this second room was really just a second waiting room, so he placed the crate on the observation table and busied himself examining the various posters and models of animal organs, bodily systems, and diseases. Just as he bent over to get a better view of a truly maniacal looking cartoon heartworm, the Room 3 door opened. Daniel turned around to see a young woman, slim though not especially tall, dressed in light blue scrubs, and holding a clipboard. Her hair, pulled back in a ponytail, fell just below the nape of her neck and matched in color the light brown, almost red frames of her glasses. *Cinnamon*, Daniel thought, *that's the color*. She pulled a pen out of the clipboard and wrote something down with a kind of rote confidence and then looked up at her patient. "Sir Walter and- ?" she asked.

Daniel could not answer. He had forgotten his name. He was with Sir Walter Scott, the kirk cat; that much was true. But his own name? In his line of work he had become so accustomed to meeting middle to elderly aged people that he was momentarily stalled by the introduction of a woman his own age – especially an attractive woman his own age. Her left hand, he immediately noticed, was clean of any jewelry.

The woman said again, "Hello, my name is Dr. Gray. I see Sir Walter is here with us today and you are?"

"Dr. Gray? Elspeth Gray?" Daniel asked. She nodded. "I was expecting someone older."

"So was I," she said, "and female. My mum usually brings Sir Walter for his check ups."

"You're Elspeth Gray's daughter?"

"I'm also Elspeth Gray, but most people call me Ellie. It's better than Junior, right? You still haven't told me what you're called."

"Oh, sorry, Daniel. Daniel Darrow. I'm the new assistant reverend at Church Street."

"That's right. Mum was telling me they were getting someone new. Someone foreign, she said."

"American," Daniel told her. "I haven't seen you at church. I think I would have remembered."

"What is that supposed to mean?" she asked as she opened the crate to coax out a reluctant Sir Walter. Given the choice between a cramped crate and a veterinarian's office full of blood samples, shots, and thermometers, Sir Walter now preferred the crate.

"I, um, no, it's just that most of the people I've met at the church are either old or married with kids," Daniel stumbled through his reply.

Ellie reached for a thermometer and Sir Walter's eyes widened when he remembered that uncomfortable stick from last year's visit. "So you're saying I'm unmarried and childless? Dear Reverend, I think that's the sweetest thing anyone's ever said to me," she said wryly.

"No, that didn't come out right," Daniel said. "I did say *not* old." He scratched his head. "Is it weird for a minister to compliment a parishioner's daughter?"

"Is that what you're trying to do?" she asked. She put the thermometer away, wrote a note on her clipboard, and pulled out a syringe.

"It's not going well, is it?" Daniel asked.

"Hold him a second. I need to take blood," Ellie instructed. Daniel held Sir Walter's head and petted his chest. Ellie pulled a vile of blood from the loose skin at the nape of the cat's neck. "Ta."

"He's been limping. That's what someone said," Daniel told her. "One of his back legs I think."

"Let's have a look," Ellie said to the cat and inspected his hind legs. "He has a cut on the paw here," she informed Daniel. "It doesn't appear to be infected and is already mostly healed. Keep an eye on it and if it looks worse, let me

45

know." She petted Sir Walter a few times and then stepped away from the examination table. "I have to go check out his blood, but he appears healthy. As fit as ever, eh Sir Walter?" Ellie said and then opened the door.

She paused before she left and turned around to face Daniel. "And feel free to try again," she said.

"Huh?"

"The compliment. I believe in second chances. Perhaps over coffee?"

Chapter Seven

George Fraser arrived in front of Hugh and Marjory Macphersons' house on Bellfield Park Rd. at 7:00 a.m. sharp. He was a man driven by punctuality who considered tardiness a sin on par with thievery and lying. Those were the consequences of tardiness after all – a theft of time and false representation of oneself. Confident in his timely piety, George Fraser leaned his cane against the car door and pulled his jacket straight before heading on to the house. His fingers lingered on the tail of the jacket, tracing the herringbone pattern of moss colored fabric. This was one of his favorite tweeds. From Harris in the Outer Hebrides, its wool was naturally fine and soft. Many years of wear had given it a further delicate, feathery touch. Its cut allowed for a range of movement without appearing baggy or loose. It was the perfect cool weather golfing uniform.

Mr. Tweed stood on the sidewalk in front of the short stone wall protecting the house's twin yards and tried to remember which door he should ring – the left or the right. Other than their paint color, they appeared identical. Before he forced a decision, Daniel Darrow stepped out of the blue door on the right. "I heard you pull up. You're right on time," the reverend shouted with a wave. Mr. Tweed smiled, considering the remark a compliment, and pushed open the gate with his cane. "Nice suit," Daniel said. Mr. Tweed had not consciously set out to impress the new reverend with his attire; yet, neither did he find this flattery unexpected. This suit deserved it. "Lighter than Sunday," Daniel observed.

"Of course," Mr. Tweed said. "We're golfing. Darks are for more serious pursuits. 'No brown in town,' and all."

Daniel reviewed his own clothing: khaki slacks, short-sleeved polo shirt, and a light windbreaker jacket. "I'm afraid I'm underdressed," he said.

"Most young people are," Mr. Tweed lamented.

Daniel followed Mr. Tweed to the right side of the car for a moment before he remembered to reverse the driver and passenger sides. As Mr. Tweed took his seat, Daniel noticed a fine, black residue covering the sides and bottoms of Mr. Tweed's shoes. This sooty grime contrasted with the otherwise impeccably dressed man. "I think you might have stepped in something," Daniel warned him as he looked around the sidewalk and nearby road.

Mr. Tweed glanced at his shoes with disgust and tapped the side of one with his cane. "A shame that," he said. "Left them close to the fireplace when I had it cleaned. Two weeks past and still stained."

Daniel replied with a knowing "Huh," and upon further reflection added, "Two weeks, wasn't that about the time of the Broonburn fire?"

"Ironic, eh? I'm having my chimney swept while theirs is burning down."

"You've worn them since then?" Daniel asked. "You mentioned golfing on Sunday."

"Amazing how the stuff lingers, isn't it?" Mr. Tweed put the car into gear and then looked at his watch. "Have you seen it?"

"Seen what?"

"Broonburn House, or what's left of her," Mr. Tweed said.

"No, just whatever's printed in the papers."

"It's really something you should see in person," Mr. Tweed said. He wrinkled his forehead, devising a plan. "We'll have less time than I'd prefer to warm up, but it's on the way. We shouldn't be late for our tee time at least."

"You're driving," Daniel answered. Mr. Tweed's impromptu proposal intrigued him. After the original newspaper he had bought at the Inverness airport, Daniel had collected several others with headlines describing the fire. Though speculation still varied, many commentators were beginning to circle around accidental electrical fire as the cause. This theory, however, could not explain the CCTV footage, obtained through unnamed sources of course, of a mysterious hooded figure entering the house shortly before the fire. Police had yet to pronounce an official assessment. As the regular

Broonburn bus stop was closed due to the ongoing investigation, Daniel had not had an opportunity to see the place for himself.

After several minutes of driving Daniel asked, "Are you sure it's on the way? You said we're going to the Torvean Club, right?" Daniel had lived in Inverness for nearly two weeks and he was still learning the streets and relative locations of its major sites. He knew how to get from Bellfield Park to Church Street. That was easy; just follow the River Ness north past the castle. He knew a few other locations and bus routes from his house calls and veterinary visit. He also knew how to look up locations online the night before. If his memory of internet maps proved true, Broonburn House lay nowhere near the Torvean Golf Club. Sure, they were both located on the west side of the Ness, so initially from Bellfield Park to the bridge, their paths coincided. Yet, after crossing the river, the two locales diverged significantly with Broonburn House just off the northeast shoreline and Torvean directly south. This fact stuck out in Daniel's mind because the Kinmylies Veterinary Clinic lay directly in between.

"Aye, they're not far," Mr. Tweed replied. Daniel was not convinced, but what could he do? He was not the one behind the wheel. They crossed the river and then the canal. Daniel watched houses and storefronts pass by as they headed toward the A862. Before they reached the highway, he noticed a woman in a long black dress walking what at first glance appeared to be a small dog along the sidewalk. The animal moved in an odd manner, causing Daniel's gaze to linger. When he realized he was watching Eliza MacGillivray with her rabbit on leash, he laughed. "What's that?" Mr. Tweed asked.

"Oh, nothing. I just saw Eliza MacGillivray walking her rabbit down the road," Daniel answered.

"Ha, you don't get much of that in the States, do you?"

"Can't say that we do."

"To be honest, neither do we," Mr. Tweed said. "But that's our Eliza. One of a kind, that one. I hear she spoke one of her prophecies to you."

"She did, two in fact. Word travels fast in Inverness," Daniel said.

"Word travels fast on Church Street," Mr. Tweed chuckled.

"Actually, I wonder if one of her prophecies might have to do with Broonburn. She certainly sounded dramatic when she brought up the subject. Something about fire and water running through the streets of the city."

"Ah, the old Brahan Seer prophecy. She doesn't usually recycle material like that. You know it's about modern plumbing and electrical lines."

"That's what I've heard," Daniel said.

Mr. Tweed turned onto the two-lane highway that wound around the coast of the Beauly Firth until it crossed the River Beauly and turned north toward Dingwall. He rolled down the car's windows so the cool, sea air could rush in. The calm bay waters mirrored the sky. Reverse cumulus clouds floated on gentle waves. "She predicted my son would be accepted to Oxford, you know. 'Eldest to eldest,' Eliza said. Collin is my oldest and Oxford is Britain's oldest university. It made sense. Of course, he always received top marks from school and I'm sure his recommendations from a few influential friends of mine helped, but still, you should not write off Eliza's gift. Perhaps it has a dual meaning – the prophecy she gave you."

"So, electricity *and* the Broonburn fire? But it's already burned down. Why would she tell me that after it had already happened?" Daniel asked.

"I don't know. Some people say Mr. Harrow had it coming."

"Who?"

"Alec Harrow, he owns Broonburn House, or did when there was still a house to own."

"That's just what she said!" Daniel said. "She didn't say his name, but she said the owner had it coming. What did he do to make people dislike him so?"

"Most people don't know or care who owns Broonburn these days. It's simply an icon, a piece of our heritage as much as the Castle or the Culloden battlefield. I know of him because I have certain friends. But I will tell you this, you don't get to be as wealthy as Alec Harrow without having a few skeletons in your closet."

That's just what people said about you, Daniel thought to himself.

Mr. Tweed put on his turn signal. "We're almost there." He slowed down and exited onto Auld Angus Rd. He drove down the narrow road until

50

reaching a tall iron gate attached to a stone fence. Behind the fence stood a row of short evergreen trees, several of which were charred in part if not entirely. Police tape hung from the closed gate, blocking the road in. Mr. Tweed pulled his car to the side of the fence. "We'll have to walk from here," he said.

"Are you sure we can go in? It looks fairly off limits," Daniel asked.

"Scotland has quite liberal outdoor access laws," Mr. Tweed said as he opened the car door and stepped out. He leaned back in and said, "If anyone asks, we were walking through the wood and became turned around. Say it with that American accent of yours and it'll sound believable."

His answer did nothing to calm Daniel's anxiety, quite the opposite. Nevertheless, Daniel exited the car and followed Mr. Tweed on foot along the outside of the stone fence. After several yards, they came to a partially collapsed section. Mr. Tweed seemed to expect this break. He peeked through and then scrambled over the loose stones. Spry, thought Daniel, for a man with a cane and wearing, in Mr. Tweed's words, "not quite the right costume for climbing." Apprehensive, Daniel followed.

On the other side he experienced the reality of what he had previously seen only in flat, newsprint images. The open blackness of the scene contrasted sharply with the blue and white sky and thick green of the Craighadrig Wood in the distance. A great lawn, once manicured and green, spread out barren and charred. Ancient trees looked like giant spent matchsticks. Some showed tiny new buds, struggling to push out some green. Others had been so overcooked they had no life left in them. The land no longer smoked as it did for days after the fire, like an old man's pipe using up the last of its snuff. Yet, with each step the two men took toward the epicenter, the ground crunched and swirled a fine ashy dust, as if the flames had sucked all the moisture out of the lush coastal soil and not even the persistent Scottish rains could replenish it.

Still a good distance away, nearly half a mile, Daniel could see the broken, blackened remains of Broonburn House. It must have been magnificent before, he thought. The front steps and stone foundation remained. Several of the old stone walls stood, cowering at significantly less than their previous stature. The collapse of the house's roof had broken them down and splayed their stony chunks about the immediate yard. The fire had so fully consumed the timber beams and support structure that only ashy splinters remained.

"They found a body," Mr. Tweed said, as Daniel stood transfixed by the sight of such massive destruction. Daniel blinked a few times back into consciousness.

"Huh, what did you say?"

"I said the police found a body. Inside, in a closet or behind the walls," Mr. Tweed repeated.

"A body? I thought it was unoccupied when the fire happened?" Daniel said.

"They thought so at first, but once investigators had a chance to really get in and have a look round, they uncovered a body. It was hard to find wasn't it – all burned up and nearly turned to ash itself. But bones nonetheless. A human skeleton. Unmistakable."

"None of the papers or anyone have mentioned anything about a body. How do you know?" Daniel asked. *Unless you put it there?*

"The police want to keep it hidden until they identify him, or her. But I have certain friends, you know," Mr. Tweed answered. "You mustn't mention I told you."

"No, I won't," Daniel assured him. "So, do they suspect murder? Or is the leading theory still accident?"

"With a body, the possibility of murder must be considered. I've always found the accidental fire thesis hard to fathom."

"Do your *friends* have additional information no one else knows?" Daniel asked.

"Certain indications sure, and my own suspicions." Mr. Tweed walked toward the ruined manor like a man strolling home from work – intentional, familiar. Unruffled by the devastation around him. He had obviously been here before. Whether he was most familiar with the place before or after the fire, Daniel could not determine.

As they approached the ruined heap that was once Broonburn House, a sudden movement startled them. A police officer appeared from around a blackened corner and spotted them. "No worries," Mr. Tweed said after a pause, with one hand blocking the sun from his squinting eyes, "I know him."

The police officer took several, swift, less than friendly steps toward them and shouted, "Oi, who's there?"

"On second glance, I don't know him," Mr. Tweed said, his voice betraying a hint of uneasiness for the first time since they had left his car. He looked at Daniel and said in a hushed tone, "I think we had best take our leave." He turned Daniel around, flipped his cane under his arm, and took hurried strides back toward the fence.

"Stop! This area is off-limits!" the police officer called out in pursuit.

As they ran, Daniel looked back and shouted, "We were out for a walk and got turned around in the woods." The officer's enthusiasm for the chase lessened the farther they retreated. When they reached the fence, Mr. Tweed scrambled through the broken part. Daniel followed him, but felt a pull on his leg just as he was nearly over. He winced, and closed his eyes, not wanting to look behind him, but knowing he had to. Knowing that when he opened them, he would see the police officer's hand around his ankle. A new newspaper headline flashed through his mind: *Evangelist or Terrorist? Foreigner caught fleeing the scene of the Broonburn murder.*

Daniel opened his eyes and breathed a sigh of relief. The leg of his slack had caught on a sharp piece of rock. "What are you waiting for?" Mr. Tweed said from the other side of the fence.

"I'm stuck. My pant leg is caught."

Mr. Tweed huffed, irritated. He pulled Daniel through, ripping the reverend's slacks in the process. Safely on the other side, the two men leaned against a cool, intact portion of fence and took deep breaths, allowing their heartbeats to return to a more normal pace. They looked at one another. Pent up adrenaline burst out as laughter.

Mr. Tweed leaned forward on his cane. "We're out for a walk and got turned around in the woods," he said, laughing, in an exaggerated American accent. "Brilliant!"

"That's what you told me to say."

"I just said that to get you over the fence."

"Well, it worked," Daniel said. "And my pants paid the price."

"Your pants. Mr. Darrow you are too much!" Mr. Tweed said, still laughing.

Daniel peeked over the fence. He saw the police officer who had chased them talking with another officer and then point. "I recall you also saying something about taking our leave. I think we have a little more leave still to take," Daniel said. Mr. Tweed followed close behind still chuckling to himself, "Got turned around in the woods, ha!"

* * *

The drive to the Torvean Golf Club occurred with no further detours. They took General Booth Rd. south through Kinmylies, passing the veterinary clinic along the way. Daniel wondered if Ellie Gray was working that morning. He replayed their last meeting in his head. It was the Tuesday morning after Sir Walter's appointment. They had made plans to meet for coffee. He arrived first. He sat, warming his hands around a mug. Rev. Calder had planned a supervisory meeting for that morning, but he had pushed it back. He did not tell her why. The coffee shop was small, but he managed to secure a table with a view toward the entrance. He waited as morning commuters came and went. Then the door opened and she walked through. Ellie did not see him immediately and he enjoyed this chance to observe her. She wore her light blue veterinary scrubs and her cinnamon hair back in a ponytail. Her presence filled the room, or rather she took the room into herself, assessing, determining – the same way she had when she'd entered the veterinary patient room two days prior. She smiled when she saw him. He returned her smile, dizzy and relieved. He waved her over.

"I see you've begun without me," Ellie said.

"Oh, um," Daniel looked down at his coffee, "I didn't know what you wanted."

"Americano."

"Really? I figured you for something a little sweeter."

"Thought I'd have a try at something new." She winked. They both laughed.

When Daniel returned with her drink and two scones, she asked him about Sir Walter.

"Good I suppose," Daniel said. "I haven't seen much of him since our visit. He kind of comes and goes as he pleases."

"That's Sir Walter."

"I guess so. Have you worked at the clinic long?" Daniel asked her.

"Not officially, no. I'm just completing my clinical EMS, em, extramural study at the Kinmylies Clinic now. It's nice to be closer to mum. But then I'm off again to Edinburgh for my final year. After that, who knows?"

"Will you return to Inverness?"

"I'd like to." She sipped her coffee. "I hope so, it really depends on job prospects."

"Well, Sir Walter and I were very satisfied with your service. I'll give you a glowing letter of recommendation if it helps."

Ellie laughed. "I'm sure you would."

Before Daniel knew it, their scones were all crumbs and only a thin dark film lined the bottoms of each of their mugs. Ellie glanced at her mobile phone for the time. She touched his hand.

"This has been fun. Thank you."

"Yes, um, oh, are you leaving?" Daniel asked.

"I'm sorry, but I must. My shift starts soon."

"Oh, of course. Um, we should do this again sometime."

Ellie smiled and withdrew her hand. She thought for a moment before standing. "Have you been up to Loch Ness?"

"You mean like the sea monster?"

Her eyes gave him a good-humored roll. "I don't know if Nessie will show, but yes, that Loch Ness. I'm off Friday. Do you have plans then?"

"No, me too. I mean I'm free." He would have to check his calendar, but an eraser and quick phone call could fix any conflict.

"Splendid. We'll make a day of it!"

* * *

A day of it. A *date* of it? Could he call it a date? She was a parishioner, or at the very least, a parishioner's daughter. He knew that caution was called for; yet caution was the last impulse he felt when he thought of her. Daniel stared absently out the passenger window of Mr. Tweed's car. He asked the driver if he knew Ellie Gray. "Everyone at Church Street knows wee Ellie, though she is not so wee anymore, is she? A picture of her mother when she was younger. Gorgeous young woman. Why do you ask?"

"Oh, no reason." Daniel did not want to admit to Mr. Tweed that he agreed with his assessment of wee Ellie. She was gorgeous. He smiled to himself. He had just trespassed, lied, and ran from a police officer. Caution could save itself for someone else. He would call it a date!

Chapter Eight

O ne of several courses in and around Inverness, the Torvean Golf Club is located on the outskirts of the city, south of the Kinmylies area, where the Caledonian Canal first meets the River Ness and parallels the river's southeasterly path into the mountainous lake of Loch Ness. It is a smaller golf course than several of its neighbors such as Narn to the north or Castle Stewart to the east, which boast striking coastal vistas, celebrity visits, and pricey greens fees to match. Yet for a small Inverness course, Torvean maintains an ease of play and view of the river and woodland that, if less dramatic than the rocky coast, add to the course's nestled charm.

On the morning that George Fraser arrived with Daniel Darrow at Torvean Golf Club, prestige was the last thing on the elder man's mind. George Fraser had chosen Torvean for two reasons. First, he had invited an unproven partner to join him. Though Rev. Darrow boasted a Carolina heritage, a land in George Fraser's mind that was second only to Scotland in golfing excellence, the young reverend had yet to translate the benefit of his birthplace into verifiable talent on the links. He could not afford to risk his own reputation by debuting a potentially unskilled, or worse, a slow, partner on a course like Castle Stewart, which hosts the Scottish Open. He did not tell Rev. Darrow this. Being a learned man of faith, Fraser thought, the reverend would understand. As the writer of Ecclesiastes had expounded: To everything there is a season. A time to be born and a time to die; a time to weep and a time to laugh; and surely, a time for municipal courses and a time for private clubs.

The second reason he had chosen Torvean, and the reason he had brought

Rev. Darrow along, as George Fraser did explain, was, "to throw off the friend of mine who will complete our threesome today. He has suddenly and quite unexpectedly lowered his handicap and I cannot fathom out how. I need a new set of eyes, so I want you to keep a watch on him – see if you notice anything unusual."

Daniel Darrow was not entirely sure what to make of his host's explanation. He took slight offence to the notion that his invitation included an ulterior motive. George Fraser, or Mr. Tweed, was not simply interested in his friendship. Regarding this ulterior motive, Daniel was further unsure how helpful he could be. Mr. Tweed had, in his indirect way, accused his friend of cheating. Yet, without knowing this person, Daniel was uncertain as to what qualities or incidents might qualify as *unusual*. Nevertheless, the prospect of spending more time with Mr. Tweed intrigued him – this man with such an inexplicable knowledge of crime scenes, not to mention fashion sense. As far as Daniel was concerned, Mr. Tweed more than met the conditions for *unusual*.

When they reached the course, Mr. Tweed glanced at his wristwatch. "Hmm, we still have time to warm up, hit a few practice balls," he said.

"Well, you did pick me up pretty early," Daniel said, only half joking. Mr. Tweed nodded as if he had received a compliment. Then he noticed Daniel's trouser leg. The broken fence at Broonburn House had ripped the seam from the knee to the cuff, fully exposing the lower half of the reverend's leg. He then looked at his own shoes, encased in mud, and made a disapproving huff.

"This simply will not do," Mr. Tweed said. "I've a spare pair of shoes in the boot and we must get you a new set of trousers." He retrieved his spare shoes and led Daniel into a small retail section of the clubhouse. "Find your size and put it on my tab."

"That's nice of you, but I can pay for my own pants," Daniel said.

The young man behind the checkout counter giggled. Mr. Tweed frowned. "Trousers. And I insist. I hauled you over that silly fence. There's a changing room back there. I'm going to switch these out and head to the practice green. We're on at 9:00 sharp. Do not be late." He turned toward the changing room before Daniel had a chance to respond.

Daniel looked through the display shelves and found a pair of pants. He took them to the cashier with every intention of paying for them himself. That is until the young man told him the price. Daniel's eyes widened. "Hold on, I need to find something less expensive."

"These are the less expensive ones," the young man said.

"Oh, um, put it on Mr. Tw- um, Mr. Fraser's tab," Daniel said.

The cashier nodded and rang them up. He handed them back to Daniel with a childish smile. "Your trousers, sir." Daniel gave him a puzzled look. "Here, *pants* mean knickers, underwear."

Daniel returned a tight lipped, blushing smile, grabbed the trousers, and headed for the changing room. When he entered, he saw Mr. Tweed, now in fresh, shiny shoes, close a footlocker door. "9:00," Mr. Tweed said as he left.

Daniel sat down on the bench near the lockers and took off his own muddy, ash -stained shoes. He tried to wipe them off with a paper towel from the sink as best he could. Mr. Tweed should understand. After all, he had shown up to Daniel's flat that morning in a pair of ash-stained shoes. Marks still noticeable two weeks after Mr. Tweed had said they'd first become stained. *What was it he had said?* That he was sweeping his chimney while the one at Broonburn House was burning down? Daniel held up his own shoes to get a better look. He tried to remember the exact color of the stains on Mr. Tweed's shoes. Had they been this dark? If they matched, it could mean Mr. Tweed had been on that lawn before. Had he been there the night it burned?

Daniel returned to the lockers. *Now, which locker had Mr. Tweed stored his old shoes in? There!* He bent down and pulled at the locker door. Locked. He gave the handle a jiggle, but it held shut. "Worth a shot," he sighed. Daniel removed his trousers and examined the tear. He shook his head. They were ruined. He was thankful his leg had not shared a similar fate. Only a thin, jagged line with a few drops of dried blood were visible on his calf. The mark had barely even broken the skin. He picked up the new pair of trousers and removed a pin that held them in a crisp, folded position. He looked for a trash bin, but hesitated. He looked at the pin, then to Mr. Tweed's locker. Another quick glance around the room told him that he was alone.

It was a simple enough looking lock. He'd seen more complicated locks picked with everything from a hair pin to a credit card a thousand times on TV shows. How hard could it be? Daniel inserted the pin into the keyhole. He wiggled and scraped it around, but nothing happened. He took the pin out, bent it at a forty-five-degree angle and tied again. This time he was more careful. He felt something inside move, then another. A final faint *click* and the locker door opened. Daniel couldn't believe his good luck.

He was about to look inside, when he heard the door to the changing room open. Had Mr. Tweed forgotten something? Daniel froze, then hurried to the far corner of the room. The row of lockers did not extend across the full length of the wall and there was just enough space for a man to squeeze between them and the adjoining wall. This position hid Daniel from view of the doorway, but it also meant he couldn't see who had entered.

"Doesn't someone clean this room at night?" a voice asked. Daniel did not recognize the speaker.

"Yes, but I'm supposed to check it before we open. I already saw two go in. One was George Fraser and you know how he can be," a second voice said. This one Daniel recognized as that of the young cashier.

"Better late than never."

"I hope so. If the night cleaner didn't do a good job, I'm sure to hear about it. Fraser once lectured me for twenty minutes on the proper way to fold and put away a shirt," the cashier said.

"That's nothing. You should've been here the day that old house was sold. You know, the one that burned down two weeks ago?"

"Broonburn?"

"Aye, that's the one. He and his mates were having a celebratory round at the bar. Seems they thought they'd bought the place. Were going on about how they were going to turn the estate into a five-star golfclub. One that would rival Castle Stewart, put our little club to shame. Then one of 'em gets a call. Seems they were outbid at the last second. Oh, you should've seen the looks on their faces. I've never seen a redder bunch of Scotsmen. Simply fuming all of them and cursing. And ol' George Fraser was the worst. Good thing that new buyer was from out of town or I'd swear Fraser would've murdered him right there on the spot!"

"And I would've been the one to have to clean up the mess the next morning!" the cashier said. They both laughed. "Well, it looks tidy enough in here to me. What you do you say, Sean?"

"Good. I say it's time for our break."

"I wish."

"Look, someone left their trousers there. Can you imagine ol' George Fraser strolling around in his knickers!" Sean laughed.

Daniel looked down at his own naked legs. He closed his eyes, praying the two young men would leave without checking the rest of the room. How could he possibly explain his being wedged in the corner behind the lockers in nothing but his shirt and boxers. He couldn't even explain it too himself. He had simply panicked when he heard the door open. He had a clear view of the sink and saw his shoes laying under it where he'd dropped them. *Dear Lord, please let these boys be as lazy as they sound and just leave.*

"Hello? Anyone in here?" the cashier shouted. Daniel held his breath. "Guess not."

"What about that mess on the bench?"

"They're not tweed so they can't be Mr. Fraser's. Leave 'em. I could swear I just sold a pair just like that to some American. Called 'em pants."

Sean chuckled. "I don't pretend to understand Americans. All I know is the thicker your *Scot'ish accent mate*," he said with great exaggeration, "the thicker they tip!" They both laughed. Daniel heard a locker door slam, more laughter, then the changing room door open and shut.

Daniel waited another minute to be certain they were not returning before he squeezed out of the corner. The door to Mr. Tweed's locker was shut. Daniel tried it, but it wouldn't budge. He scanned the floor for the bent pin when a clock on the wall chimed 9:00. Late! He would have to find another time to examine the shoes. He slipped on his new trousers not bothering to tuck in his shirt or tie his shoes. He hurried out the door to find Mr. Tweed, hoping his tardiness would not put his host in another murderous mood.

Chapter Nine

At the clubhouse, George Fraser gave their names to the Starter who warned them that he had nearly given their tee time to another group. "I've held your time, Mr. Fraser, but we mustn't delay our other players," he said.

George Fraser took this as an insult to his character and reprimanded the man. "You know well enough I have arrived precisely at the time scheduled. True, I was not early, but neither was I late and a man should not be shamed simply for being punctual. It is my colleague here who was delayed." He glowered at Daniel then returned to the Starter. "I should hope in the future you will direct your criticisms to the appropriately guilty party. In all my years as a member of this club, I have never missed a tee time, have I?"

"I- if you say so. I'm not certain," the Starter stammered, taken aback by this verbal blitzkrieg.

"Of course I haven't."

Daniel offered the poor man an apology that he knew was insufficient and then followed Mr. Tweed to the first tee. Their third member, Mr. Tweed's suspect friend, had already arrived, hit several practice balls, and was waiting for them at the tee. He was stocky, bordering on rotund. He wore a flat hat similar to Mr. Tweed's, a sporty looking sweater (as sporty as it is possible for a sweater to look), and blue trousers. He appeared irritated.

"There you are!" the man said. "You'll have no time to warm up. We're on next."

"That's entirely my fault, I'm so sorry," Daniel said.

"Let's not make a habit of it," Mr. Tweed said. He straightened his jacket and adjusted his hat. "Mr. James Hall, this is Mr. Daniel Darrow, our new Reverend at Church Street." The two shook hands.

"Nice to meet you. Have we met at church?" Daniel asked.

"I shouldn't think so," Mr. Tweed interjected. "James here is a papist."

"St. Mary's," James Hall clarified. "Religion aside, we're up." The last member of the group in front of them hit his ball and started down the fairway after it. "First to arrive, first to tee?" James Hall said, more an assertion than question.

"Fair is fair," Mr. Tweed agreed.

The three men gathered their clubs, Daniel borrowing an old set from Mr. Tweed, and took their places. Daniel and Mr. Tweed stood back while James Hall aligned himself in the middle of the tee box. He took a few practice swings while waiting for the previous group to move a little farther down the fairway.

"Watch him now," Mr. Tweed whispered to Daniel. "I know he's cheating; I simply can't work out how."

Mr. Hall pressed a ball and wooden tee into the soft, manicured ground. He adjusted his stance, bent his knees slightly, and pulled back his driver. Just when the club reached its zenith, he stopped and scurried back to his bag. "Almost forgot," he said. He unzipped a pocket to reveal two white golfing gloves.

"Come on James, it's not cold enough for those," Mr. Tweed said. His friend ignored him and, with a little difficulty, put on his gloves. He took another practice swing. "See his feet?" Mr. Tweed whispered. "He'll slice right." His friend swung and the ball soared through the air, straight.

"Did you see her?" Mr. Hall exclaimed. "Down the middle. A perfect beauty!"

"Aye, we saw. Nice shot, James," Mr. Tweed said. To Daniel he muttered, "I simply can't fathom it." Mr. Tweed took his place on the tee box and hit his ball nearly as far as his friend but much closer to a sand bunker on the right of the green. When Daniel stepped up, he paused for a moment, took a breath, and entrusted his fate to muscle memory. He considered saying a quick prayer but figured God had already done him one favor that morning and was likely too busy fielding requests from football, basketball, and all manner of other sports fans. He straightened his feet, pulled back the driver, and swung. The club scrapped the top of the ball, causing it to slide clumsily off the tee and roll a few feeble yards forward. *At least it rolled straight*, he thought.

"Don't be afraid to get some earth in your swing," Mr. Hall said. Mr. Tweed said nothing. He simply nodded in approval of his own decision not to have booked a game at a more prestigious club. Daniel hit his ball twice more to get it near the green alongside the other two. As they walked down the fairway, Mr. Tweed's friend asked them about their late arrival that morning, or near late, as Mr. Tweed corrected him. "It's just that you're usually more prompt than that," he said.

"We had an impromptu walk in the wood," Mr. Tweed said with a wink at Daniel.

"Ah, out on a wee walkabout as they say? Where to?" Mr. Hall asked.

"He's from America, not Australia," Mr. Tweed said.

"No worries, mate," Daniel joked. "We were out around Broonburn House," he said, "or what's left of it."

"Broonburn House, aye, our local mystery. That's become a favorite topic of George's," Mr. Hall said. "Has he told you about the body?" Daniel nodded. "I didn't believe him at first, but he has a way of finding things out. It's a wonder no official police report mentions it, though."

"In these types of cases, you don't want to show all of your cards prematurely," Mr. Tweed said. "But I'm certain they'll say something before long."

"What about you, Reverend? Who do you think did it?" Mr. Hall asked Daniel.

Daniel glanced at Mr. Tweed then quickly down at the grass, trying to avoid staring at Mr. Tweed's shoes. "I think it's too soon to say. If Mr. Tw-uh, Fraser, George, is right and there is a body, then we don't even have all the evidence before us to make an informed judgment," Daniel responded.

"Oh, don't give me that. Everyone's got a theory – electrical short, gangs, some secret vendetta, lone wolf terrorism, and now murder, maybe a cover-up. My money's still on electrical. With all the builders' equipment running on those ancient lines, bound to be a short somewhere," Mr. Hall said.

"What about the CCTV footage?" Daniel asked. He had seen a news story showing leaked closed-circuit security footage from the night of the fire. It showed a grainy, shadow of a figure appear from behind a hedge, climb the front steps, open the door, and enter the house. No images existed of the figure exiting. The camera had stopped recording by then. The video had sparked a fervor of new speculation and conspiracy theories amongst those interested in the case, a group that made up the majority population of Inverness. "If the fire was just caused by a freak electrical short, how do you explain that person entering the house just before the whole place went up in flames?"

"Humph, that video. Doesn't show anything. People make a big deal about the man entering and then never exiting. Humph. I'll tell you what happened: some builder left his phone or wallet or what have you and didn't notice until that night. So he goes back, uses his key to enter - the video did not show forced entry. He retrieves the forgotten item and leaves. There's no video of him leaving because the fire fried the lines. Only reason we have a video is because their security system stores its files off site," Mr. Hall said. He thought for a moment. "You know, that video actually supports my theory of an electrical short. What else would cut the video feed? These things are rarely as fantastic as people make out."

"A person could cut a camera cable," Daniel said.

"I see why you like him, George. He thinks like you," Mr. Hall laughed.

The Broonburn fire continued to occupy the three men's conversation until they reached the green on the first hole. Daniel and James Hall continued their attempts at persuading Mr. Tweed to divulge the source of his secret information. Mr. Tweed continued to refuse, only answering their pleas with evasions or further questions. Once on the green, Mr. Tweed's attention refocused on more immediate concerns. Mr. Hall was furthest out, so he took the first putt. With his friend occupied, Mr. Tweed pulled Daniel close and whispered, "Any thoughts yet? See anything unusual?"

"Too soon to say. This is only the first hole, and unfortunately, I've hit more than either one of you," Daniel replied. He had, however, noticed one irregularity that he was not yet ready to mention. It was the small matter of Mr. Hall taking off his gloves when he went to putt. The weather that morning did not especially mandate gloves, so perhaps he had simply changed his mind about wearing them. Yet, when they teed up at the second hole, Daniel noticed that the gloves were back on. And once again, James Hall hit a long, straight shot that landed perfectly between a midway bunker and the tree lined out-of-bounds. This pattern continued throughout the game: gloves on the tee, bare hands on the green. By the time they reached the eleventh or twelfth hole, Daniel was certain this pattern was no coincidence.

Just then, a small boat passed them, floating along a section of the Caledonian Canal that bordered the golf course on its eastern side. Several of the men on deck waved and shouted incomprehensible words at the golfers. The threesome waved back and Mr. Tweed took this distraction as an opportunity to whisper his question again to Daniel.

"First, I need to ask *you* a question," Daniel whispered back. "What specifically in your friend's game have you noticed change? I mean, is it his long game or short?"

Mr. Tweed thought for a moment. "Long," he answered, just before the boat passed out of sight behind a border of trees. "He's been gaining on his drives, but still makes rookie mistakes on the green. That's the only way I've been able to keep up lately."

"And you're sure he's not just been practicing more?"

"Certain."

Daniel thought for a moment, absently grinding the head of his club into the grass. "That is a puzzler," he said. "I have an idea, but you'll have to let me think on it."

"The round is nearly over," Mr. Tweed said impatiently.

"An investigation takes time. Surely your secret sources have told you that."

Chapter Ten

A sudden downpour caused Daniel Darrow and Ellie Gray to hide under the protection of a long-ruined castle on the bank of Loch Ness. Rain poured over the ancient stone ledge that was once a great tower overlooking the loch, or lake. The outer wall of the room where the couple sheltered was exposed, having succumbed to the decay of time and weather long ago. This forced its present occupants to huddle close in one of the surviving, semi-sheltered corners. They had been caught off guard by the shower; wet beads dripped from their hair, rolled off the tips of their noses, and met the lingering drops that covered their entwined hands. Wet, though not drenched, they could still laugh at their predicament and the sudden, nervous intimacy that it precipitated.

They considered themselves lucky to find what drafty shelter they could. Had they taken a right instead of a left when they crossed the wooden gangway leading up to Urquhart Castle, they would now be as soaked as if they had gone for a swim in the loch that surrounded the castle on three sides. To the right of the gatehouse, only foundation stones and waist-high walls stood. When the storm clouds broke, visitors on this side of the castle roosted under their outspread umbrellas or fled up the hill to the dry safety of the Visitors Center.

* * *

Three centuries earlier another rain had fallen on Urquhart Castle. Though, instead of a sprightly afternoon shower, this storm laid siege to the castle.

Weakened from centuries of warfare and decades of neglect, the stone and mortar of its walls shook under the force of the storm winds. The entire southwest side of the castle's great tower collapsed, exposing its inner rooms.

Crippled and uninhabitable, much of the castle's remaining structures were slowly dismantled by local residents of the glen and used to shore up and repair their own homes. Thus, when the great storm struck, it met with little fortified resistance. The demise of Urquhart Castle, the crashing of its walls and slow evacuation of the stones that had given it strength for so many centuries, foreshadowed the larger devastation that would come to the Highlands in the form of the great Clearances. Nearly twenty miles north of the castle, the unrest of one such Clearance would spark the fall of another great icon of power and privilege – Broonburn House.

* * *

"You knew him?" Daniel Darrow asked Ellie Gray as they finished their lunch in the café adjoining the Urquhart Castle Visitors Center. The day before, police had finally disclosed their discovery of a body within the charred remains of Broonburn House. They had simultaneously released the name of the body. That name, Tom Shaw, now appeared on the fronts of papers in all the local newsstands.

"Not well, but I remember his name. I might have met him at a party once. I didn't even notice until I read he studied at Edinburgh," Ellie said. She put her fork and napkin on her plate and pushed her chair back. Daniel understood her cue and stood.

"Ready to go?" he asked.

She nodded. "Hard to fathom it. Tom Shaw, killed, burned up in that house. Must have been terrifying." She shook her head to rid her mind of the image. Daniel wanted to put his arm around her, in part to comfort, in part to simply be nearer to her. Out of her veterinary scrubs, she appeared more beautiful than he remembered. Her familiar ponytail, a practical piece of her uniform, was now transformed into straightened locks parted down the middle and resting just below her shoulders. She wore a slim green striped sweater, dark coffee colored trousers, and a light rain jacket. The outfit was sensible, appropriate to the day's task, yet it possessed a sense of casualness and conviviality reflective of its wearer. Dreary dispositions do not lend themselves to green striped sweaters.

Though Daniel and Ellie had met on casual terms previously, the meeting had been brief. Their coffee date must not have gone too poorly, otherwise they would not now be spending the afternoon together. Daniel tried to keep the nervous sweat on his palms to himself, for while he might appear witty and agreeable in small doses, he was uncertain whether he could sustain such charm over the length of an afternoon. He found a morbid comfort in discussing the Broonburn fire. It provided a wealth of common interest in addition to a welcome distraction from his nerves.

"I heard that Tom Shaw is now the prime suspect for starting the fire. Though police are still working on a motive," Daniel said as they waited in line for admission to the castle.

"Really? They think Tom was an arsonist? I had my money on someone with a vendetta against the owner. Oh, what's his name?" Ellie asked.

"The owner? I don't know. Mr. Tw-, uh, Mr. Fraser, seems to know him. Do you know George Fraser? From Church Street?"

"Of course. He's always so smartly dressed."

"Yes, I've never seen him without a suit. Mr. Tweed is what I call him in my mind to help me remember," Daniel said.

"Ha, Mr. Tweed!" Ellie snorted. "Or Sir Tweedy. The Earl of Tweed. I've only ever said hello to him in passing, but he seems like the kind of man who would be an earl of something. Not something very important, mind you, but just enough so that he could hold his nose a little higher than everyone else."

"I think you've about summed him up. Of course the nickname must stay between us."

"You don't want people thinking their shiny new reverend makes up names for them behind their backs?" she teased.

"It's only a mnemonic device."

"Hmm, sure."

"Eight pound fifty," the elderly man behind the ticket desk said. Daniel fished for his wallet. He fingered through a small collection of colorful bills and pulled out a light purple one with a picture of Sir Walter Scott (not the cat) on the front.

"Two please," Daniel said.

"You don't have to," Ellie said. "This trip was my idea."

Daniel handed her a ticket stub. "The price for your silence."

"I see," she laughed. She entwined her arm in his and ushered him out the Visitors Center door.

The early afternoon sun shone brightly in contrast to the dark clouds that waited in the distance. When his eyes adjusted to the brightness, Daniel gazed down upon a scene of green and gray and blue. A green cropped lawn stretched down the hill from the Visitors Center. It held fiercely to the memory of summer despite ochre indications in the surrounding forests. The lawn halted in a ringed indention around the castle, evidence of its late moat. Bridging the dry moat, a wooden gangway led visitors to the castle's arched gatehouse. A broken stone wall stretched out to the right and up another short hill. To the left, he could see more crumbling wall and a tower on a piece of shore that jutted out into the loch. Beyond the castle ruins lay the loch, another strip of green hills, and finally the blue darkening sky.

Daniel paused to take in the picture. Ellie, whose arm was still entwined in his, was pulled to an abrupt stop. "Right," she said, "I forget. You haven't seen this before." She stood beside him. "I took loads of family trips here as a kid."

"It's beautiful," Daniel said. He waited for Ellie to agree, but she seemed unimpressed. The ruined castle reminded him of Broonburn House. "We can keep going."

"No, you're right. It is beautiful. It's just that being here, it made me think of my mum. She hasn't seemed herself lately," Ellie said.

"Really? Is she sick?"

"She seems in fine health."

"You said your dad passed away. I don't mean to bring up bad memories, but could the anniversary of his passing be near?" Daniel asked.

"No, my da died in spring - March. Of course Mum took it hard then. We all did. How can you not? But that was," she hesitated, "six years past." Daniel put a comforting arm on her shoulder. She leaned into him. "Hard to believe," she continued. "Time is weird that way – sometimes it seems like just last Sunday, Da and I walking along the Ness. Sometimes it feels like ages ago."

"I'm sorry I brought it up," Daniel said. "I haven't experienced it myself, but I don't think losing a parent is something you really ever get over fully."

"No. Nor would I want to. But this thing with Mum now – it's different. I can remember her grieving. This isn't like that. It has some other element to it I can't figure out. It's more like depression – emotional, social withdrawal. Like, she's skipping afternoon tea with her ladies, these old mates of hers; it's usually the highlight of her day. But lately she never leaves the house."

"I saw her last Sunday at church. She's the one who introduced me to Sir Walter," Daniel said.

"Well, the kirk is the only place she does go and she stays longer. Have you noticed that?" Ellie asked.

Daniel thought for a moment. "At the end of the service, she did linger in her pew, though I don't think that's anything to be concerned about. Some people prefer to wait out the crowd as everyone's leaving. I haven't noticed her for tea afterward, though. Do you think she's simply developed a distaste for tea?"

"Hmm." Ellie smiled. "That would be a worry, wouldn't it. No, it's not that. Maybe more of a paranoia? But she's too young still for her mind to be slipping. She's sharp when I talk to her. But, there's something, like she's worried of someone watching her – stays in, checks the windows often. And then the gloves. Have you noticed the gloves?"

Gloves again, Daniel thought. First with Mr. Tweed's golfing friend and now Elspeth Gray. "Yes, I've seen them. Reverend Calder commented how nice they look on her. She said they were fashionable."

"Mum's never gone in for gloves before. Perhaps it *is* her health. Poor circulation can make your extremities colder."

"You mentioned depression. That can produce physical symptoms as well,"

Daniel said.

"I don't have much expertise in that area. Veterinary school didn't offer any classes on depression. Though I sometimes wonder if it should; I've seen some animals, especially pets whose owners have died or moved, that lose their appetites and exhibit a general listlessness that really has no other medical explanation. Or other social animals like horses. You know they need a stable mate to keep their spirits up? Anything will do really – another horse, donkey, even a cat. They just need to be with someone."

"I'm sure," Daniel said. "I can look in on your mother if you'd like. Visitations are a normal part of my job. Maybe she needs someone to talk to. An outside set of ears can sometimes help."

"Could you? Thank you. I'm not trying to pry, or keep tabs on her; I'm just worried. I'm her daughter."

They left the overlook from the Visitors Center and continued down the lawn that led to the castle. Before they reached the dry moat, they passed a giant wooden trebuchet that, at its zenith, reached to a height of at least five grown men. Using its long throwing arm and counterweight to hurdle projectiles, this massive medieval war machine now stood docile – a mere replica for wide-eyed tourists. Daniel and Ellie paused to examine it. "Do you think a good person could do a bad thing for a good reason?" she asked him.

"Like should you hurtle a big rock at a castle?" Daniel asked. "Do the ends justify the means? You're mighty philosophical all of a sudden."

"Philosophical perhaps, though not so Machiavellian – more domestic. I was just thinking, what cause might warrant an illegal or immoral action? Or could a good end make the immoral means moral? Doesn't your theology have anything to say?"

"There are the classic examples or thought experiments, such as God ordering Abraham to sacrifice his son Isaac. Would a good God truly ask for human sacrifice or even the willingness to kill another human for faith's sake? Ultimately, so the biblical story goes, an angel provided a ram to take Isaac's place on the alter, but the intent was still there. Or, if you lived in Germany during the Holocaust, would it be ok to lie, a sin, in order to save the life of a Jewish person hiding in your basement? Different theologians would give different answers. St. Augustine, for example, took a strict stance against lying for whatever reason."

"Hmm," she reflected. Her finger traced a crack along the wooden railing of the trebuchet. "I'm not so interested in a lecture in moral philosophy. I want to know what would you do?"

"I think I would need more information," Daniel said. "I would need to know the story behind the situation. I think we run into trouble, morally, when we abstract such questions from history or the people they affect. Not that morality is all just situational, but I do think the larger narrative needs to be considered," Daniel said.

"You're no help."

"Sorry," Daniel said. "I have a feeling we're not just talking about trebuchets. Is this about Tom Shaw?"

"Maybe," Ellie said. "I'm not sure. Arson just doesn't seem to fit his character. What's his motive? Granted, I didn't know him well, but I know he studied film. Why would an arts student destroy such a beautiful old house like Broonburn?"

"You know before the police decided on Tom, I had a few suspicions of my own. I suppose everyone did," Daniel said. They crossed the gangway over the moat. Its dark wood held on to the moisture of a recent shower. Daniel looked up at the clear sky. "Huh, it doesn't look like rain."

"This is Inverness. If it's not presently raining, you can be sure it just finished or is about to start," Ellie said. Then she pointed to the dark clouds waiting behind the hills on the far side of the loch.

"Do you think they'll get us?" Daniel asked. Ellie shrugged. They passed through the gatehouse and Daniel felt the temperature drop a few degrees in its ancient shade. He ran his fingers along the cool, hard stone. On the other side of the gatehouse, the remains of Urquhart Castle fanned out before them. The walls, crumbled rectangular traces of once grand rooms and halls, now stood waist high at their tallest. To the left, the castle's tower beckoned them.

"You had suspicions?" Ellie asked Daniel. "About Broonburn House?"

"Oh, yes. I'm sure it sounds ridiculous to anyone else, but I thought I noticed suspicious behavior from a few people at Church Street. I know I don't really have much to compare to, having only just met them." They entered an ancient room open to the sky and grass. "What do you think this was?" Daniel asked.

"Are you trying to change the subject? You can't just say you suspected someone of murder and then not tell who!"

"Well, not murder necessarily. No one officially knew about Tom Shaw until yesterday."

"Arson then. You must tell," Ellie insisted.

Daniel stretched to peek over the edge of the outer wall in the small open room. He watched a motorboat speed by, cutting the loch's gentle waves. "That'll sure scare away any Loch Ness Monsters."

"Monster," Ellie corrected. "There's only one – Nessie. And you're still stalling."

"Ok. The most obvious is Eliza MacGillivray, the, I don't know what you would call her? The prophetess, the seer of Church Street?" Daniel said. Ellie laughed. "Seriously. You've met her?" Daniel continued. Ellie nodded. "Well, then you must know what I mean. She's not as frail as she appears. She carries that rabbit of hers around in a bag – it can't be light and she has a surprisingly strong grip. I was talking with her and the subject of Broonburn House came up; she had no kind words. She sounded almost threatening – suggested it was deserved."

"Eliza MacGillivray's odd, but she's no arsonist," Ellie said. "Having an extra perceptive intuition doesn't make her a criminal. She knew that I would take my degree in veterinary sciences. Back when I was a wee child, she told me. I wish I could remember her exact words. They sounded so mysterious and wise then. Did she give you a prophecy?"

"Everyone keeps asking me that. Yes, two in fact. They were both very vague, or mysterious as you say. Something about furry feet and love and fire and water running down the streets of Inverness."

They exited the open room and continued toward the castle's tower. A couple with a small child passed them, having already toured the tower. The child hopped along with his arms outstretched and made buzzing noises. When he decided to walk a balance beam on the edge of the walking path, the child's mother took one of his hands for stability.

Ellie paused to bend down and wave at the child. "Did you glimpse Nessie?" The child nodded.

"Really? Where?"

The child looked back at the tower. "I don't know," he said and continued buzzing along the edge of the path.

"Bonny lad," Ellie said to the couple. They smiled, thanked her, and continued down the path. Ellie sat on a wooden rail bench located near the tower entrance and motioned for Daniel to join her. "If Eliza MacGillivray's your number one suspect, I'm glad you didn't go to the police. That would have just been embarrassing."

"Ok. How about George Fraser, Mr. Tweed?" Daniel asked. Ellie raised her eyebrows. "I'm serious. Here's my reasoning: Fraser somehow knows things about the case that regular people shouldn't know. He knew about the body before the police released it. I don't know if he knew Tom Shaw's name, but he knew there was a body. He also seems to know the owner of Broonburn House and they're definitely *not* friends. A Mr. H- it started with an H. What's his name?" Daniel looked at Ellie who could offer no help. "Harris? Harrow? Anyway, Mr. Tweed knows him while no one else around here does."

"So, he knows a man? That doesn't mean he would burn down Mr. H's house," Ellie said.

"No, but combined with other things it starts to look kind of suspicious. Earlier this week, he invited me for golf. But we had a little detour first. He took me to Broonburn House. He parked his car out of sight and led me to a broken part in the wall so we could climb over and get a closer look. He seemed to know exactly where he was going, like he'd done it before. Oh, and he had soot stains on his shoes! He claims it was from a messy chimney sweep, but- " Daniel shrugged suggestively.

"George Fraser, setting fire to Broonburn House and then fleeing over a wall in the middle of the night? Did he break the wall himself to make his escape easier – maybe with his cane?" Ellie teased.

"Mock if you will, but when you add up all the pieces it kind of makes sense."

"That'd be the scandal of the century, wouldn't it," Ellie said.

While Daniel and Ellie talked, the dark clouds waiting on the horizon made their silent advance upon the castle. The storm announced its arrival with a loud clap of thunder that felt as if it might shatter Urquhart's remaining walls. Within seconds a volley of heavy, wet projectiles fell from the sky. Gasps and cringed shock issued from those tourists too slow to don their waterproof gear as cold rain cut through their cloth garments. Used to such sudden downpours, Ellie acted instinctively. She grabbed Daniel's hand and rushed him into the tower. Following her lead, other tourists quickly piled into the tower's protective entrance. The steam of so many confined, wet bodies stifled the air so Ellie ushered Daniel up a narrow corkscrew stairwell. The steep incline and slick stone steps made them grasp at the claustrophobic, cylindrical walls for support.

The stairs eventually opened into a cavernous, vacant room. They breathed in the cool, rain soaked air. This was made easy by the room's lack of an intact ceiling and southwesterly walls. Those had fallen centuries earlier from a similarly sudden, though far more destructive, storm. From the exposed side of the tower Daniel and Ellie could see people below huddled under umbrellas or scattering toward the roofed protections of the gatehouse and visitors center.

Daniel and Ellie stood close together in the corner of the room to take advantage of its narrow cover. Rain poured off the exposed stone all around them and lingering drops ran down their faces. A burst of spontaneous laughter erupted from them both. "Wow," Daniel said, catching his breath. "What just happened?"

"Welcome to Scotland," Ellie said. "When you're tired of sunshine, we've got you covered." They both laughed again.

Their laughter quickly turned from exuberant release into nervous realization of their physical closeness and the sudden privacy the storm allowed them. Ellie still held Daniel's hand from when she first led him up the tower. With his free hand, Daniel reached tentatively toward her face and brushed aside a wet lock of hair that clung to her cheek. White fog began to form inside the auburn frames of her glasses. His hand hesitated at the back of her neck. She gave a slight nod and he leaned in to kiss her. Her lips tasted like honey lip gloss and rain.

Chapter Eleven

A damp chill lingered in the London cellar. The room's climate never strayed from the cooler side of the temperate zone, but on this frosty fourth night of November in 1605, the cellar seemed especially cold to its lone inhabitant. The sweat on his brow did not help. Though his nerves needed more cooling than his body, the physical effect remained the same – involuntary perspiration. He pulled his cloak tightly around his tall, athletic frame. From his perch atop a stack of lumber near the entrance he surveyed the room. It was tight for a cellar. The low ceiling required that he remove his hat, high and wide brimmed in the fashion of the day. Still, the room had space enough for his purposes. It had space enough to hold thirty-six barrels of gunpowder.

Guy Fawkes, or Guido as he liked to call himself, though for his present venture he had assumed the innocuous alias John Johnson, recalled the events that had led him to this damp cellar with a flint and steel in one pocket and a long fuse in the other. He had grown up in England, York specifically, at a time in European history when many Christians felt war to be the most expedient solution to their conflicting interpretations of Scripture. He spent the majority of his twenties fighting on the continent for the Catholic Spanish against the Protestant Dutch in a conflict that history would eventually dub the Eighty Years War. On the battlefield, Fawkes quickly established a reputation for which he was quite proud: military strategist and munitions expert.

It was the latter skill that led him to his current position sitting atop thirty-six barrels of gunpowder in a cellar beneath the English Parliament buildings.

While fighting in Flanders, a fellow Englishman recruited him for a plot back home against the Protestant King James I of England (born James VI of Scotland). For eighteen months, Fawkes and twelve others worked out their plan. They rented a cellar that lay beneath the Parliamentary House of Lords. Directly above, separated only by a thin layer of board and brick, sat the chair that would eventually seat King James as he presided over Parliament's opening day. Throughout the summer and fall they filled the cellar with explosive barrels – enough to reduce the building to a smoldering heap – more than sufficient to kill a king. Fawkes assumed the most dangerous role in their gunpowder plot. When the king entered Parliament on the fifth of November, Fawkes would put flame to fuse and in his words, "blow you Scotch beggars back to your native mountains!"

Ten minutes before midnight on November 4th, Guy Fawkes, aka John Johnson, reviewed the kindling he had arranged earlier that evening. Anxiety made him restless and he still had several hours to wait. A surprise inspection of the cellar by the Lord Chamberlain that afternoon had nearly pushed his already frayed nerves over the edge. Fawkes uttered a quick prayer of thanksgiving that the gunpowder barrels had been sufficiently concealed.

Five minutes to midnight, he froze silent at the sound of– yes, he definitely heard footsteps. He groped his side at the belt and cursed the empty place where his sword should have been. When the king's men entered the cellar, he was unable to defend himself with words and excuses a second time. They discovered the gunpowder and arrested him. By morning Fawkes, in shackles, faced the king he had attempted to assassinate and heard his sentence: death by hanging.

That night, and every year after, the inhabitants of London lit bonfires throughout the city in celebration of the foiled gunpowder plot. The celebratory Bonfire Night tradition quickly spread throughout England and eventually made its way into Scotland, homeland of the plot's intended victim. Over the centuries the night's original religious zeal and barrels of gunpowder were replaced with civic festivity and fireworks so that every royal subject would forever, as the old rhyme goes, "Remember, remember the 5th of November."

* * *

Over four hundred years after the gunpowder plot and roughly the same number of miles north from Fawkes's London cellar, Daniel Darrow waited in a small, windowless room attached to the gathering hall of Church Street Kirk, Inverness. The kitchen area was partitioned off from the main room by a half wall and counter. It doubled as a laundry room. Ten minutes remained on the drying cycle of the combination washer/dryer in the corner. Daniel used this time to review his notes for a future sermon. He found concentration elusive, however; his mind kept wandering back to his first Sunday at Church Street Kirk when he washed tea and coffee stains from mugs in the room's sink and was later caught by Eliza MacGillivray at the larger room's exit. His left shoe still missed a small chunk of heel from where her furry, long eared companion had taken a nibble. Was that really only a month ago? He felt like it had to have been longer. He looked at the date on his mobile phone – November 5th, roughly one month from when he had first arrived.

He wondered about Eliza MacGillivray's prophecies and the faith in their efficacy that others at the kirk seemed to have. People questioned her odd, out of time, appearance or unusual social interplay, but they never questioned the truth of her visions. In fact, her personal peculiarities seemed to only add to her prophetic credibility. Even Rev. Calder, who as the spiritual leader of the church would seemingly have the most obvious cause for objection, displayed no ill will or even suspicion toward Eliza. Daniel had to admit that his own skepticism had begun to falter as well.

"From across the sea shall a shepherd come

Professing grace divine,

Not to lead but to be led

By fur and feet toward love terrestrial."

Eliza MacGillivray's first, or second, prophecy for him had initially seemed like gibberish. Though, as William MacCrivag had pointed out, after they had discovered his missing Scotch, the first bit could easily be read to describe Daniel's coming from America to Scotland. The second bit remained, in

MacCrivag's words, "wonderfully enigmatic." At least it had seemed that way until recently. After their kiss in the ruined tower of Urquhart Castle on the shore of Loch Ness, Daniel wondered if Ellie Gray might be his "love terrestrial." The cause of their first meeting was, after all, due to Sir Walter's yearly check up and, other than Eliza MacGillivray's own pet rabbit, no other member of Church Street had more fur or feet than the kirk cat.

The washer/dryer interrupted Daniel's musing with a high-pitched buzz. Rev. Calder had warned him that this dual machine was more adept at washing than drying. So, after the dryer announced its completion, he pulled out its contents one by one and laid them on a wooden-railed drying rack to finish the job. When Rev. Calder had given him the task of washing the communion cloths, she had spoken of the machine's inefficiency as a near virtue. It never reached sufficient heat to shrink the cloths or set any overlooked stains, she boasted. Hanging them up for their second round of drying, however, seemed to Daniel like just the kind of salvation through an abundance of work, good or not, that the Protestant Reformation had tried to get away from.

Just then, a second high-pitched sound interrupted his thoughts. Outside the kitchen/laundry, on the opposite wall of the large gathering hall, an old, unlevel door creaked open. Laughter and shouting preceded raucous footsteps into the room. "Oi! Oi! Anyone home?" From their voices and laughter, Daniel could tell the intruders were young boys, teenagers.

From his position in the back of the kitchen/laundry, Daniel's presence was concealed from the youths. At this late hour in the afternoon, he had not expected anyone else to be present in the kirk, other than perhaps Rev. Calder. The youths' sudden entrance surprised him and he did not immediately respond to their calls.

"She's not here," one of them said.

"Of course she is. We planned to meet here. Where else would she be?" a second boy said.

"Where's the supplies – the wood and such? Brodie, you've heard wrong," a third boy said.

"We're just early," the second boy, Brodie, suggested.

"No, you've got the wrong room. Anyway, we're late."

"How much petrol do you suppose it'll take? For such a big fire it must be loads!" a fourth boy said.

"You're daft. No one uses petrol for a bonfire."

Ignoring the insult, the fourth boy continued, "It'll be the biggest bonfire in Scotland. We'll make that ol' Broonburn House seem a wee matchstick!" The other boys laughed in agreement.

"I know where she'll be. Come on then," one of the boys took charge and led the others out of the room.

Daniel had no conscious intent to follow them; nevertheless, he left the laundry and crossed the gathering hall in pursuit. In a further unconscious move, he found his pursuit to be surprisingly stealthy. He measured each hasty step for minimal sound. He opened the door slowly, pulling up on the handle to ease pressure on the hinges and prevent its creaking. In the hallway, he kept plenty of space between himself and the boys. If this had been a car chase, he would have allowed another vehicle to move in between them so as not to arouse their suspicions.

Thinking back on the event, Daniel realized it must have been the boys' Broonburn reference that compelled him. With the release of Tom Shaw's name, the victim, or perpetrator depending on whom you asked, Broonburn House had surged once again to the head of the local news cycle. In a live interview, one of the police inspectors, to the visible consternation of his nearby colleague, openly questioned the viability of Tom Shaw's masterminding the arson that killed him – or at least Shaw could not have done it alone. The off-script inspector then asked members of the public to come forward with any information that might aid in their investigation. Daniel knew this to be an act of desperation for such a high-profile case that had gone for too long unsolved. He also knew that, secretly, he wanted to be that member of the public to uncover the decisive clue.

As a member of the clergy, he was more used to picking up the broken pieces of parishioners' lives after the fact of a tragedy than playing any preventative role in to why or where those pieces fell in the first place. Surely, he thought, men and women of the cloth must actively pursue the mitigation of people's suffering whenever possible. Christ, after all, had been no idle bystander to the suffering of others. When they hungered, he fed them. When disease ravaged their bodies, he healed them. The least Daniel Darrow could do, so he told himself, was prevent a copycat arson and its subsequent human suffering. And if that prevention gained him some heroic popularity amongst the citizenry of his adopted city, and one cinnamon haired citizen in particular, so much the better.

The gang of boys turned a corner and Daniel heard another door open and close. Daniel hurried to the corner and in his haste to catch up with them he failed to pay attention to his steps. Within an arm's length of the door, his foot caught on a furry, blond obstacle traveling at matching speed in the opposite direction. Sir Walter Scott let out a yowl and spun around with claws unsheathed to face his surprise attacker. Daniel let out a yowl of his own when his shoulder met the corridor's stone floor. "You stupid cat! Where did you come from?" Sir Walter hissed and swiped with one paw before turning around to continue his feline pursuits. Leaving his assailant alone on the floor, a heap of bruised body and ego.

Daniel staggered to the door. He opened it to a small garden and footpath that branched out in two directions. A gang of fire-happy youths was unlikely to obey the polite boundary of the flagstone pavers, he thought. They could have gone anywhere, jumping the garden's short wall and escaping into the city. "Why did I ever take that stupid cat to the vet?" he asked the empty garden as he lamented such an embarrassing interruption to his heroic ambition.

Rubbing his injured shoulder, Daniel returned to the room at the back of the kirk gathering hall to hang the last of the not-quite-dry cloths. There he dreamed of how the city, how Ellie, would admire him for catching a hoodlum gang of copycat arsonists, or, if he were lucky enough, the original Broonburn arsonist.

Had he stayed in the garden and followed the path down its right branch, Daniel could have found the boys, still scheming in another room of the kirk.

Chapter Twelve

While Rev. Daniel Darrow was busy with the laundry in the back of the Church Street Kirk gathering hall, a spirited meeting was taking place in a nearby part of the building. Around the corner, outside, and at the end of the right branch of a small garden footpath, stood the thick wooden door to Rev. Sarah Calder's study. Inside the study, squeezed into a narrow couch and spilling over on one of its arms, sat four boys in excited conversation with the Reverend.

"And we get front positions for the bonfire, right?" Brodie asked.

"I don't know about front, but we'll save good spots for you," Rev. Calder said. Brodie frowned. "Remember lads, this booth is for the good of the kirk. The roof is in desperate need of repair and our Bonfire Night booth is a great fundraiser. People come from all over to see the Inverness bonfire. It's the largest in Scotland."

"That's what I told them," one of the boys said. "And they light it with petrol, right?"

"I couldn't say what they use, but petrol seems as good as anything," Rev. Calder said. The boy elbowed his friend and made an I-told-you-so face. "Finn, your sister's class won the Guy contest this year?" Rev. Calder asked. "Perhaps she would know. They created such a realistic model. With his tall hat and beard and mustache. It looks just like the real Guy Fawkes. I'm almost sad to see him hoisted up there and burned. What did they use for the mustache?"

"Goose feathers, I think," Finn replied.

"Shouldn't we be off if we're going to set up the booth? People must already be arriving for the funfair. Will it even fit on a bus?" another boy asked.

"What about Reverend Darrow? Couldn't he help? This'll be his first Bonfire Night," one of the others said.

"Aye, I've been meaning to mention it to him. But you won't need help building the booth as it's already up. All you four have to do is man it," Rev. Calder said to four relieved faces. "But you are right, we really should be on our way. I've got to fetch the cashbox and a few other things – find Reverend Darrow. But you should go on ahead. And don't take the bus. It's such a short walk to Bught Park and a fine day. We won't have many more with winter settling in. Get out and enjoy it!"

The boys left Rev. Calder's study through the small outdoor garden. They reentered the main kirk building by the same door where Daniel Darrow had earlier lost their trail due to an unfortunate encounter with Sir Walter Scott. The boys could have left from the garden directly, but that would have required a longer walk around the kirk to put them on the correct path down Church Street toward Bught Park, the location of Inverness's Bonfire Night festivities. Despite their willingness to volunteer their time, they could not pass up the opportunity of a shortcut.

On their way through the kirk, they passed the gathering hall where Daniel was just finishing the laundry. Despite his position at the far end of the hall, Daniel heard their passing. The boys could equally not pass up the opportunity to romp through an empty kirk corridor at full volume.

Daniel tossed the last drying cloth on the rack and hurried to the hall's exit. He could not believe his luck. The arsonist gang had returned! Fate had given him a second chance to play the hero. He could see his name in tomorrow's paper already. He would be hailed as the reverend who, despite being a foreigner, heroically stopped these would-be copycats of the infamous Broonburn House fire. Daniel waited at the door until he was sure the boys had progressed a sufficient distance down the corridor that they would not notice they had a tail. Their rowdy procession around the corner and toward the kirk's front entrance was enough to scare away any small animals. Still, Daniel kept an eye out just in case. With no feline appearances to impede him, he followed the boys outside and onto Church Street.

In the mess of pedestrian and motor traffic, he no longer feared the gang would notice him. Yet, that same crowded camouflage made pursuing them far more difficult. Daniel had no professional tracking experience to aid him. He had over the years, recovered many stray golf balls, though golf balls had a convenient habit of lying still and waiting to be found. His current prey, annoyingly, kept on the move, twisting through other groups of pedestrians, around bus stops, and over shop signs and small trash bins. Daniel's only saving grace was the blue and white St. Andrew's cross stitched across the Scotland rugby hoodie worn by one of the boys. It served as a target for Daniel to lock onto as he pursued them through the crowd.

Before long, the teenagers reached the River Ness and took a left down the Ness Bank, a narrow one-way road typically traveled by sparse, unhurried traffic. Daniel had himself walked this road several times going to and from Church Street Kirk to his flat at Bellfield Park. He usually enjoyed the Ness Bank with its raised pedestrian path shouldering the river. A string of pleasant, double-floored houses covered its opposite side. At its northern termination, the red sandstone towers of Inverness Castle stood tall. A lovely view of the river persisted through its brief southward journey until the road branched off toward Bellfield Park and only a pedestrian path remained to follow the river.

When the boys took this path, Daniel worried his steady presence behind them might become obvious. On this evening, however, the human population of the Ness Bank dwindled only slightly from what it was closer to the city center, which, now that he thought of it, seemed unusually crowded as well. Daniel refused, however, to let such oddities deter him from his course. If this gang of would-be-arsonists meant trouble, he meant to find them out and stop them.

Then they started singing, or rather chanting in an off-key, singsong manner: "Remember, remember the 5th of November." The nursery rhyme seemed vaguely familiar in a way Daniel could not quite place. Had he heard something like it before? Anyway, it was a clever rhyme masking an alarming message. These boys had been planning their crime for some time and they meant it to be so shocking the world would forever remember the day.

Daniel quickened his pace to keep up with them. Without notice, the group of tourists he had been using as a buffer between himself and the gang stopped to gaze at some landmark in the way that tourists often stop to gaze at landmarks and they unwittingly caused a pile up of pedestrian traffic in their wake. Daniel bumped into the one holding up her mobile phone for a selfie. In any other country and perhaps even in other parts of Scotland such as in Glasgow, this would have resulted in a rude exchange of profanity. Yet, in Inverness, the wounded party assumed responsibility, rightly or not, with a surprised, "Sorry, oh, sorry." Daniel's Southern upbringing, not to be outdone, instinctively followed with, "No, I'm sorry ma'am. My fault entirely."

By the time all the apologies had been said and he managed to get around the stalled tourist group, the Scotland rugby hoodie and its three companions had progressed a considerable distance. Instead of continuing south along the shore, the boys took a white cable footbridge across the river. Daniel jogged to catch up with them. Once he regained his distance, he noticed that their chant had changed:

"The Guy, the Guy,
Poke him in the eye.
Put him on the fire
And there let him die!"

Though they had adopted a more cheerful cadence, their words had taken a decidedly deadlier turn. If they were planning on copycatting the Broonburn House fire, this latest tune might be an irreverent reference to that fire's victim, university student, Tom Shaw. Or, Daniel shuddered, they might have murderous intentions of their own. God only knew what guy they sang of. As he crossed the bridge in pursuit, he took extra caution not to be noticed.

The boys, laughing and singing their morbid rhymes, turned south once more to follow the river's opposite bank. One of them, the one wearing the Scotland rugby hoodie, started in the opposite direction at the end of the footbridge and was called back to the group with a shout and an insult. "Oi, Bught Park's this way! Your head's as loose as the Guy's!"

When Daniel reached the end of the bridge, he knew his pursuit had taken him further than he dared go alone. He had heard of Bught Park. It lay to the south of Inverness between his flat in Bellfield Park and the Torvean Golf club just past where the Caledonian Canal forks off from the River Ness. Though he had yet to take the time to visit the park himself, Daniel knew it to be a popular destination for youth rugby and football, or soccer. As much as he enjoyed the idea of playing the lone hero, he knew that if these four arsonists were going to carry out their plot in such a populated area, he would need help. Daniel ducked behind a wide tree and retrieved his mobile phone from his jacket pocket. He pressed 999 on the call screen.

"Hello, my name is Daniel Darrow, and I need to report a crime. Or prevent a crime. The point is a crime is about to occur and a lot of people could be seriously hurt." The voice on the other end asked him to slow down and enunciate more clearly. This was a busy night for emergency services, she explained and could he remain calm and be more specific about the nature of the crime. "Arson. Or murder. Maybe both," Daniel said trying to tighten his Carolina drawl as best he could. "In Bught Park, sometime tonight. Probably sooner than later." The voice on the other end gave an irritated huff and asked him to be serious. She did not have time for prank calls. "I am serious," Daniel insisted. "Look, I am a minister at Church Street Kirk. I am phoning in a real threat here and am concerned about the safety of anyone in that park. I have no reason to lie about this." Daniel did not like pulling religious rank like that, but this woman clearly needed convincing. "I think it might be related to the Broonburn House fire. A copycat or something." With a reluctance Daniel could not understand, the 999 voice assured him that she would send a patrol car to investigate and then promptly ended the call.

Daniel put away his phone and continued his pursuit of the four boys. He might be on his own in stopping them after all. During the phone call he had lost sight of them. But catching up would not be difficult now that he knew their destination. Four rowdy teenagers would easily stick out on such a calm, empty road. Except that today it wasn't. Daniel panicked when he gazed out on the river of pedestrians, several of whom wore Scottish rugby attire. In his excited single-mindedness, Daniel had not regarded the unusual number of people crowding the banks of the Ness that evening. Nor had he, until now, considered the way they all seemed to be heading in the same direction – toward Bught Park.

Daniel pushed his way through until he reached the edge of the park. He stood as a stone while the crowds streamed around him. Before him, crowding the whole of the park, families gathered. Parents chased after children who chased after themselves. Queues waited impatiently around various booths selling refreshments and Highland curio. At one end of the park stood a small mountain of logs and kindling. Behind the unlit bonfire, a team of men made their final checks on a large fireworks display. A bagpipe band was warming up over the rumble of festive voices. Like Saul of Tarsus, scales fell from Daniel's eyes and he could finally see the truth of that which his pride had blinded him. He recalled the dismissive tone of the 999 woman and his stomach turned. He had so arrogantly thrown about his name and moral credentials to convince her.

Before he could find a suitable place to release the sick embarrassment from his gut, Rev. Calder approached him. "Reverend Darrow! I'm glad you could make it!" she shouted. Daniel gave a weak wave. Approaching him, she said, "The Inverness Bonfire Night celebration is truly a sight. One of our biggest tourism draws."

"Looks like it," Daniel said.

"I meant to invite you along, though I can't recall actually doing so. Anyway, you must have gotten my message because you're here. It's good for us to be involved in civic activities such as these."

The soft whine of police sirens diverted the reverends' attention. It grew louder, more deafening by the second. Pedestrians crowded either curb of the narrow road leading to Bught Park to make way for the approaching patrol car. It sped past and came to a screeching stop just a few yards from where Rev. Calder and Rev. Darrow stood.

"Oh my, I wonder what this is about?" Rev. Calder said.

Daniel pressed his forehead just between the eyebrows. He felt dizzy and lightheaded. "Yeah, that would be for me," he said. He watched the two uniformed officers exit the car. He looked down at the green ground, wanting to somehow melt away into it.

Chapter Thirteen

A mass of white mist conjured forth from the cold cauldron of the North Sea and bombarded Scotland's northeastern coast. It rolled down the Moray Firth and, like a sheet of wet linen fresh out of the wash, it hung over the golfing community of Castle Stuart before continuing south toward the city of Inverness. Early morning tee times were canceled with a single word: *"Haar."* This deep guttural word, whose rolling *-rrr* sounded as if it came from the depths of the maritime phenomenon it described, was well known by all who lived on the eastern coast. No one ever seemed particularly surprised when the haar arrived and blanketed their towns in its frosty cloud that was truly more sea than cloud; yet no one ever expected it either. The haar blew in like an old, grumpy uncle or stray, wet dog that shook and sprayed its wetness all over one's just swept entryway.

Daniel Darrow met this early morning haar midway between his flat and William MacCrivag's house, nestled at the end of Telford Gardens, west of Church Street Kirk, between the River Ness and the Caledonian Canal. These two corridors of moving water seemed to direct the sea cloud's rolling swell through the city. Hints of the haar, or more accurately forewarnings, had greeted Daniel at his door. The outside world had changed from the previous day's clear sun-filled brilliance. It was now damp and muted and became increasingly opaque the nearer his journey took him to the sea. The red sandstone of Inverness Castle hid itself away like a blushing bride behind her veil.

Once he crossed the river, the world seemed to complete its cold, white transformation. Daniel moved in a small sphere of semi-clarity, only a few feet in diameter, beyond which his vision could not penetrate. He continued to walk the remaining distance to William MacCrivag's house despite the weather and the weight of the duffel bag on his shoulder because he did not trust a double-decker city bus to avoid colliding with him as he waved his arm out into the haze beside a bus stop. Deep within their individual, limited spheres of vision, a bus could no more distinguish the curb from the street than he. Yet, more than his wariness of public transport, Daniel continued on foot because he felt he must.

The icy chill of the haar was a penance for his behavior the previous evening on the 5th of November. It offered a doleful comfort. In the same way that a recently broken heart despises the cheerful sound of songbirds in the morning, Daniel felt at home in this miserable weather. He had wanted so desperately to earn the respect of his new congregation, his first real ministerial post. He had desired so vainly to play the part of the underdog detective, the unsuspecting hero. Instead he had faced the most complete public humiliation he had ever known.

When the police vehicle burst through the crowds at Bught Park, sirens blaring, he had felt sick. Two uniformed officers stepped out, scanned the scene, and approached four youths. Their descriptions matched those Daniel had given to the 999 operator. Realizing the officers' gait was directed toward them, the boys' eyes widened. One of them bolted. The other three froze on the spot. Daniel was frozen as well, his legs lead, but he somehow forced himself forward. A cold dread filled his stomach with each step.

He gave the officers his name and stumbled through an attempt at an explanation. His cultural ignorance. The misunderstanding. His severe apologies for wasting their time and not knowing his congregation better. The officers looked him over through narrowed eyes, trying to determine if he was toying with them or telling the truth. If he was truly that daft. The look reminded Daniel of a family road trip when he was a child - his father driving through the Appalachian Mountains. The family had just stopped for a toilet break. Not more than ten minutes later, he informed his parents that he needed to go again. His father looked back at him with that same stare.

One of the officers questioned the remaining boys about their booth and their connection to Daniel. The other wrote in a small pad and reminded the gathering crowd to stay back. By this time Rev. Calder had joined them. She also reluctantly claimed Daniel. She apologized on behalf of herself and the entire Church Street Kirk community. Her face was such a rosy color, a shade that even the bitterest of Scottish winters couldn't hope to produce, that Daniel could not determine if it was from embarrassment or anger or both. After a very public reprimand from the officers and another private one from Rev. Calder, Daniel quietly retreated from the park and the evening's festivities.

Now, the next morning, the gloom and isolation he felt inside had taken form in the blinding sea mist. He embraced it with shivering, slick, nylon covered arms. When he finally arrived at Telford Gardens, the gray-white coloring of the houses made for such a perfect camouflage with the surrounding precipitation that Daniel had to squint to identify the house numbers. In his concentration, he collided with a small green car parked with two of its wheels up the curb in front of William MacCrivag's house. Daniel rubbed the side of his leg, readjusted the bag on his shoulder, and then with a sigh patted the car. He was glad for the opportunity to get out of town for a bit. As he walked the mostly paved path through William MacCrivag's disorderly front garden, the fog around him began to thin.

Daniel rang the bell. The light above the door flickered on and off, staying lighted for longer intervals than when he had first pressed the ringer weeks ago. The stuttering chime repeated its same two notes and nearly made it to a third before a pop from inside the wall silenced it. This time Daniel noticed an added fizzling sound after the pop. Wary of pressing it again, he waited. His lack of movement made the cold around him more evident and he began to shiver. He marched in place to keep warm and was about to chance the ringer again when he heard a muffled voice from inside shout, "Coming!"

Minutes later William MacCrivag open the front door and Daniel felt the warmth of the house's busy radiators. Mr. MacCrivag nearly shut the door upon opening it, trying to keep the outside weather from rushing in. He left only a narrow opening through which Daniel might squeeze. "The haar's thick this morning!" Mr. MacCrivag exclaimed.

Shortly after Daniel had first met William MacCrivag and aided him in the "great whiskey hunt," as the visit had come to be known between them, he had invited Daniel along on this trip to the Hebrides – a string of islands off the northwest coast of Scotland. He made the trip on an annual basis, his own Mecca. This was not a very Presbyterian analogy, Mr. MacCrivag had joked, but then Presbyterians had never been big on pilgrimages. The allure of the islands, therefore, came from a place other than religious zeal. They pulled on him like some ancestral lodestone. Though he had grown up in Inverness, Mr. MacCrivag's ancestors originated in the islands. Some ancient force within him never let him stray too long nor too far from them. The farthest south he had ever been in his life was Aberdeen, less than thirty miles south of Inverness.

It was while in Aberdeen as a university student that William MacCrivag met his regular Hebridean host, Philip Morrison. William had a natural attraction to Philip, who hailed from the Lewis side of the isle of Lewis and Harris. Island blood knew its own and the two soon became inseparable. After graduation, they sustained their relationship though Mr. MacCrivag's annual pilgrimages. He visited during the summers, due to the harsh nature of Scottish winters, made particularly acute on the unguarded, windswept shores of the Outer Hebrides. A trip in early November, therefore, constituted an aberration in William MacCrivag's usual migration ritual. Though unseasonable, the impromptu trip was nonetheless absolutely necessary, he insisted, due to events that transpired a few weeks earlier.

William MacCrivag explained this to Daniel as he tossed their bags into the boot, or trunk, of his little green car. Neither man's luggage required considerable space, each consisting of only two days' worth of clothing and a few toiletries. Any longer on the outer isles at this time of year, Mr. MacCrivag claimed, amounted to kind of natural mortification of the flesh that he was not inclined to endure. Though he remained an islander in spirit, he could not deny the creature comforts of home.

From his experience of that morning's bitter haar, Daniel questioned the hospitality of the entire Scottish landmass and suggested a more southerly holiday locale, perhaps someplace tropical. "It might come to that," Mr. MacCrivag conceded, though his voice lacked any timbre of credibility.

Beside their bags, Mr. MacCrivag placed two cartons of cigarettes in the car. "I didn't know you smoked?" Daniel said.

"Oh, I gave it up years ago. These are for Philly. I bring him a box or two every visit. It started as a bad pun when we were at university together - Philip Morrison you know," Mr. MacCrivag laughed. "Seemed much cleverer back then, didn't it." He scratched the short half circle of stubble on the back of his head. "Philly still gets a kick out of it I ken. We have a laugh anyway." Further, Mr. MacCrivag claimed with a wink, the cigarettes served as barter for the best scotch in all of Scotland. Philip Morrison always kept several bottles on reserve from a local distillery and what they could not drink during their visit, Mr. MacCrivag carried back home with him to Inverness as sustenance until the next summer.

When his last bottle went missing behind the recycling bin a few weeks earlier, Mr. MacCrivag had simply written it off. He was not unused to things disappearing from his house, as they tended to do from time to time. Telford Gardens, he had once heard from an Inverness old timer, was built atop an auld faerie hill and faeries, as everyone knows, enjoy a bit of mischief and thievery. This seemed as good an explanation as any to William MacCrivag. When items went missing or turned up in places other than where he recalled leaving them, he simply tipped his metaphorical hat in acquiescence. Once, in an attempt to preserve more of his possessions, he had written down a plan to better organize his house. But the faeries spirited away that as well.

On the morning of Daniel's first visit, William MacCrivag had phoned Philip Morrison to lament the faerie-snatched bottle of scotch and arrange a midyear meeting for its replacement. When Daniel miraculously recovered the bottle, Mr. MacCrivag was delighted but also disappointed. He couldn't simply cancel his trip. No, Mr. MacCrivag explained to Daniel as they loaded his car, canceling on a mate as old and steadfast as Philly would constitute the height of rudeness. He was not as boorish as that. For recovering the prize, Daniel had won himself an accompanying ride to the bottle's birthplace and, if he did not mind the hardship, a bed of Philip Morrison's sofa.

What Daniel had at first accepted as a merry Scottish adventure, he now took as a welcome retreat from the previous night's humiliation and brief delay in facing its inevitable fallout. For the next two days at least, he would *not* have to *remember remember the fifth of November.*

This was not to be, of course. While Inverness had, over the centuries, grown from village to town to true city status, it remained a smallish city and felt even more so within its various pockets. One of those pockets, that of the community of Church Street Kirk, remained quite small indeed. Rumors and gossip, whether ill or well intended, flowed like milk and honey in such a community. One had only to wait until the next formal Sunday morning gathering to have confirmation of what one already knew through the informal streams of hearsay.

Thus, William MacCrivag knew of his new reverend's misadventure well before Daniel arrived at his door that morning. He allowed the reverend a few minutes of quiet reprieve before broaching the topic. A good rumor, after all, like a good whiskey, can only sit on the shelf for so long before it must be uncorked and enjoyed.

Mr. MacCrivag breathed in the aroma and began with only a palate-whetting sip. "Did you make it out for the bonfire last night?" he asked. Daniel squirmed in his seat and looked out the passenger window. Mr. MacCrivag did not want to be cruel, but he could not help himself taking some pleasure in the exchange. "Rather exciting display this year."

Daniel turned to face him. "So, you were there?"

"No, but I heard," Mr. MacCrivag said. "You didn't really think those lads were going to burn down the park did you?"

"I'd rather not talk about it."

"And to phone the police. I'm sure they had a laugh! You must feel a bit silly, eh."

"Silly doesn't even come close to describing how I feel. Stupid, humiliated, profoundly sorry, wishing I could somehow dissolve away into this crazy fog – that gets a bit closer," Daniel said. "I am actually looking forward to this trip so I can forget the whole mess for a couple days."

"I can see you're still rather sore about it," Mr. MacCrivag said. He pulled onto the North Kessock bridge, the suspension bridge separating the Moray and Beauly Firths and connecting the Inverness harbor to the northern Highlands. "There," Mr. MacCrivag said, "it's all left behind us now. There'll be plenty of time to fret about it when you return, wont there. For now – to Lewis!" Mr. MacCrivag pointed enthusiastically forward as if leading an expeditionary army.

"Thank you," Daniel said. "I really am looking forward to this trip, and not just to get out of town for a while. I've heard the Hebrides are beautiful."

"Aye, now beautiful doesn't come close to describing them," Mr. MacCrivag said with a wink.

"And this scotch you've been going on about, I can't wait to finally try some."

"That's right, I never did share a dram, did I? That was awfully rude of me. Not to worry though. If I know Philly, there'll be plenty for us both when we arrive."

Daniel looked out his window. The haar had already passed by here, leaving a sparkling dew on the yellow, heather-covered hill of the Black Isle peninsula. Daniel had only ever seen the Isle from a distance across the firth. "Oh, I almost forgot," Mr. MacCrivag said. "Would you open the glove box there and fetch my driving gloves." Daniel opened the compartment. He shuffled through a heap of paper – receipts, napkins, grocery lists, parking tickets, and a tattered owner's manual.

"I don't see any gloves in here," he said.

"Eh?" Mr. MacCrivag scratched the ring of hair on the back of his head. "Ah," he said and reached behind his seat. The distance was too great for his arm, so he leaned back. This caused his other arm, the one holding the steering wheel, to pull back as well. The car leaped to the left and invaded the other lane. The vehicle behind them slowed and swerved to avoid a collision. The driver let loose his horn and a barrage of words laced in an English accent whose meaning Daniel presumed was not as polite as they sounded.

"Mr. MacCrivag!" Daniel shouted. Mr. MacCrivag yanked the car back into its lane. "Let me look for the gloves. You focus on the road."

"Aye, that's a good idea. Check back there, though they should be in the glove box."

Daniel maneuvered around his seat to better search. Behind the driver and passenger seats he found other odds and ends: a bit of fishing tackle, one hiking boot, an old issue of *The Scotsman* newspaper, a corkscrew, and several plastic CD cases – but no gloves. He returned to a proper seated position and gave Mr. MacCrivag a shoulder shrug look. He then noticed a leather fingered bulge poking out from the driver side sun visor. "I think I found them," Daniel said and pointed.

Mr. MacCrivag retrieved the gloves and chuckled. "You seem have a knack for uncovering things." Unlike most gloves that lay limp when independent from their hands, these held their shape around the wrist and palm. Some structure woven inside the leather provided the gloves and, Daniel assumed, their wearer stiff support. Mr. MacCrivag noticed Daniel eyed the gloves. "Orthopedic. I'm supposed to wear them whenever I take a long drive – Bad wrists, you know." Mr. MacCrivag put on the gloves, pulling them down forcefully to fit his hands.

Daniel flashed back to the morning a few weeks past when he golfed with Mr. Tweed at the Torvean Club. Mr. Tweed's golfing mate had put on his gloves in the same labored way. At the time, Daniel had thought the man's inconsistent use of the gloves odd. Now he wondered if they were more than a mere idiosyncrasy. If the man had required them for warmth, he would have worn them the entire game, but he only put them on when driving the ball. The gloves were always stuffed away by the time they hit the green.

Perhaps the gloves were not meant for warmth at all. Perhaps, like Mr. MacCrivag's driving gloves, their true purpose was support, to steady the wearer's wrists. Keeping a straight wrist during one's backswing prevented the ball from slicing to the left on a long drive. He knew this because the trick seemed always just beyond his ability to successfully execute. If Mr. Tweed's friend had purchased wrist-restricting gloves, illegal in professional play, the sudden improvement in his game could be easily explained.

Cheered by solving the puzzle, Daniel's mind jumped to another pair of curious gloves – those of Elspeth Gray, the mother and namesake of Ellie Gray, whom Daniel desperately hoped was not as well connected to the gossip channels of Church Street Kirk as William MacCrivag. When Daniel had first met Elspeth Gray, Rev. Calder had approved of her gloves as a lovely, new fashion accessory. Ellie had also mentioned the gloves at their trip to Loch Ness, though she seemed more troubled by their sudden addition to Elspeth's wardrobe. In Ellie's mind, the gloves appearance coincided with her mother's recent social reclusiveness.

Daniel placed the approximate timing of Elspeth Gray's new fashion choice on a mental calendar. She had begun wearing her new gloves around the same time as the Broonburn House fire. *What better way to hide a fresh burn?* Daniel shook his head to clear away the unwanted thought. The gloves' appearance could just as easily be explained by the change in season. Combined with the poorer blood circulation of an aging woman, winter's approach made the addition of gloves to her wardrobe perfectly reasonable.

Speculation about the Broonburn House fire had brought Daniel nothing but humiliation and a sorely battered reputation. He felt foolish enough for suspecting the kirk's youths and flying off on a half-baked chase through the city without any real proof. Now he was suspecting the frail mother of the woman with whom he had recently become involved. If he continued down this path, he knew public humiliation would be the least of his troubles.

"Would you mind putting on some music?" Daniel asked Mr. MacCrivag. "I saw several CDs behind the seat."

"Not at all. What do you want to listen to?"

"Anything," Daniel said. *Anything to drown out my own thoughts*, he said to himself.

Chapter Fourteen

The next morning, Daniel woke to the clamor of ceramic utensils clanking their way out of cupboards and across countertops. A half wall divided the kitchen from the living room and prevented him from seeing the unquiet cook. Soreness from a fitful night's sleep on Philip Morrison's sofa prevented Daniel from sitting up too quickly. Accustomed to only one occupant, his bachelor's sofa wore unevenly in a way that Daniel now felt in his neck and lower back. He stretched painfully, heard a few spinal clicks, and turned his head in the direction of the kitchen.

"Good morning," Daniel said groggily.

A mess of orange and gray-flecked hair popped out from behind the kitchen wall. "Ah, morning tae you," Philip Morrison said with more cheer than was warranted by that early morning hour. He wore a short beard that matched his hair in color and disarray and accorded him a strong resemblance to a middle-aged lion. His eyes, used to early morning waking, were wide and bright. "I'm just making coffee. Would you like a cup?" Daniel nodded gratefully. "Willie's in the bath."

"Oh, Mr. MacCrivag. Ok," Daniel said. He looked around the room, still slightly disorientated from waking up in a new location. His makeshift bed sat against a long wall connecting the living room and a short entryway. The opposite wall contained a rough, stone cut fireplace that appeared much older than the surrounding room – an ancient vestige upon which the modern drywall and wallpapered façade had been attached. On either side of the fireplace, at the approximate height of a raised whiskey glass, upside down bottles of scotch bolted to the wall like sconces. The bottles' mouths connected to tiny spigots for easy dispensing. Philip Morrison called again from behind the kitchen wall: "Beans?"

Wondering if a night on the unbalanced cushions had affected his hearing as well as his back, Daniel stood and walked to the kitchen. He instantly smelled a strong and not altogether appetizing combination of scents: coffee, gas, baked beans, and burning toast. "Sorry, I'm fresh out of bacon," Philip Morrison said with a joviality that, like the cooking odors, required some waking up to appreciate. Philip handed Daniel a bowl and a mug.

"Coffee and toast are fine, thank you," Daniel said handing back the bowl. His stomach could not handle the heaviness of a Scottish breakfast, even without the bacon. Thankfully blood pudding was also left out of the mix. Caffeine was all he really needed. He sat down at the table with his empty mug and listened to the coffee drip one slow drop after another into the pot.

"We've a big day ahead. Willie said this is your first time to the Outer Isles. He asked me to play tour guide and I know the best places. You'll need your strength," Philip Morrison said as he stirred the pot of beans.

"Really, toast is plenty. I'm not much of a breakfast person," Daniel said. He wanted to say that he had never considered a can of baked beans a welcome part of any meal, much less breakfast. Before he could ask what exotic locales his host had in mind for the day, William 'Willie' MacCrivag entered the room. He wore thick trousers and a wool jumper, ready to take on the harsh Hebridean climate. Mr. MacCrivag fished a mug out of the cupboard and sat down opposite Daniel.

"Guid mornin'," Mr. MacCrivag said. Not waiting for a reply, he stood and said, "Philly, I cannae smell bacon."

"Aye, I jest said to the Reverend here I'm fresh out," Philip Morrison replied.

"Bangers?" Mr. MacCrivag asked.

"Are ye deaf? We've got no ham on the premises. You'll find a couple eggs in the fridge, but you'll have to fry 'em. I'm busy with my pot here."

"Och, my mate the five-star chef. He can cook up a feast as long as it's from a wee tin!" Mr. MacCrivag said.

When they had arrived the previous afternoon, Daniel noticed that Mr. MacCrivag's accent thickened the moment they stepped foot on the island. Daniel recalled a similar phenomenon himself during his seminary days. Whenever he returned home for a visit, he found that his Carolina drawl lengthened in the presence of family. Once he had brought a New England girlfriend home and the relationship never recovered. A foreign vocabulary of 'y'alls', 'ain'ts', and 'fixin's', quickly unraveled their ability to communicate. His family's insistence on calling her "the Yankee" was the straw that finally broke their brief romance's back. Daniel hoped now that a similar communicative devolution would not occur – otherwise this had the makings of a very long two days.

He excused himself from the breakfast table for a quick shower. Passing by the fireplace with its upturned whiskey sconces, he smiled with a reassuring thought. His family gatherings had never had the benefit of scotch on tap.

* * *

The first stop on Philly's island tour was the Calanais Standing Stones, an ancient megalithic site on the northwestern coast of the Isle of Lewis. Long before Christianity found its way to Scotland, before even Abraham was called out from the Mesopotamian city of Ur, a unique religious zeal fell upon the natives of Lewis. The result was a series of large standing stones, similar to, though likely older than, those at Stonehenge. Like gray bony fingers, the Calanais Stones reach out of the green earth to measure the sky and the moon. In the center of their grip, they hold a tomb, welcoming the dead back into the earth.

Mr. MacCrivag pulled his little green car into the visitor center parking lot. Before exiting the vehicle, the three men zipped their coats and Philip Morrison passed around a flask for warmth. "The winds can be bitter cold out here. We require fortification both inside and out!" he said.

After several minutes strolling amongst the stones, Philip Morrison paused to pour out a dram from his flask for his ancestors. He then called Daniel and Mr. MacCrivag to his side and, in a more modern ritual, pulled out his mobile phone for a group selfie. Their visit sufficiently commemorated, the men enjoyed coffees in the warmth of the Visitors Center before heading off to their next destination. While Daniel ordered, Willie and Philly secured a table by a window with wide views of Loch Roag.

They swapped stories and updates about their respective lives and locales. Stornoway airport wanted to expand, but concerns over the environmental and community impacts of another runway had stalled the proposal. Philip Morrison couldn't see the benefits of another runway outweighing the destruction of farmland and the potential nuisance of larger planes flying over his house. "We're not as hustle and bustle as you are down in Inverness or Edinburgh," he said. "Our wee airport serves our needs fine." William MacCrivag agreed and added that he preferred the ferry to air travel anyway. If you are going to an island, he insisted, you should feel the rhythm of the sea and its wet, salty breath. Daniel sipped his coffee, offered the occasional polite nod, and enjoyed the window's scenic view.

Daniel tuned back in when the conversation turned to Broonburn House. He was surprised the case had made such an impression so far north as Stornoway. He was also concerned that Mr. MacCrivag might divulge his Bonfire Night embarrassment. After Mr. MacCrivag had exposed the kirk's high-speed gossip lines the previous morning, Daniel dreaded returning to Church Street. This dread made Philip Morrison's so far unsullied impression of him a prized commodity that Daniel knew would all too soon be in short supply. Philly and Willie reviewed the commonly known facts and speculations of the case: the house's complete destruction, the suspicion of arson, the body of Edinburgh University student Tom Shaw, and the police's apparent lack of suspects or motive. At the mention of suspects, Daniel gave Mr. MacCrivag an anxious glance. Mr. MacCrivag returned a wink and a smile and wondered aloud why no one had answered the police's call for information from the public.

Philip Morrison noticed the exchange. "What's that?" he asked. "Are you two holding out on me?"

"It's just our Reverend here has been rather silent. I ken he fancies himself a detective. Have any theories about who done it, Reverend Darrow?" Mr. MacCrivag asked.

"Oh, I don't know about that," Daniel said with eyes firmly on his tormentor.

"It's an intriguing case. Fires have a way of getting people excited, but I don't really know anything more than what I read in the papers."

"No thoughts at all?" goaded Mr. MacCrivag.

"None that've panned out," Daniel replied wryly and then in an attempt to shift focus from himself he added, "But I think if we knew more about the present owner of Broonburn House, we'd be much closer to a motive."

"Och, so serious!" Mr. MacCrivag laughed.

"I dinnae ken, Willie, the lad has a point," Philip Morrison said. "That's all been rather secretive. Tom Shaw's name is all over the headlines, but I haven't read a word on the laird – other than he wasn't at home for the fire."

"I've heard he's English," Daniel said. He wanted to say more – that he had learned the name of Broonburn House's owner from Mr. Tweed – but he stopped himself. He wasn't certain of the confidence with which Mr. Tweed had given him that information and he was still sore at Mr. MacCrivag.

"And he had big plans for the place too," Mr. MacCrivag said, having been taken in by Daniel's deflection. "Was turning Broonburn House into some hotel or tourism hot spot. Sounds good to me. I can't fathom why someone would want to destroy such a grand auld house – plus all the local jobs it promised?"

"Insurance fraud?" Daniel suggested. The two older men nodded thoughtfully, considering the idea.

"But to buy up a big house just to burn it down?" Mr. MacCrivag said.

"Be wary of Englishmen in big houses making promises," Philip Morrison said. Daniel and Mr. MacCrivag looked at him quizzically. "I'll forgive the young American Reverend, but Willie here should know better. Wealthy southerners don't exactly have a history of benevolence when it comes to their dealings in the Highlands. If there *is* something dodgy about the laird of Broonburn House, well, it wouldn't be the first time we've been burned by the English."

Daniel looked at Mr. MacCrivag for an explanation. "You've heard of the Clearances?" Mr. MacCrivag asked. "Sure you have. 1800s, when the wealthy lairds – not all of them English mind you – drove us off our land." He directed the latter sentence toward Philip Morrison who simply shrugged his shoulders. "Crofters weren't as profitable as sheep farms," Mr. MacCrivag continued. "Why do you think there are so many Scottish surnames in the States? It's no recent immigration."

"Nor were they all voluntary," Philip Morrison added. He then let out a sudden burst of laughter. "Burned!" he said. "I've made a pun. Wouldn't be the first time we've been *burned* – Broonburn – the fire – *burned!*"

Mr. MacCrivag shook his head. "How much fortification have you put in your coffee?"

"None," Philip Morrison said, "That's why it's so brilliant!" To Daniel he said, "You get it don't you – *burned.*"

"Yes," Daniel said, trying his best to sound genuine, "that's very clever."

"Och, the both of you, you've no sense of humor," Philip Morrison said. He stood. "Anyway, we should be off. Part two of Philly's island tour is a bit farther."

"Bernera?" Mr. MacCrivag asked.

"No, farther still. You'll have to wait and see. Tis a bit 'off the beaten path' as they say." The three men exited the visitor's center and piled back into Mr. MacCrivag's little green car. Philip Morrison at the wheel, they headed south, crossing the mountainous boundary that separated the island's northern half of Lewis from its southern half of Harris.

Chapter Fifteen

Philip Morrison drove across the midsection of the island. They continued south into Harris, farther than Mr. MacCrivag could see the sense in. "If it's tweed you're after, we could've stayed in Stornoway. They sell it there too," he said. He was referring to Harris Tweed, one of the most well known and popular brands of tweed in the world.

"You're only half right, Willie, mate," Philip Morrison said. "You've been living in Inverness too long. The big Stornoway mills may do the finishing and stamp the orb mark, but tweed is created out here amongst the mountains and lochs and heather. It must be woven by strong, rural hands. Real Harris Tweed is as much a part of this place as the grass that feeds the sheep and the air that fills the weavers' lungs." He dramatically raised one hand to the car window.

"Why Philly, you're a poet, a regular Robbie Burns," Mr. MacCrivag said.

"Robbie Burns?" Daniel asked.

"Scotland's national bard, laddie, Robert Burns," Mr. MacCrivag explained. "O my Luve is like a red, red rose, that's newly sprung in June," he continued, reciting a poem.

Not to be outdone, Philip Morrison recited another. After several more recitations and partially remembered rhymes, they arrived at the village of Leverburgh. A few neat, modest houses and shops dotted the main road. They could see mountains to the north and to the south the strip of sea between the Isles of Harris and North Uist. In less time than it took to recite a Burns chorus, they were through the village and turning onto a narrow, unpaved side road. At the end of the road stood a wide white house roofed with dark gray shingles. Philip Morrison stopped the car and got out. "Here we are, lads!"

The noise from the car drew out the house's occupant. She was a young woman with rosy cheeks and dark brown hair. She wore a long dress under a thick, striped shawl. Philip Morrison stayed near the car and looked around. "Is Robbie about?" he asked the young woman.

"The poet?" Daniel whispered to Mr. MacCrivag.

"I hope not, he's been dead over two hundred years," Mr. MacCrivag whispered back.

"He's down the village just now," the girl shouted back to Philip Morrison. "I'm Bridget, his daughter. Can I help you?"

"I'm Philip Morrison. I was here a few months back and I've been extolling his skill to my mates here. They're from out of town and we were hoping to see what he's been up to. Em, will Robbie be around soon?"

"He's out most of the day, I'm afraid. But I ken he won't mind me giving a wee tour," Bridget said. She directed them to a door on the far side of the house. "Here's where the weaving's done. The finished rolls are against that wall."

A large metal loom took up the majority of space in the crowded room. A multitude of fine, black and white yarns fed into one side of the loom. Out the other end, where the weaver's chair and foot pedal were located, the yarn had been woven into a sharp houndstooth pattern. On the wall that Bridget had indicated, stood several tall columns of woven cloth. "Mind your hands," she warned Daniel as he approached the woven tweed. "It's greasy. Those are waiting to be sent out for finishing."

"Freshly woven tweed still holds oils from the die. It has to be darned and washed before it can be sold," Mr. MacCrivag explained.

"I see you know some of the trade," Bridget said approvingly.

Mr. MacCrivag nodded to Bridget and then to Philip Morrison he said, "Don't look so surprised, Philly. I may live in Inverness, but my blood's still Hebridean." To Bridget he added, "You wouldn't have any finished product around, would you?"

"I've a few scarves, but for anything more you'll have to go to a shop," she said.

"I've never seen you in tweed, Reverend," Mr. MacCrivag said to Daniel.

"No, I can't say that I own any," Daniel said. "Though Mr. Tw- um, Mr. Fraser, you know, George Fraser from Church Street, he's recommended it. I don't think I've ever seen him *out* of tweed."

"Aye, that's a sight only Mrs. Fraser would be privy to!" Mr. MacCrivag said with a chuckle.

Philip Morrison held up a moss and tan colored scarf. "Take a look at this one. And so soft. I think it would suit our Danny quite well, wouldn't it."

"Your accent – Canadian?" Bridget asked Daniel.

"American. And I think my Scottish friends here are conspiring against me," Daniel said.

"Just trying to improve the local economy," Philip Morrison said as he hung the scarf around Daniel's neck.

"Och, a truer Scotsman mine eyes have never beheld," Mr. MacCrivag said with dramatic flare. "He'll take it!"

"I guess I'll take it," Daniel said. He pulled out his wallet hoping he'd brought along enough cash. A price for the scarf had never been stated.

"Don't let these two bully you," Bridget told him.

"It's ok. This is very nice, and I've needed a good scarf anyway." Daniel paid for the scarf and they exited the weaving room. The fresh sea air and rugged Harris landscape gave them pause. They looked out upon the mossy grass that covered the island. Centuries of sheep grazing had made it a thin garment and so ragged in places that Harris's rocky bones poked through. An equally patchy sky of gray and blue hung low overhead. When the wind picked up, it carried with it a light flurry – insufficient to whiten the ground, but enough to mottle their view.

Mr. MacCrivag rubbed his bald head. "Wanna borrow my scarf?" Daniel asked.

"Cheeky," Mr. MacCrivag said and then shoved his hands into his coat pockets.

Daniel laughed and then turned to Bridget. "This is a really beautiful spot you've got here."

"Even in winter – incomparable," Philip Morrison agreed.

"It is. Some prefer a sea view, but I like being amongst the hills. Every time I see Mount Roineabhal there, I'm filled up with pride," Bridget said. She pointed to the mountain that dominated the landscape. The clouds hung low, obscuring its peak. "We're lucky she's even there to be seen. It was almost quarried. A whole mountain dug up and sold. Turned into roads for Europe and America and we left with nothing but a crater."

"Aye, but we showed that mining company," Philip Morrison said. "They underestimated us, didn't they. That wee row made us world famous for a bit."

Bridget nodded. "My da's a skilled weaver, but saving the mountain – that's work that will truly outlive him. I was a wee lass at the time, but ask any old timer and they can tell you stories," she said. Philip Morrison frowned. "Sorry, em, a personage of greater experience?" Bridget said with a smirk.

"So this mountain, Mount Roine- uh, it was going to be quarried?" Daniel said.

"Well, they made a lot of big promises, the mining company – money, jobs, and the like. Most of the community was for it at the start. Then we took a closer look – saw their track record, found out how much wealth would leave the island and how little would stay, found out the actual number of jobs and how temporary. We may be known for our tweed, but this mountain- " she paused. All four stared at Mount Roineabhal in silence. The mountain so dominated the landscape, the soul of the place, its absence was unimaginable. "Choosing to preserve this over a quick profit, seeing that money is not the sole determiner of value – that is my family's, our community's, true legacy."

* * *

Philip Morrison, William MacCrivag, and Daniel Darrow left Harris before the snow flurries had a chance to gather into a storm. They thanked Bridget for her hospitality and promised to return in warmer weather when they all, including her father, could enjoy an afternoon's hike up Roineabhal. The return trip to Lewis was colder than their drive down. Wind whistled through the cracked seals of the windows in Mr. MacCrivag's little green car. The drive seemed to last longer than the two hours it had taken them to drive down. By the time they arrived in Stornoway, the sun had long set and they were all quite hungry.

Philip Morrison parked the car around the corner from their final destination of the day. When they entered the pub, the smell of beer and hot food made their stomachs groan. A large stone fireplace warmed the room and they grabbed a table as close to it as possible. A folk band, consisting of an accordion player, fiddler, and guitarist, occupied the corner of the pub opposite the fireplace. Daniel, Mr. MacCrivag, and Philip Morrison reminisced on the day's highlights in between rowdy choruses. When their food arrived, they ate in silence for several minutes, being fully consumed with the need to fill their empty stomachs.

Two thirds through his smoked salmon, Mr. MacCrivag said, "Philly, you must mail me a copy of our photograph at Calanais."

"I'll print it when we get home," Philip Morrison said.

"Have you got a new printer?" Mr. MacCrivag asked.

"No, same old one."

"I can wait."

Philip Morrison turned to Daniel and said, "This one refuses to use email. I have to pop by a shop to develop photos for him. Those are hard to find these days. I keep- " The band started up again and Daniel could not make out the rest of his speech.

When the song ended, Daniel said, "If you send me the image I could just upload it to the Church Street website. I've been working on a section for community involvement and outings. A pic of us at the standing stones could be a fun addition. It might distract from," Daniel paused, "other things." He had nearly forgotten about the Bonfire Night fallout that surely awaited him upon his return to Inverness.

"What 'other things' might you be referring to, Reverend Darrow?" Mr. MacCrivag asked. One of his bushy eyebrows raised in a mischievous manner – payback for the bald jab back at the weaver's house.

"Nothing that would interest Mr. Morrison. Oh, I think the band is starting up again," Daniel replied.

"No, they're not," Philip Morrison said. "They've taken a break."

"Um, are you sure? It looks like they're getting ready for another song," Daniel said as he watched the fiddler put down his instrument and head for the bar. "Mr. MacCrivag, have you been to the church website lately? I've really put a lot up there since Reverend Calder asked me to update it."

"Och, I can't see why the kirk wastes money on that. We have a perfectly adequate corkboard in the kirk hall that goes unused," Mr. MacCrivag said.

"But it's not expensive at all. I've put all the photos and sermon audio files on a cloud service that's practically free. Just look for the little cloud icon with an arrow on it. If the arrow's green, it means I've recently added something."

"All these webs and clouds! How does that work – messing with the static electricity like lightning? Our Scottish winters aren't dreadful enough, now all the kids are putting their photographs up in the clouds. No thank you, I can wait for Philly's letter."

"Willie, even you can't be that daft," Philip Morrison said.

Mr. MacCrivag swallowed what remained of his beer. "I need a top up," he said and headed to the bar.

"Willie's always been a bit intimidated by technology, but we'll get him there," Philip Morrison said to Daniel. "I'll text you the photo."

When Mr. MacCrivag returned, he distributed three small glasses of Scotch. "Reverend Darrow, now you'll see why we traveled all the way out here." He raised his glass. "Cheers, mates." They all took a drink of the smoky single-malt. Unused to its strength, Daniel coughed and shook his head. "Whew," he uttered, "too much of this and I won't be able to see anything!"

"I've been thinking," Mr. MacCrivag said. "Perhaps that web photograph isn't such a bad idea." Philip Morrison winked at Daniel. "Could set some people straight," Mr. MacCrivag continued. "You may not know, but I've got a bit of a reputation as a hermit. Elspeth Gray, you know her, she once called me altogether antisocial. Now she's one to speak! She's become the recluse of late."

Daniel's interest piqued at the mention of Elspeth Gray. He had been unable on his own to discover much about her. Perhaps now he might uncover something useful to pass on to her daughter, Ellie – something that might make her overlook the Bonfire Night incident. "Do you know Mrs. Gray well?" Daniel asked.

"The Grays have been at Church Street for as long as I can remember. I knew her husband, the late Mr. Gray. He was an electrician, you know. Brilliant, wasn't he and always gave the kirk a good rate. But Mrs. Gray, she never took much interest in her husband's trade. I asked her once, this was after Mr. Gray passed, if she had any thoughts on my doorbell. She said she didn't know enough to fix anything, just enough to really muck things up – and she'll tell you that herself. It's true. She came to look at the doorbell and it's never rung right since. Philly, you should hear the blasted thing. It's like a dying pig!"

Daniel laughed, "I was careful to wear rubber soles before pushing it."

"Why the interest in Mrs. Gray?" Mr. MacCrivag asked. He took a sip from his glass before washing down his own question, "Or is it the young Ms. Ellie Gray that you're interested in?"

"Um, well, I've met Ellie, yes," Daniel answered. Then evasively he added, "I have an interest in all the members of the church."

"Aye, an interest!" Mr. MacCravig said. "You see, Phillie, our new Reverend here has taken a liking to the young lass."

"What? Why would you say that?" Daniel said, startled. He most certainly had taken a liking to Ellie, though he hadn't realized that anyone else had noticed. He wasn't even entirely sure how much Ellie had noticed. They had gone out a couple times since their sudden, stormy kiss under Urquhart Castle, but had never again repeated that encounter. Her affections seemed as elusive as Loch Ness's famous monster.

"Don't be shy. She's a bonnie lass. You'd make a better match than her old boyfriend – that boy who worked the till at my chemist. His family's from Glasgow aren't they. I swear he always shortchanged me."

"Not everyone from Glasgow is trying to cheat you," Philip Morrison said. "We went to *one* pub there and the bartender mistook his tenner for a five.

He's been prejudiced ever since."

"Anyway," Mr. MacCrivag said, "you are taking her to the kirk ceilidh next week?"

"That's the dance, right? I was planning on going, but I didn't know I needed a date?"

"Is that the dance!" Philip Morrison laughed. "What the lad needs is some courage." He tapped his empty whiskey glass. "I'll be back with more." Just then the band started up again. Mr. MacCrivag mimed a few dance moves. Daniel shook his head but could not keep from smiling. When Rev. Calder had first mentioned the ceilidh, Daniel of course had hoped that Ellie Gray would be in attendance, but he hadn't before thought to ask her. He was now more nervous than ever to return to Inverness.

Chapter Sixteen

Daniel dressed for the Church Street Kirk ceilidh in what he believed to be an appropriate outfit – pressed trousers and shirt, necktie, blazer, and the green and tan tweed scarf he'd bought during his recent trip to the Hebrides. Leaving his side of the duplex at Bellfield Park, Daniel noticed a brief slant of light caused by the Macphersons' front window blinds opening and quickly closing. Before he could exit the short garden path to the street, Hugh Macpherson, dressed in shined shoes, kilt, and formal jacket, caught him.

"You're not off to the ceilidh like that, are you?" Hugh Macpherson asked. Daniel quizzically assessed his clothing and informed the older man that he owned nothing nicer. "Ah, that may suit an American dance, but this is a proper Scottish dance and for that you must dress like a proper Scotsman!" Hugh Macpherson said.

"But this is all I have," Daniel said.

"Speak up lad."

"I said, this is all I have and I wouldn't have time anyway. Ell-, um, my ride will be here any minute. I was just going out to wait."

"What's that? This young generation, you are always in such a hurry. But we must make time to dress properly, mustn't we," Hugh Macpherson said. "The young Ms. Gray will not mind a wait." Daniel was disheartened to hear that the church gossip lines had reached even the nearly deaf Mr. Macpherson. "Come inside and we'll get you sorted." Hugh Macpherson ushered Daniel into his own side of the house. "I'm sure we have some of Young Hugh's things stored away. You seem his size."

When Daniel returned outside to find Ellie's car waiting, he was dressed in full Highlands costume: kilt, sporran, white knee high socks, and a black Prince Charlie jacket. Hugh Macpherson had much overestimated his son's likeness to Daniel, so the whole ensemble fit snuggly – too snug at places. The socks felt more like arthritic support hose and the jacket, already high cut around the waist, seemed almost childish. Partly from design and partly from size, he couldn't have closed its shiny, silver buttons if he had wanted to. As for the kilt, Daniel doubted that its length above his knees would pass any school dress code.

Having his date pick him up only added to the awkwardness he felt. Neither he nor Ellie owned a vehicle. She had borrowed this one from her mother. Still, it seemed better than taking public transportation. His American sensibilities would not allow them to arrive at their first dance via double-decker bus. When they pulled up two blocks away from the kirk, he insisted on preserving some semblance of Southern chivalry by walking around and opening the door to escort her out of the driver's seat. Ellie told him he needn't bother – she was neither a great lady nor a southern belle that required such pampering.

Daniel walked around the vehicle with an unease that naturally accompanied a man not wearing trousers. He kept one hand down at his side to hold the kilt in place. Though the heavy fabric did not require his help, he could not get the image of Marilyn Monroe standing over a street vent out of his mind. Despite Hugh Macpherson's spirited extolment of traditional Scottish dress and the traditional way of wearing it, Daniel had succeeded in keeping at least one article of his own clothing on that night. He was after all still an American at heart and, though he might happily sample haggis or blood pudding, walking around in a kilt without underwear was a step too far. After Bonfire Night, he could not afford another embarrassment of a more intimate nature.

Ellie, on the other hand, appeared quite comfortable in her attire for the evening. She wore a flowing dark green skirt and a white blouse with a tartan sash. She wore her cinnamon hair down at shoulder length. Her usual ponytail, she said, was too dangerous for a ceilidh. With all the twirling and spinning, someone might lose an eye. Daniel had expected her to be slightly taller, though she remained her normal height in comfortable flats. Heels, she informed him, were utterly impractical for Scottish dancing – simply a cruel tool invented by a man, or the English.

"Wait," she pulled his arm before they entered the kirk hall. "I know it's traditional to wait until the date has ended, but," she looked around in all directions, "what the hell." She kissed him. It was a small kiss at first, but then he leaned in and extended the embrace.

"Now don't be getting any ideas, but, well, someone had to make a move and it sure didn't seem like you were ever going to," Ellie said.

"I wanted to. After that afternoon in the rain at the castle. I just didn't know if *you* wanted me to. I've never been good at reading signs."

"I thought you went to graduate school," Ellie said. "Aren't you supposed to be smart?"

"Well, studying ancient Greek is not always as useful as one might think."

"Urquhart Castle – that was a sign."

"And this?" Daniel said. "Another sign?"

"I think he's finally catching on."

Hand in hand, Daniel Darrow and Ellie Gray entered the kirk hall as the band was warming up. Fisher, the choir director, hovered around them. Though he technically had no authority over the band, he could not help himself offering advice to these unknown musicians within his own musical jurisdiction. The band largely ignored him, tuning, and practicing short refrains over his admonishments.

Daniel and Ellie milled about the room engaging in the small talk required during such occasions. They also endured the little, needling comments that sometimes accompanied such gatherings of family or old friends – small slights that masquerade as friendly banter. "Don't light up while Reverend Darrow's watching, he might phone the police" or "Have you caught any more criminals lately? I saw some suspicious characters building a nativity scene." Ellie received a few exaggerated "Welcome backs" or "I thought you might've converted, it's been so long." While Daniel responded with a forced smile or self-deprecating laugh, Ellie returned in kind: "Are you sure you're in the right place? The pub's a few blocks south still" or "If I'd known you were coming, I'd have stayed away longer." Daniel was impressed by the quick ease with which she engaged them. "'Do unto others' and all – that's the Bible," she told him. "Anyway, it's just good fun, isn't it."

Daniel was relieved when Rev. Calder finally stepped up to the mic. She thanked everyone for coming and encouraged contributions to the silent auction set up at the far end of the room. Proceeds and ticket sales for the ceilidh would be split between the ongoing roof repair fund and the kirk's annual Christmas donation to a local homeless shelter. Small items had been generously donated by church members and a few local businesses. The largest auction of the night was an all-expenses paid four-day Highlands tour – an unexpected donation from the Philarguria Energy Co. Rev. Calder kept her greeting short because she could tell everyone was eager to dance. Further, she had seen the disregard the band had given Fisher during their warming up and she did not want to be cut off when they decided they had waited around long enough.

The moment she stepped aside, the band fired out lively chords. Dancers gathered in formation around the center of the room. Ellie pulled Daniel to her side amongst the growing crowd. The accordion player, doubling as vocalist, began the dance by calling out brief instructions, though the majority of feet on the floor already knew what was expected of them. The dancers separated into gender specific rows and without warning, at least as far as Daniel could tell, they all at once rushed toward one another, collided in a swing of interlocking arms and rushed away free in opposite directions. Further collisions, spins, and circlings occurred, prompted by calls from the accordion player. Daniel was reminded of a southern square dance, but played in fast motion on a carnival carousel.

When the music stopped, he was sweating and a little dizzy. Ellie was right – that would have been impossible in heels. He and Ellie made their way to the periphery of the dance floor. "You haven't said much of your trip to Lewis," Ellie said.

"It was certainly an experience. Mr. MacCrivag and his friend Mr. Morrison are quite a pair," Daniel answered. "I don't see him here tonight.

Do you?" Before she could answer, the accordion breathed out new chords. The fiddle and guitar joined in and dancers regained the floor.

"You up for another?" Ellie asked. This song had a less frantic tempo and the dancers were arranging themselves by couples, so he agreed.

"Ok, but after I'll need to catch my breath."

When the song ended, Daniel and Ellie continued their conversation near a table where drinks had been set up. "So, you've met the infamous Philly Morrison, have you?" Ellie said. "Anyone who's known auld MacCrivag long, has heard stories of Philly, but no one as far as I can tell, has ever actually met him. He's a phantom, people doubt he truly exists."

Daniel pulled out his phone. "I have proof of his existence – a photograph."

"We've all seen photos of mythical creatures before. Nessie is quite photogenic," Ellie said.

"Ha, the Loch Ness Monster, Bigfoot, and now Philip Morrison. This photo will fuel conspiracy theorists for years to come!"

They retrieved two drinks from the table, said polite *Hellos* to passing church members, and found two unoccupied chairs near the edge of the dance floor. "You know your mother came up in conversation on the trip," Daniel said. "Evidently she once took a look at Mr. MacCrivag's doorbell and, so he claims, it has never rung the same since."

"That sounds like Mum. After Da died, she tried to help people out – I think as a way to still feel a connection to him. But she had only seen him work sometimes. She has no real training."

"How is your mother doing?" Daniel asked. "Does she still seem depressed?"

Ellie stared into her cup as if into a magic eight ball, searching for an answer. "I'm really concerned about her, Daniel," she said. "She seems to have slipped farther away and I don't know how to bring her back. She refuses to see a doctor or talk to anyone. She hardly talks to me. Have you been able to speak to her?"

His eyes turned down in a flash of guilt. His failed detective fantasies had so preoccupied him, he had forgotten his promise to look in on Ellie's mother. "She is difficult to reach. I was planning on stopping by this week if she's in." It wasn't a complete lie. He had intended to see her; he simply hadn't yet set a date.

"She's always in," Ellie sighed. She shook her head. "Let's talk about something else. This is a party after all. And I haven't fully complimented you on your Highlands dress. I'm impressed, even if your kilt is a bit, em, short above the knees."

"It's a loaner." Daniel tugged at the plaid fabric. "Are miniskirts not in style anymore?"

"Come on, let's show off those sexy thighs!" She stood, grabbed his hand, and led him back to the dance floor. When the song ended the band took a short break. Ellie made her way to the ladies' room and Daniel refilled their drinks. While he waited for her, he overheard a conversation that would change the course of their relationship.

"So, they're sure, are they?"

"Quite. Definitively *not* accidental. The electrical box showed signs of tampering and certain wires had been crossed."

"I don't see how anyone could possibly know that. The whole house is an ashtray."

"Forensic science has come a long way since our day."

"And the boy, the university student? The police still think he did it?"

"He wouldn't have had the know-how, would he? No, the arsonist knew exactly how to muck up the wiring to cause a fire."

"Arson *and* murder – this Broonburn business is providing more intrigue than Inverness has known in a long while. A bit grim though."

Ellie appeared from behind a crowd. "Penny for your thought," she said. Daniel looked up, surprised. *Penny for my eavesdropping more likely*, he thought.

"Oh, nothing," he said.

Then a thought did enter his mind, or a more a memory. He was transported back to the Hebridean pub with William MacCrivag and Phillip Morrison. He heard Mr. MacCrivag say: "She didn't know enough to fix anything, just enough to really muck things up." Daniel tried to stamp down the thought. He did not want to think it, but once the thought had seeded, he found it impossible to ignore and with it a question he could not help but ask.

"Ellie, when did you say your mother's condition started?"

Chapter Seventeen

D aniel walked along Lilac Grove, a curved, almost circular road in the Merkinch part of Inverness. William MacCrivag's house with its broken doorbell was only a few blocks away. Today, though, Daniel had an appointment with Elspeth Gray. With each step he thought of how she lived much farther from a bus stop than any older woman should. His legs, his entire body, still ached from the previous night's ceilidh. He had never before experienced such energetic dancing. He woke up this morning feeling as if he had just run a half marathon. No wonder Ellie had worn sensible footwear. He now wore a bandage on the heel of his right foot where his borrowed shoe had rubbed through the skin.

He was hungry and could have eaten an early dinner before catching a bus here, but he had already put off this visit too long. He had promised Ellie that he would look in on her mother. He didn't mind that. Visiting elderly church members was just part of the job. They usually had funny stories to tell - if you didn't mind hearing them more than once. They often offered snacks. Tea and biscuits seemed a common mark of British hospitality – a dram of Scotch if you were lucky. If this had been a typical home visit, he might be looking forward to it.

If only he hadn't overheard that conversation at the ceilidh. If only his mind hadn't formed a connection between what was said in the kirk hall and what was said at the pub in Stornoway.

A one-on-one visit with the mother of the woman he had just begun a relationship with would have been difficult enough on its own. But add this ulterior motive, this needling suspicion. The walk from the bus stop to her house was agony. Daniel thought back to Ellie's answer to his question. She wasn't exactly certain when her mother had started showing signs of depression, but it had hit quite suddenly. "Maybe it's you," she joked. "Her depression started about the same time you arrived, but it really got worse a week or two after." *Just about the time when police released information about a body found in the ruins of Broonburn House*, Daniel thought.

If his terrible suspicion was correct, Elspeth Gray would not have displayed any unusual behavior immediately after the fire. What person is saddened by success? But the body – that might not have been expected. Daniel hoped it hadn't been expected. Perhaps guilt had overcome her? Elspeth Gray did not seem like a murderer; but then, she did not seem like an arsonist either.

He arrived at her door and paused. He thought of Ellie and the time they had spent together the past few weeks: their meeting at her clinic, the early morning coffee get-togethers, their kiss at Urquhart Castle, the ceilidh. He remembered of the smell of her hair and the green of her eyes behind her glasses. He thought of her smile and the taste of her lips. If he was right about Mrs. Gray, even if he was wrong, he knew that these might be the last memories he would have of Ellie. Nothing puts the brakes on a new relationship like accusing her mother of murder.

Daniel took a long breath and, remembering William MacCrivag's bell, gave the door a cautious ring. A pleasant, wholly unbroken tone sounded. For a moment he hoped. Perhaps there was no connection with the fire? Elspeth Gray opened her door and invited him inside. He noticed that she still wore her silk gloves. She seemed surprised to see him even though he had phoned ahead. When he entered the house his pupils widened, taking in whatever light they could find. The whole place seemed as if under a shadow. Curtains covered the windows and the main lights were switched off. She showed Daniel to the sitting room where a single lamp tried its best to illuminate the modest sized room.

"I'm sorry, I wasn't expecting company," she said.

"I phoned."

"Tea?"

"No thank you," Daniel answered. "I'm fine. It's a little dark in here, though."

"Yes. Well, what was it you wanted to see me about?"

Daniel got the impression that his presence was not particularly welcome. "I just wanted to stop by and say 'Hello' – see how you are doing. We haven't had much of a chance to get to know one another," he lied. The darkness and her curt manner unnerved him. Besides, one cannot simply ask another person outright if she is an arsonist and murderer. A degree of subtlety was needed and a pleasant lie seemed as good a place as any to start.

Daniel looked around the shadowy room. "Your house looks, um, nice. I can see you have a nice fireplace, I think. Do you ever use it?"

"Yes," she said.

Perhaps too subtle. Daniel decided on another route. "Oh, Sir Walter seems in good health. Your daughter's a fine veterinarian."

"Aye," Elspeth Gray answered.

"She's attending the vet school in Edinburgh, right? Doing a, I forgot what she called it, E M something, here in Inverness – like an internship," Daniel said.

"EMS, Extra Mural Studies. I suppose it is like an internship," she said.

Daniel smiled. He had gotten more than a one-word response from her. He decided to capitalize on it. "Edinburgh University, that place has been in the news a lot lately."

"Has it?"

"Yes, in connection with the fire at Broonburn House. The body, the boy they found there, he was also a student at Edinburgh."

"How do you know my daughter?"

She hadn't taken his bait. Had he pushed too soon? "Actually, Sir Walter introduced us. She gave him his yearly checkup, if you remember." Daniel wondered why Ellie had not mentioned him to her, but that question could wait. He decided to cast another line – play a hunch. "I like your gloves – they look very nice."

"Thank you."

"Are they fashion or therapeutic?"

"It's just something I'm trying."

No bite. Daniel decided to abandon subtlety. "It seems like everyone is talking about that Broonburn fire. Have you noticed? Everyone at Church Street seems to have their own theory of what happened or who did it. My favorite is that a mouse got into the wiring. Ms. MacGillivray, Eliza, says it was more likely a cat. But I think she and her long-eared companion might have a prejudice. What do you think? Do you have any theories?"

"Eliza MacGillivray is most certainly prejudiced against cats," she answered.

"I mean about Broonburn House."

"It was an old building."

Strike three. But who was counting. "Mrs. Gray, I need to confess something to you," Daniel said. "My visit today is not purely conversational. I'm concerned about you. I've noticed that you seem rather, um, reserved. And from what I hear, that is not you at all. I know the kirk doesn't really have anything like a confessional, and please forgive me if I'm being presumptuous, but I am here to listen if you ever need to talk – for whatever reason."

She offered no response this time save a blank stare. Daniel had hinted as much as he dared and he now began to doubt himself. He had been wrong before – humiliatingly wrong. Maybe he was wrong again. A lightness came over him and he nearly laughed out loud. How could he think this depressed, but clearly not malicious, old woman before him could possibly be an arsonist and murderer. He promised himself to give up his ridiculous infatuation with Broonburn House. It had caused him nothing but anxiety and disgrace. His job was to minister to the people of Inverness, to trust them – not to suspect them of murder.

Just as he was about to change the subject, Elspeth Gray looked down at her gloved hands. For several minutes she remained in that bowed position. Without warning she burst into tears. "I didn't know. I didn't know," she repeated.

"You didn't know what?" Daniel asked.

"I didn't know he was in there," she said, tears soaking her gloves.

"Who?"

"Tom Shaw."

Chapter Eighteen

When Daniel Darrow stood to give the closing blessing at Church Street Kirk, he could feel the cold tension that had been building in the air all morning. Heavy and thick. Like a social haar. The stares, the judgment, the standoffishness coming from row after row of church pew – all palpable. He had a newfound sympathy for Judas and how the erstwhile disciple must have felt the morning after his infamous kiss. If Daniel had hoped that, after Bonfire Night, a correct allegation could redeem him in the eyes of his congregation, he now knew otherwise. The emotions he felt emanating from the men and women all bundled up in their woolen overcoats, tweeds, and laces chilled the very stones of the kirk building.

Elspeth Gray was no saint. No one could deny the culpability of her alleged actions. But she was still one of them. She had been a member of Church Street long before the kirk hall's 1990s remodel, back before the leaky roof had expanded from a few drips to a steady stream on especially rainy days. The kirk had seen her daughter grow from diapers to high heels. After her husband's death, the kirk, now their only family, had mourned with her and wee Ellie. Sure, the congregation enjoyed a juicy bit of gossip and playful teasing with regard to one another, but as in a family, these were privileges allowed only to members. Their new minister had not yet earned these rights. That he might cause the ruin of one of their own, whatever her actual guilt, was indefensible.

Ellie Gray was not present at the morning's service. Daniel had hoped he might see her there, despite knowing that he would not. Days earlier, immediately after her mother had confessed, he had wanted to call Ellie. He had wanted to spare her the pain of first hearing about it from the morning news. Yet, Elspeth made him swear to wait until after she had turned herself in to the police. She had insisted that he not speak to anyone, especially Ellie, until after she had given her official testament to the police. Daniel did not understand the elder Gray's request, but he honored it. What else could he do in the presence of a weeping, broken woman?

When Daniel finally was able to call Ellie, she did not answer. He called repeatedly, but connected to nothing more than her jovial answering machine voice. Assuming she was screening his calls, he tried again from a borrowed phone. She picked up, but upon hearing his voice, ended the call before he could say, "I'm sorry." Daniel understood Ellie's evasions. Elspeth had mentioned in her tearful police report that only after consulting with her new minister did she feel she must confess to the fire that destroyed both Broonburn House and the life of poor Tom Shaw. It had not taken long for the local papers and news outlets to connect the dots between Elspeth Gray, her long membership at Church Street Kirk, and their new American minister, who had recently made a bit of news himself.

Bonfire Night Buffoon Leads to Broonburn Breakthrough

Killer Gran's Clergy Confession

Yankee Doodle Murder

Daniel understood Ellie's evasions. Irreverent and badly punned headlines aside, the media had left little suspicion that he was the impetus to her mother's confession and subsequent imprisonment. He just wished she would let him tell his side of the story.

If she would only stay on the line long enough, he would tell her that he had gone to see her mother out of a mutual concern for her well-being. He would remind Ellie that she, herself, had asked him look into her mother's unusual reclusiveness.

Daniel had run through their imagined conversation many times in his head. Of course, he would leave out the part of the story where he asked Elspeth Gray certain leading questions. The part of the story he would tell was nonetheless true. He would tell Ellie that, though her mother had been reluctant, her confession was inevitable. Her guilt had made her ill in both body and spirit. Just as a body may faint to relieve itself of intense pain, Elspeth Gray had confessed out of sheer spiritual necessity.

* * *

"I went out for a drive," the old woman told Daniel. "I didn't mean to drive past that," Elspeth paused, "that House. I didn't have a destination at all actually. I was thinking about – em, that's not important. I was just driving to clear my head."

"You drove by Broonburn House the night of the fire?" Daniel asked. Elspeth Gray wiped her eyes with a cloth.

"Aye, before I knew it, I found myself at the front gate," Elspeth said. "I drove past a bit and parked. I got out of my car. I don't know why. My body just moved on its own – like in a dream where I can watch myself acting. I -" A flush of new tears prevented her from continuing. Though Daniel had cobbled together enough curious circumstances to make him suspicious - her recent reclusive behavior, her ever-present gloves, her amateur knowledge of household electrical systems - he was unready for such an outpouring of guilt. Her tears made him uncomfortable.

He looked around the room for a tissue, but found none. Compassion and decorum told him he should do something to calm her crying, but he felt foreign in her living room, and helpless. He shifted his weight in his chair and moved his hands from his lap to the chair's arms and back again, unsure of what to do with them. "Can I, um, get you anything?" he asked her and immediately felt silly for offering such an inadequate response. Elspeth made no indication of hearing him. "I can see this is hard. You don't have to continue," Daniel said, though he hoped she would and he felt guilty for that.

"I watched myself scramble over the fence. It's quite short actually, and the rough stones made easy footholds," Elspeth Gray said. She did not bother drying her tears. "I remember pulling my shawl over my head. There was a chill in the air."

Of course, Daniel thought. CCTV had shown a hooded figure enter the house just before the fire. Everyone had assumed the grainy, lowlight images had been that of a youth in a hooded sweater.

"I walked up the front steps. The door was open. Can you believe it?" Elspeth continued. "A great house like that and with all the expensive builders' tools – just open to anyone." She spoke now with greater calm, as if she were recounting an overheard story or a program she had seen on television.

"I had visited Broonburn House once as a girl for a school trip. I was so enamored with it then. I had never before seen such gilded grandeur – perhaps in a museum or gallery down in Edinburgh on holiday. Aye, that's what it reminded me of. But in a home? And one rarely ever used by its owner? It was difficult for my young mind to comprehend.

"Little had changed since then. I walked about from one room to another, admiring the displays of wealth and pomp. I can see now that a darkness was in me too, deep in my stomach. I saw more in those old walls than the princess playhouse of my girlhood. I knew now-" Elspeth's voice gave out.

"Yes?" Daniel said.

"Em, well, I don't know what possessed me to stop at the house, much less walk about. I was about to go to the upstairs, when a small cracked door in the hall distracted me. I knew instinctively what it was. I had seen similar when I accompanied Mr. Gray at his work. The covering to the electric box came off easily enough. I recognized a few of the switches. Those old wirings are difficult to mend, but surprisingly easy to muck up. One can do a great amount of damage with just a little knowledge."

That's exactly what William MacCrivag had said about her at the pub in Stornoway, Daniel thought.

"Gave me a nasty shock though," Elspeth Gray said. She rubbed her gloved hand. "I put a salve on every morning and evening, but the burn doesn't want to heal."

"When I had finished, I carefully replaced the covering and took a look around the library. I wanted to visit the conservatory, but my hand hurt badly and it had gotten quite dark by then. Before I left, I switched on an electric saw some builder had left out on a table. That's all that was needed. That wee surge of electricity. I thought I might see fire trucks on my way home, but I remember the traffic being unusually light." The old woman, tears partly dried on her face, offered a hollow chuckle.

After several long, silent minutes, Daniel asked, "And Tom Shaw?"

The old woman's face changed. She looked right at Daniel, but she did not focus on him. She looked through him, past him toward a memory or some hope for understanding. Perhaps she thought of her own daughter, also a student at Edinburgh University. "I didn't know he was there. I didn't know anyone was there. The house seemed abandoned for the night. I know it was."

"But Mrs. Gray," Daniel said, "Tom Shaw *was* there. The police found his body in the ashes."

"He shouldn't have been there. It wasn't about him. I was-" She stopped herself again.

"You were what?" Daniel asked. "Why did you mess with the electrical system? Mrs. Gray, why did you burn down that house?" All the while she had been telling her story, Daniel kept asking himself that question. *Why would this small, shy woman, lifelong member of Church Street Kirk, mother to his adored Ellie, intentionally set fire to Broonburn House?* She had confessed to the act, but still withheld her motive.

"I dinnae ken," she said with her face now in her hands.

"Huh?"

"I don't know. I hadn't intended to. I just – I can't explain it."

"But you drove to the house. You walked in, changed the wiring, and drove away. You knew what you were doing," Daniel said.

"Did I?" she asked. Daniel was uncertain whether her question was rhetorical or meant for him. "I am getting old," she continued. "I do not remember things as well as I once did. Maybe it was an episode of early dementia or Alzheimer's."

"You killed a boy. Even if you didn't know he was there, he still died because of a fire you set. You must tell the police. You owe it to the boy's family. Everyone thinks he set the fire. They think he's a criminal."

"A criminal," Elspeth Gray repeated. Her composure sunk with the weight of such a title applying to herself. "You cannot tell Ellie. I cannot bear her thinking badly of me. Promise me you will not tell her."

"She will find out eventually."

"Then let it be from the police – someone she doesn't know, disconnected. Promise me that."

* * *

As people left the service, few shook Rev. Darrow's hand. Of those that did, most did so out of some holy obligation or habit – they did not meet his eyes. A few, three perhaps, offered firm shakes and hushed praise. That made him feel somehow worse than the majority's coldness. He forwent tea and biscuits in the kirk hall. After changing out of his clerical robes, Daniel decided to wait out the crowd in the little garden outside of Rev. Calder's study.

The air outside was cold and damp. Daniel welcomed it. The cold would keep everyone else inside. The garden's only other occupants were a small bird that had forgotten to fly south for the winter and a light orange cat happy for the bird's absentmindedness. Sir Walter Scott crouched behind a stone bench watching the bird hop from one branch to another in a mostly leafless tree. He wiggled his hindquarters on occasion, but seemed content to simply observe. "You've got the right idea," Daniel said to the cat. "If only I'd been happy to sit back and watch like everyone else. Let the police do their thing and gossip about it later over tea. That would have been the sensible thing."

The cat gave Daniel a sideways glance and flicked its tail. "Don't worry, Sir Walter, I won't scare away your little friend. I've scared away enough of my own." Daniel sat softly on the bench's edge, careful not to spook the bird. Untrusting of this human who had once carted him to the vet for shots and later kicked and tumbled over him in a hallway, the cat put the length of the bench between them and returned his attention to the bird.

"What was I thinking?" Daniel said. "Why couldn't I have just stuck to the job I came here to do? No one asked me to find out who burned down Broonburn House and killed Tom Shaw. Sure, it was all anyone talked about, but that was just it – talk. I was the only one dumb enough to actually go and try to solve it. And what's that gotten me?"

The bird flew away behind the kirk's towered spire. Sir Walter Scott gave Daniel a quizzical, accusing look and jumped onto the opposite edge of the bench. The cat sat and stared at the patch of sky just before the spire where the bird disappeared.

"I'll tell you where it's gotten me," Daniel continued, "It's got me avoiding my congregation and sitting out in the cold with only a cat to talk to. Not quite the tickertape parade I'd envisioned. And Ellie, what am I do to about Ellie? She's completely shut me out. Just when things were beginning to go so well with us." Daniel had a thought and looked at the cat. "What do you think, Sir Walter? Want to help me out and exaggerate that limp of yours? We can get in to see her at the clinic."

The cat made a throaty chirp and jumped down from the bench. "What a pal," Daniel said. "Et tu, Scotte?" Daniel remained on the bench outside Rev. Calder's study, listening to cars drive off and thinking of investing in a dog. Except for the business of arranging the morning's service, he had hardly spoken with Rev. Calder since Elspeth Gray's arrest. After the cold reception he had just received from the rest of the congregation, he dreaded their inevitable meeting. Still, despite his trepidation, he knew that she was his best shot at finding a way forward.

Chapter Nineteen

Mary Monroe stood at the front window of her small living space with her eyes fixed on the horizon. The weather was overcast that last Sunday in May, 1819. Mary strained to see through the fog. On any usual Sunday morning, she would be readying her family for church. She would be patching the hem of her daughter's best dress, worn bare from so many Sunday walks to the parish kirk a few miles away. She would be yelling at wee Duncan to wash his hands and face before breakfast, after he had helped his father tend their three milk cows. Mary's husband would come in from the cool morning full of physical warmth and hunger. He would place a fresh pail of milk on their table and wait for her to finish cooking their eggs and oatmeal. They would discuss the weather and the state of their animals and crops and whether or not the Campbells would be in attendance that Sunday as Mrs. Campbell had lately been in poor health.

But this was not a usual Sunday morning. Instead of mending her children's best suits, she had packed their clothing along with her own and whatever bedding that would fit into a trunk. This morning the milk pail sat in the corner of the kitchen because her husband and son were busy dismantling their table. Her grandfather had built that table from trees he and other men from their village had felled from the nearby forest. Her husband said it would be easier to transport in smaller pieces. She looked back from the window to their small home and offered a silent prayer that their fates might change, that unlike Pharaoh the laird's heart might be turned back from stone. She wanted to scream to the heavens, but she knew no help would come. In the months after her family and neighbors had received their writs of eviction, she had screamed. She had cried, prayed, and pleaded, but hearts remained hardened and she was now being driven out of her promised land.

"Maybe they won't come," she said to her husband.

"They'll come. Perhaps not today, but they'll come," he said.

"But how do you know? Didn't you ask her to reconsider?"

"Aye, the Reverend wrote a letter on behalf of the village. But you've heard the stories from the west. The whole country's being turned into sheep walks. The lairds have no use for us anymore."

"The lairds have no use for *us*?!" Mary Monroe shouted. "Well, I have no use for the lairds! Haven't we always paid our rent? Even when that old cat raised it, we had to sell a cow, but we paid her. Monroes have farmed this land since there was land to farm – your father, his father, his father before him, on and on, all while her ladyship flits away her fortune down in England."

"You're too hard on her ladyship. She's offered us an allotment in Helmsdale. That's a lot more than folk on other estates got."

"Helmsdale," she huffed. "That's far off on the coast. Are you to become a fisherman? Which of us knows the first thing about fishing? And for what? So she can replace us with sheep? Are our lives worth so little?" Mary paced the room. "How can you be so calm? We have a right to stay in our home, a right to stay and farm this land as we always have!"

Her husband laid down his hammer and ran his hands through thinning hair. Without notice he slammed his fists on the table and cursed. The old wood creaked under such violence. The boy jumped back in fright. "Of course I'm angry, Mary! I nearly died fighting the French for her. Of course she owes us our farm. I know the plots in Helmsdale cannot sustain our crops or animals. But what can we do? The people fought back in Roth-shire and see what good it did them. They still lost their farms and now where are they – imprisoned, scattered."

"But we-" Mary Monroe stopped. The startled cawing of a crow turned her attention back to the window. She saw the outline of two men on horseback and a few more on foot. They carried with them the instruments of her eviction: axes, hammers, and fire. "They've come," she said. Her husband met her at the window. "Why have they brought torches?" she asked.

"I'd hoped it wouldn't happen like this, but I've heard rumors – the same from all across the Highlands. They mean to make it so we can never return. They mean to permanently clear this land of us," her husband said. "Gather the children and whatever you can carry. I'll harness the animals."

Mary recalled that today was Whitsunday, Pentecost, a celebration of the day the Holy Spirit descended upon Jesus' disciples with tongues of fire. On this unusual Sunday morning, Mary witnessed what seemed to her an advancing league of unholy spirits, shrouded in smoke and fog. For her children, she kept her composure as she wrapped them in wool blankets and ushered them outside. With their backs to the approaching gang, she told her children to look at their home and farm. She instructed them to take in their small portion of the glen and the surrounding hills and to hold it in their hearts. They would not understand now, she told them, but this vision, this memory, was their inheritance. They must pass it on to their children and grandchildren and to their children after them.

* * *

When the last car drove away from Church Street Kirk, Daniel Darrow knew the time had come for him to face Rev. Calder. The cold stone bench he had been sitting on together with the damp air of Inverness in November had sapped all the warmth from his body. He knocked on the door to her study and winced at the impact of his frozen knuckles on hard wood, feeling as if they would shatter. Like a swaddling blanket, he pulled his coat tight. He knocked again, this time with the toe of his shoe. A muffled cry came from inside, but Daniel couldn't make out its intention, so he waited another few minutes until the door opened to him.

"Why Daniel, I wondered where you'd gone off to. Made yourself scarce after the service did you," Rev. Calder said.

"Can you blame me?"

"Not really, no. Come in, come in, you're letting in the chill."

Daniel sat down on her couch, the same couch upon which earlier that month a hoody gang of teens had sat. Rev. Calder hung her stole in a narrow wardrobe before taking her place in a nearby chair. She looked around the room. "I'm sorry, but tea is over in the parish hall."

"That's fine," Daniel said. A cup of hot tea would have warmed his body, but he did not imagine it could do much for his spirits.

"I've got some homebounds to see – my regular Sunday engagements, but I'm glad you didn't run off. We're due for a talk. I wish you had come to me sooner about Elspeth Gray. Especially after our wee embarrassment on Bonfire Night," Rev. Calder said.

"I know. I'm sorry, I should have spoken to you when I first suspected something."

"I've had a few assistants before you, but none that have made quite the same, em, impression as yourself. Not that the police shouldn't have been notified if Mrs. Gray really is guilty of what they say she is. I'm still trying to wrap my mind around that. Sweet Elspeth Gray setting fire to that grand house – and while that poor boy was trapped inside." Rev. Calder sighed. "If you suspected her, and I'm not sure why you believed it your place to investigate the matter, but since you did, there had to be a way to handle it with more decorum. How am I expected to mentor you if you're not more open with me?"

"I'm here now," Daniel said.

"So you are. What are we going to do about all this?"

"I've been thinking," Daniel said, "and her story just doesn't seem to add up. You said it yourself – why would Elspeth Gray, who's never shown any criminal— much less, murderous— tendencies, burn down Broonburn House? When I talked with her that afternoon, when she confessed, I got the feeling she wasn't telling me the full story."

"She said as much to the police. She suffered from an acute bout of dementia – that she wasn't fully aware what she was doing," Rev. Calder said. She reached to her desk for a copy of the local paper.

"I've been wanting to ask you," Daniel said, "did Mrs. Gray display signs of dementia or that kind of disorientation before? I've only met her a few times, but I did not get that impression. Neither did Ellie or anyone else

I've talked to. Never even a suggestion about her mind slipping. Mrs. Gray wasn't telling me the whole story, but not because she couldn't remember it. When she confessed to me, it felt like she was withholding because she didn't want me to know – like she was concealing something."

"Do you think she was lying?"

"I don't know. She seemed to have an intimate knowledge of the house's interior and there was her burned hand. I think it's reasonable to believe she did start the fire, but she may not have done so for the reason she claimed."

Rev. Calder ran her fingers along her collar as she thought. "I can't recall anything. Actually, Elspeth's always struck me as quite sharp."

"Any family history of dementia?"

"I don't know. Well-" Rev. Calder went over to a closet door. She opened it to reveal shelves stuffed from floor to ceiling with thick, old books. Their combined weight, which Daniel imagined must be considerable, bowed the shelves. "Before long, we'll have to find another place to keep all these," Rev. Calder said. She stooped to one of the lower shelves, pulled out a volume, and placed it on her desk. "These are the kirk's records. Births, weddings, deaths – they're all recorded here. Sometimes brief commentaries accompany the entries. I've lent my study to many a parishioner wanting to investigate their family history."

"And the Grays are in there?" Daniel asked.

"I don't know how far back the records go, but I'm fairly certain Elspeth's parents were buried here. I haven't time to go through these with you just now, but you're welcome to them if you like. If you think there might be something there that could help her, I know she, as well as the rest of the kirk, would be grateful."

"Thank you," Daniel said. "I don't think I could take another Sunday morning like this one."

"I know everyone felt a bit tense this morning. It's one thing for the police to arrest one of their own, but to be aided by their own minister – they feel betrayed. I'm glad that you came to me this morning, because if you are to remain with us, if you are to regain their trust, you cannot hide away and pretend like nothing happened or wait for people to forget. We have long memories here in the Highlands. If there's any redemption to be found in the midst of this tragedy, it's your task to find it." Rev. Calder gave him a heavy pat on the shoulder, collected her purse and coat, and exited the room.

Left alone, Daniel opened the thick book and searched for Elspeth Gray's name. Near the back he found it, along with that of her husband and her daughter, Elspeth Gray II (Ellie). Records showed that Elspeth Gray had been both married and born in Inverness. Daniel traced the branches of her parents and both grandparents. He flipped through evidences of births, marriages, and deaths. He read brief commentaries summarizing the lives of the deceased. Elspeth's maternal grandmother had been a schoolteacher and lived until the ripe age of 92. Records of the paternal branch of her family tree went back further. Her father had won commendations for his service in the second world war. His surname, Elspeth's maiden name, was Monroe. Elspeth's grandfather had moved the family to Inverness from Dingwall where he had, at different times, been a member of two local rugby leagues and later a bowling league right up until his death at age 86.

The record ended there, so Daniel went to the closet to employ other, more fragile and musty volumes. The records in these older books were sparser and more difficult to read, many of them handwritten. Daniel felt strange going through Ellie's family history without her there, but, he told himself, if she wasn't going to talk to him, what else could he do? Besides, the smell and feel of these old tomes was too strong for him to resist. They reminded him of his seminary days researching ancient scriptures and early church documents.

As he read on, he was able to piece together much of the family's origins. Before Dingwall, the family seemed itinerant, with brief mentions of a son or cousin or great great grandfather residing in towns and villages Daniel had never heard of and could hardly pronounce. One record placed a Monroe clan in the coastal town of Helmsdale with an accompanying note about a failed fishing enterprise. The historical trail ended just before that in 1819 with a writ of eviction for Duncan Monroe, Sr. and Mary Monroe. They had once lived, it seemed, on a croft near Kildonan in the hill country of the Sutherland estate.

When Daniel finally closed and reshelved the last of the record books chronicling the Gray/Monroe clan, he felt an ache in his stomach. Looking at a clock, he was surprised to find that he had worked through lunch and nearly into dinner. He sighed as he locked up Rev. Calder's study and headed down Church Street in search of food. For all he had learned about Elspeth Gray, he felt no closer to understanding why she had set fire to Broonburn House. He had found no historical traces of mental decline. From all accounts the Grays and earlier the Monroes were all of strong and long-lived stock.

If there was something else in the historical record, some long hidden motive, Daniel would need more than books to uncover it. Elspeth Gray was in jail and seemed to have told him all she was willing to tell. If she was holding something back, Daniel knew he would have to look elsewhere for answers. He would have to speak with Ellie.

Chapter Twenty

Daniel left his half of the house at Bellfield Park later than usual for a Thursday morning. After word got out of Elspeth Gray's arrest and of his own part in urging a confession out of her, he found he had more free time. His usual home visits to parishioners had become less welcome and therefore less common. In the four days since he had sat with Sir Walter Scott, the kirk cat, in a chilly garden to avoid after church tea, he had had only one home visit. He spent this extra time preparing for the next week's service, updating the kirk website, and trying to decide how many times he could still attempt to contact Ellie Gray without seeming a stalker. He had concluded that three unanswered calls in as many days was sufficient, more than sufficient, to obtain that title. So, today he would cease. Rev. Calder had implied it was up to him to repair what he had helped break in the kirk community, but he was only one man. If Ellie wouldn't talk to him, he didn't know what else he could do for them.

Marjory Macpherson was outside trimming back her dormant rose bush. "Good morning Mrs. Macpherson," Daniel said as he passed her.

"Eh? What?"

"I said, 'Good morning, Mrs. Macpherson,'" Daniel repeated, more loudly this time.

"Eh, oh, good morning Reverend," she said. "I'm glad you stopped by. I've a message for you."

"Well, I was just heading out," Daniel said, slowing his walk, but still moving away. Marjory Macpherson's impromptu greetings had a way of turning into lengthy, rambling conversations if he wasn't careful.

She did not appear to hear and continued as if he were standing right next to her. "A woman called for you yesterday. A young woman actually. I don't know why she didn't just ring you herself. Doesn't your phone work over there on your side? You must let Hugh know if things are not working properly."

"What's the message, Mrs. Macpherson?"

"Right, the message, yes. I don't know why she didn't just ring you herself. Surely she has your number. She didn't say much, just to ring her back."

"Ring who back? Who called?" Though he was on no strict schedule, Daniel feared that this conversation might eat up the rest of his morning.

"Wee Ellie Gray, dear."

"Ellie? Ellie called for me?" Daniel asked.

"Aye, that's what I said. Did you not hear me? Perhaps you should get your hearing checked – young lad like yourself should have better ears. Now Mr. Macpherson, that's an altogether different story. He won't-"

"Mrs. Macpherson," Daniel interrupted her, "if this little fence wasn't between us, I could kiss you!" He blew her a theatrical kiss and hurried back to his own door. Marjory Macpherson blushed and cut a stem of her rose bush several inches too short.

Once inside, Daniel called Ellie's cell phone but went straight to voice mail. He tried her at the Kinmylies Veterinary Clinic.

"Ms. Gray is assisting with a patient just now," the receptionist said.

"Ok, um, can you leave a message?"

Daniel gave the receptionist his information. While he waited for Ellie to call back, he attempted to write a homily for the upcoming Sunday. He made little progress, distracted with rehearsing what he would say to Ellie and checking his cell phone to ensure its volume and reception were active. When Ellie finally called him back, she said they could meet at her mother's house shortly after lunch when her morning shift ended.

The bus let Daniel out with plenty of time to spare. He could have taken a later bus, but he didn't want to risk arriving after Ellie and giving her more time to change her mind. The walk down Lilac Grove also took less time than expected so that when he arrived in front of Elspeth Gray's house,

Daniel had at least half an hour to wait. He rang the bell just in case. When no one answered, he sat on the concrete step in front of the door. At this level a narrow sticker attached to the flap of the door's mail slot caught his attention. In block lettering, the sticker read: "GRAY ELECTRICAL." Elspeth Gray must have been unable or, more likely, unwilling to remove it after her husband had died, Daniel thought. What must Ellie be going through now? No wonder she had been so standoffish. Her father had passed away only a few years ago and now she was effectively losing her mother.

In the days that had passed since Elspeth Gray's confession, Daniel dwelt considerably on what the arrest had meant for him. The amateur thrill of solving a mystery quickly soured, as did the initial ministerial goodwill of his parish. He had lost the thrill of a nascent romance. Until now, however, he hadn't considered, in any depth at least, the impact the arrest had had on Ellie. He now felt ashamed for his selfishness. Ellie had needed time to process and to mourn – time which he had refused to grant her. The memory of Bonfire Night flashed before him. Self-absorption clouded his thinking then as well. *Dear Lord*, he thought, *let me have learned my lesson this time.*

He wished he were Catholic so he could confess and receive specific instructions for absolution. Along with a few Hail Marys, he imagined, penance for this vice of the ego must require some act of selflessness. What exactly that might be, however, he was unsure. His own Reformed tradition taught him that forgiveness rested in divine grace alone. He could only hope that Ellie was as generous.

When she arrived, driving her mother's car, Ellie smiled at him. *That's a good sign*, Daniel thought, *and more than I probably deserve.* "I'm sorry I haven't called you back sooner," she said.

"You have nothing to be sorry for. I was being selfish. You needed some space. I should've realized that. I just really wanted to see you. I had a few questions and, well, I missed you."

She unlocked the door and invited him into the house. "Do you want tea?"

"No thanks, I'm fine."

"Well, I'm putting the kettle on if you change your mind."

Ellie went to the kitchen and left Daniel in the front sitting room. He felt strange being back in that room. He did not want to sit in Elspeth's chair and sitting in the room's other chair, where he had sat the evening she had confessed, did not feel quite right either. So he stood. He looked around the room at the burgundy checked wallpaper and the framed photographs of the Gray family. There were likely Monroes in there as well. Elspeth Gray smiled brightly at him in one picture. Young and dressed in white. She and her late husband stood hand in hand in the sanctuary of Church Street Kirk. Next to this hung a faded photograph of what Daniel assumed to be Elspeth's parents on their own wedding day. Daniel saw an infant Ellie, wearing curls and a lace dress, then a family picture of the three of them in front of the deep blue water and green hills of Loch Ness. A map of Scotland hung on the far wall. It recreated an engraving of the land as it had appeared generations ago, with many more hills than highways.

"Please sit," Ellie said when she reentered the room. She took a seat in her mother's chair and motioned for Daniel to take the other. He hesitated and then sat down.

"I'm not sure what to say," Ellie said.

"Me neither." They sat in silence for a few long minutes. "How is Elspeth? Have you seen her since-"

"I visit her every day. Well, I didn't yesterday. I hate seeing her there, in those, those prison clothes. And with guards or cameras watching everything we say. It's so impersonal. Can't they let her keep her own clothes?" Tears began to well up in Ellie's eyes. "I'm sorry, I told myself I was done."

Daniel fidgeted and glanced around the room, still no tissue in sight. He pulled his chair closer and took her hand in his. The tears and the green of her eyes reminded him of Loch Ness and their first kiss. She was beautiful. He couldn't think of any appropriate words of comfort. "I'm so sorry Ellie."

"I'm fine. I'll be fine. She should be coming home soon. I can't see why they've detained her this long." Ellie wiped her eyes with the back of her hand. "She's just an old woman with her family and home here in Inverness – not exactly a flight risk."

"I'm glad she's coming home," Daniel said. "Can I . . . I wish I could do

142

something to help. I can't help but feel somewhat responsible."

"Well-" Ellie said with a look on her face that said, *That's the understatement of the century.*

"I know. If I hadn't been so obsessed with Broonburn myself, I would have never brought it up with her and-"

"No," Ellie interrupted, "you only brought to light what was already there, I know that. It's just hard to take in. I shouldn't have shut you out like I did. I just needed some time to process."

"I shouldn't have been so stalker-y."

"You were a bit." Ellie smiled and dried her eyes once more. "I actually," she laughed, "I actually deleted you from my phone. I was just so angry and upset at . . . at you and Mum and everyone I guess."

"Ouch," Daniel said, feigning a shot to the heart.

"I know, a bit dramatic, but my mum had just been arrested for arson and murder." She paused. "Sounds so bizarre to say out loud."

"That's why you called at the Macphersons' this morning?"

"Yesterday. I knew you were renting there. I tried the kirk, but no one answered. Here," she said and pulled out her phone. "You can put yourself back in."

"So, are we ok?"

"I don't know about ok, but we're not *not* ok. Does that make any sense? With all this I just can't be in a relationship right now."

"Of course," Daniel said, trying to sound sympathetic, hiding his disappointment. They both turned, hearing the kettle squeal from the other room.

"I'll be right back," Ellie said.

Daniel typed his number into Ellie's phone as she went for tea. "Can't be in a relationship right now," Daniel repeated to himself. *Sounds about right with my luck*, he thought. Once he entered his information, the phone's screen returned to its home setting. Glancing at the screen as he walked to the kitchen, he noticed a familiar icon.

"Hey, CloudFile. That's what I use for the kirk's website," Daniel said and handed the phone back to Ellie.

"I know. I follow it. I liked your pic by the Lewis standing stones. That may be Mr. MacCrivag's first internet appearance."

"Yeah, I think he's still waiting for a hard copy."

Ellie poured herself a cup and motioned for a second. Daniel nodded. They waited in silence for the tea to cool. Ellie held her cup close to her face and breathed in the aromatic steam. She went to the refrigerator. "Forgot milk."

While she searched for it, Daniel hugged his fingers around his own cup. He hadn't realized how cold they were. He looked around the tidy, unused kitchen. An island of unopened mail on the small table disrupted the otherwise orderly scene. It reminded him of William MacCrivag's entire house. Ellie noticed him staring. "Please excuse the mess. I've just been piling them up there since Mum-" she trailed off. "It's amazing the amount of junk mail she receives."

Ellie picked through the pile. She held up a few restaurant menu fliers, "Rubbish," and tossed them to the side. "Bill," she said and placed an envelope on a not yet covered corner of the table. "And these, ugh," she said while adding two identical envelopes to the "rubbish" pile.

"Wait a second," Daniel said. He reached for one of the envelopes. "I've seen this before." He tapped the parcel against the table, searching his mind for the correct memory. William MacCrivag's house once again came to mind. "Philarguria Energy, where have I seen that before?"

"Oh, seems like everyone in Inverness is receiving them," Ellie said. "I haven't heard much about them, but I remember Mum getting upset whenever she saw one. Would rip it up, throw it immediately in the bin, and mumble something about greedy Southerners. I guess with my da being an electrician, she always preferred Scottish power. She has some peculiar habits."

Daniel stared at the envelope another few seconds. "I've got to go," he said suddenly.

"What?"

"I'm sorry," he said and left the kitchen.

"Wait, why?" Ellie said, confused. "I thought you said you wanted to talk. You had questions you needed to ask me?"

"Oh, you've been a great help. Thanks for the tea!"

"But you haven't even had any," Ellie called out after him. "Where are you going? Daniel!" But he was already out the door. Daniel shouted something back from the road, though she couldn't make out what he said. She stood at the open door with a cup of tea still in one hand, watching his hurried figure grow smaller.

Chapter Twenty-One

From Ellie's house, or rather her mother's house on Lilac Grove, Daniel rushed to the first eastbound bus he could find. Thanks to several weeks without a car and the aid of a clever mobile phone navigation app, Daniel had become quite competent at deciphering the city's maze of public transportation. After crossing the River Ness, he changed buses and took a short walk to his destination.

When he arrived at the prison, Daniel had to check the signage to make certain he was at the right place. He expected the high walls, chain-link fences, razor wire, and possibly a gun tower common to the architecture of American prisons – or at least American prisons as portrayed on popular television. Instead, he found himself in front of a plain brick building, one that he must have passed on multiple occasions without granting it a second thought. Sure, the walls were high and solid, but no higher than a typical two-story house. He approached the unimposing pedestrian door and pressed the buzzer. When he gave his name and credentials, the door's lock clicked open. After passing through a metal detector and x-ray machine, he arrived at the front desk.

He told the uniformed guard behind the desk that he needed to speak to Mrs. Elspeth Gray and that, no, he did not have an appointment. The guard informed him that one cannot simply show up and expect to see a prisoner. One must follow procedures and make a proper booking with the offender for a specific date and time. If he would like to do that now, he might be able to schedule a visit for a day the following week.

"You don't understand," Daniel said. "I really need to speak to her today.

You see, I'm her minister and what we need to discuss might have a big impact on her case." He tried his best to sound professional and if that did not do the trick, supplicating. The guard asked to see his ID again. He studied the picture and then Daniel.

"Och, that's right. You're the American priest who phoned in those lads at the Bught Park bonfire, aren't you."

Daniel's hopeful disposition drooped. "Thanks for remembering," he said. *Oh, the joys of local celebrity,* he thought.

"We all got a good laugh out of that! Wait, watch out," the guard mocked, holding up his hands, "you didn't come here to arrest me, did you?"

"No, I seem to only accuse members of my own parish," Daniel said.

The guard slapped his hand on the desk. "That's right, you got the old woman to confess didn't you. It's highly irregular to simply pop in like this, but since you seem intent on keeping us at the prison in business, I'll see if Mrs. Gray can visit with you. Keep it brief, though, I've got a proper booking for the visits room shortly." The guard shook his head as he buzzed Daniel through. "This is highly irregular," he repeated.

Daniel thanked him and proceeded to the visiting area – a plain box of a room containing a single table and two chairs. He did not have to wait long for Elspeth Gray to join him. She must have been eager for a visitor, though she seemed surprised when she saw him. *Probably expecting Ellie,* Daniel thought. She seemed older and more frail in the oversized prison uniform. Without her silk gloves Daniel could see a gauze wrapping around her right hand. She hesitated and glanced at the CCTV camera in the corner before approaching the table and empty chair.

"Thank you for meeting with me, Mrs. Gray. You look well," Daniel lied. "I hear you're getting out soon?"

"Just until the trial," she said.

"Still, it will be nice to be back in your own home."

"I suppose."

Gathering that she was not in the mood for small talk, Daniel decided to jump straight away to the reason for his impromptu visit. "Well, we don't have a lot of time, but I just couldn't wait until you got out to talk with you."

"Go on then," she said, looking all about the room but never quite meeting his eye.

"I've been thinking about our last conversation, running through it over and over in my mind, and I keep coming up against the same question – Why? Why did you stop at Broonburn House that night? Why did you go in? Why did you tamper with the wiring?"

"I've already told you – you and the police."

"You told me about that night, but I don't think you told me everything. And I'm not buying the dementia story. You're holding something back, Mrs. Gray. I've been racking my brain trying to figure it out. I've gathered a few pieces, but I need you to put together the complete puzzle. That's why I came here today."

"I'm sure I don't know what you mean," Elspeth Gray said. "I've already told you I was just out driving, and I don't know why I stopped or did those things."

Daniel ignored her evasion. "Your family's not originally from Inverness, is it?"

"I was born in Inverness. My parents as well."

"But further back. Your family comes from the north, surname Monroe, right? They moved around and lived in several different places before finally settling here in Inverness, but they were originally from Sutherland. Am I right? They were evicted from their farm?"

Elspeth Gray offered no visible response.

"I did a little research into the time period," Daniel continued. "It's known as the Clearances. A lot of Highlands families were cleared off their farms then. It seems that southern aristocracy believed the land might be more profitable with sheep than farmers. That's probably where my own family came from – Darrow. My father's family were immigrants from Scotland, you know."

Elspeth Gray stared at him through narrowing eyes. She did not answer, so Daniel kept talking.

"I didn't think much of it. A sad historical note, but nothing more. Lots of people are moved or displaced from their homelands, their *promised lands* –

that's the plot of much of the Old Testament. But then, earlier today, I met with your daughter, Ellie. She's clearly torn up about all this, but she's strong. Given time, I think she'll be alright. Anyway, I noticed on your kitchen table a mess of unread mail: letters, bills, catalogues, advertisements. But one envelope in particular caught my eye, two actually, from a company called Philarguria Energy. You see, I've seen that same envelope before at a few other parishioners' homes.

"That fact on its own wouldn't mean much. A lot of companies send out mass mailings. It's simple advertising, like TV commercials. Most people simply toss them in the recycling. But that wasn't your reaction, was it, Mrs. Gray? You got upset, angry even. Ellie said you ripped the letters up, complaining about greedy Southerners. Your daughter chalked it up to the peculiarities of old age, but that phrase, *greedy Southerners*, that gave me pause. I don't think it would have except that I had just been looking into your family history – no signs of dementia by the way – and now I can't help but feel that there's something there. This English company, your family, some kind of bad blood?

"But there's one thing I'm missing, that I can't seem to figure out. What's the connection to Broonburn House and Tom Shaw? There's got to be one. A sane woman does not just go burn down a house with someone in it. Tell me *why*, Mrs. Gray."

Elspeth Gray closed her eyes and hung her head low. She looked as if she were praying. She sighed and glanced around the room once again, pausing when her eyes met the security camera's blinking red light. She adjusted her chair so that Daniel's body obstructed the camera's direct line of sight. She leaned across the table closer to him.

"They burned our house to the ground. And the outhouses for the animals. Everything. They wanted to ensure we could not return, that no one could live there again. Did you find *that* in your research? Monroes had farmed that land for so many generations – it was a part of us. We were not wealthy, but we were content and proud. The lairds and their English cronies didnae care. They were too busy with their gambling and balls and foreign wars. Our rents paid their debts. That is, until they devised their sheep scheme.

They could be rid of any responsibility to their tenants while continuing to fill their own purses.

"Whole villages, whole clans, were erased and replaced with more profitable sheep farms – less labor, less responsibility. So, they came with their writs of eviction and their torches and they left us with nothing. My inheritance, passed down to my parents from theirs and on, all that couldn't be burned away, is the memory of our home and our land taken, betrayed for a few pieces of silver. You see, I know my scripture too."

Elspeth's emotional response reassured Daniel that he had hit upon something, but he was still unsure of exactly what. What did all this have to do with Broonburn House?

"So, the Philarguria Energy company?" Daniel asked. "Is it somehow related to the Clearances? Descendants of the lairds who evicted your family?"

Elspeth frowned. "No," she paused, "but in spirit they are. Did you read the letters they are sending everyone?"

Daniel shook his head.

"If you had, you would understand what I'm saying," Elspeth said. "Philarguria Energy is not just some utilities company wanting us to switch providers for a lower rate. They want to produce energy. They can't get at the North Sea oil, because others got there first – most, by the way, owned by the English and more than happy to funnel the majority of profits south. But Philarguria found another source right under our soil. Do you know anything about natural gas extraction, Reverend Darrow?"

Daniel shook his head again.

"Perhaps that is what you should have spent your time researching. The letter they sent out informs residents of the natural gas deposit they've discovered under Inverness and of their plans to drill it. The letter says this will be a boon to our economy; that they have our best interests in mind, that only minor traffic disruptions may occur whilst they construct their wells outside of town. But it does not tell everything, Reverend Darrow. What they fail to inform us is that when they are done, they will have taken much more than underground gas. Our water will be poisoned, our air sullied, our very land left quaking.

"They don't want something sustainable like tidal or wind energy, of which you may have noticed, Scotland has plenty. That's all too local, too hard to sell off. They want quick, cheap energy. They want sheep farms. The characters may have changed, but tis the same old story."

"Ok," Daniel said, trying to plumb her line of thinking, "If you feel that way, I can understand your reaction to the letters, but how does this all connect to Broonburn House? Broonburn presumably uses the same water and air as you."

"Aren't you paying attention?" Elspeth Gray said, impatiently. "Philarguria Energy *owns* the Broonburn Estate, or at least its CEO does, an Alec Harrow from London. He bought it shortly before the letters began showing up, though you wouldn't know that from the media. He's kept his name out of all press about the House's conversion into a grand hotel and its big plan to be an elite springboard for Highlands tourism. That's all just smokescreen. People like him have always wanted fancy residences to show off their wealth and keep them separate from commoners. Tourism was a distraction. People were so happy about the promised jobs they didn't ask questions. But when I hear that a piece of the Highlands has been sold off, I take notice."

Daniel ran fingers through his hair, rubbing the back of his head as he listened to Elspeth's story. "So you stopped at Broonburn House that night because you found out it was owned by the Philarguria company, which you say plans to steal or destroy the land here around Inverness," Daniel said, summarizing her tale for himself. "But you couldn't truly think that by burning down that House you would get them to stop?"

"They threatened my house, my home – the home where Ellie grew up. Threatened to buy out my mortgage from the bank if I didn't keep quiet. Drive up my rate until I can't afford to pay. They threaten all our homes!" Elspeth paused, collecting herself. "No," Elspeth continued more calmly, "No, I didn't think that would stop them. But I wasn't lying when I said I didn't know what I was doing that night. Well, I knew what I was doing, but I didn't know it until I was actually doing it. I was angry that night, out for a drive in the country to calm myself. I had only recently uncovered the connection between Philarguria and Broonburn House. So when I drove past Auld Angus Road, I exited. I'm not sure why. Perhaps to simply drive past; perhaps to give Alec Harrow a piece of my mind."

"But no one was home, except that student, Tom Shaw," Daniel said.

"No," Elspeth Gray said emphatically. Then softly conceding, "Well, yes, but when I entered the house through its unlocked doors, I thought it was empty. I wasn't quiet about my being there. I shouted 'Hello.' I wanted a confrontation. I had no idea the boy was there. I've never lied about that! How could I have crossed the wiring had I known someone was present?"

"But he was there, Mrs. Gray."

"How? What was he doing there?" she asked.

Just then, a sharp knock sounded against the door. Through the door's window, the front desk guard held up his wristwatch and tapped it, indicating their highly irregular meeting was over.

"I'm sorry," Daniel said and stood. Elspeth Gray looked from the window back to Daniel with a fresh desperation in her eyes. "I can come with Ellie to pick you up when they let you out if you want," he said.

"You connected the dots with my family," Elspeth Gray said in what sounded to Daniel like an accusation. "But that boy had no reason to be there. Why don't you investigate that? Why was Tom Shaw ever at Broonburn House?"

Chapter Twenty-Two

Daniel Darrow sat on the floor, with legs crossed, in the center of Rev. Calder's Church Street study. Around him stood three stacks of old newspaper pages. The stack on his left contained stories referring to the Broonburn House fire generally; in front of him were pages with highlighted passages pertaining to Tom Shaw; to his right lay articles he had yet to read. Ellie Gray sat at Rev. Calder's desk with her back to Daniel. She sifted through her own Internet search for any mention of the boy who, according to her mother, should have never been at Broonburn House.

Daniel wiped a bead of sweat from his brow and placed a freshly highlighted page down in front of him. "He seems to have had a record of being places he wasn't supposed to be."

Ellie turned her head slightly to hear, but kept her eyes on the computer screen.

"He's had a few trespassing charges before," Daniel continued, "in Edinburgh and Dundee. Maybe it was just a case of being at the wrong place at the wrong time. If he knew he wasn't supposed to be there, he's unlikely to have spoken up when he heard someone else enter the house. There's not much to this article, but it does interview an Inverness police officer who says as much."

Ellie didn't respond.

"You find anything over there?" Daniel needed a conversational reprieve from research.

Ellie held up a finger and after a pause, she spun her chair around to face Daniel. "No." She blinked and rubbed her screen-weary eyes.

"Did you hear what I said? Wrong place, wrong time?" Daniel asked.

"I did, aye."

"So?"

"If Mum says no one was in the house, then I believe her. No one else was there."

"And she hasn't said anything else since she's been back home?"

"No, she's gone quite silent again about the whole thing actually."

Daniel straightened his legs on the floor and leaned back. "Ok," he said. "Your mother rings the doorbell, goes inside, shouts around for Alec Harrow or anyone who's home. Then she goes into most of the downstairs rooms, even turns on a loud electric saw before she leaves, and nothing? No signs of anyone else there. How could Shaw not have heard any of that?"

"*If* he was even there in the first place," Ellie said.

"But he was there. Or at least his body was."

"Do you think someone could have put his body there after the fire?"

"I don't know, I don't see how," Daniel said. "His body was badly burned. The evidence seems pretty clear. Tom Shaw died in the fire. Unless your mother is mistaken. Maybe she didn't make as much noise as she thought?"

"No, my mum is not lying. She's already confessed to setting the fire. If she says no one else was there, then no one else was there!" Ellie stood, ready to pace the room.

"I don't see how that's possible. Unless the reports are wrong or the police are lying. But why would they do that? Who would have reason to frame your mother? And why kill some random university student to do so?" Daniel asked.

"Ugh, we're getting nowhere," Ellie said, frustrated. She walked to the couch near where Daniel was still sitting on the floor. She reclined with a long sigh. "I need to see that report."

Daniel gave her a quizzical look.

"The postmortem," Ellie clarified. "I need to see the full report. That might shed some light on all these questions. What our solicitor showed me was mere summary."

"Well, give him a call," Daniel suggested.

"Her, actually. And I should, shouldn't I?" she said with growing confidence. "This is my mum's life here. We should have all the evidence we can get." Ellie scrolled through the contacts list on her mobile phone. "Here she is." She pressed the number and waited for it to connect. Instead of a receptionist, she got soft jazz music. "This could take a while," Ellie sighed.

Daniel stood and stretched his arms. "I could use a coffee. Do you want anything from the place around the corner?"

"Tea for me, please."

"With milk?"

"Ta."

Daniel stepped out the garden entrance of Rev. Calder's study. Sir Walter Scott emerged from behind a bush and meowed. The cat rubbed against the door, wanting to be let in. "Stay here and I'll bring you back a little cup of milk." He reached down to pet the cat, but Sir Walter avoided his hand and again nuzzled the corner of the door. "Suit yourself," Daniel said and exited the garden onto Church Street.

The crisp afternoon air refreshed him. Though they had only been laboring for an hour, the somber work, combined with the church's enthusiastic heating system, made the atmosphere in Rev. Calder's study oppressive. Daniel was thankful for the break and did not envy Ellie her lawyer's phone call. He took his time walking the half block to the corner café.

Light from a pale sun muted the stone and brick of the surrounding buildings to placid hues. The ambient sounds of traffic and sea birds stimulated contemplation. The city, he reflected, seemed calm, steady. It had weathered enough storms throughout its centuries long life to be untroubled by his own current crisis. Its stalwart indifference was at once comforting and heartbreaking. Passersby offered rote smiles or, weary of surveyors and leaflet distributers, kept their eyes steadily on the pavement in front of them. Most people simply ignored one another, wrapped up in their own affairs – all seemingly alone in their personal joys or troubles.

When Daniel returned, Sir Walter was nowhere to be seen. Daniel left a small open cup filled half an inch high with milk on the ground. He left the door to the study cracked open to allow in the cool outside air. He was surprised to see Ellie standing next to the computer desk with her purse slung over her shoulder, ready to leave. The screen behind her displayed what looked like a hospital's website. "Right, we're off," she said, not a minute after Daniel had entered the room.

"What?"

"You can clean this up later, can't you?" Ellie said, indicating the stacks of newsprint spread across the floor.

"Yes. Wait. What's going on? Where are we going?"

"I'll tell you on the way. Now come on, we haven't all day," Ellie said as she stepped out the door Daniel had just entered. "Oh, and thanks for the tea." Ellie grabbed her cup and headed to her mother's car which was parked on the curb outside.

Daniel locked the study door and followed her. Once inside the vehicle, coffee cup securely stowed in a cup holder, and seatbelt latched, Daniel said, "Now, will you please tell me what we're doing? I thought you were talking to your lawyer? Is that where we're headed?"

"Not quite," Ellie said. "Hold on." She turned to join the stream of vehicles traveling down Kingsmill Rd. "I did talk to the solicitor, but it was utterly unproductive. She was a bit rude actually. Because Mum is not denying that she set the fire at Broonburn House, she said there's not much to be done for her case. The evidence is quite obvious, she said, and besides, Mum would have to request a more in depth report because I, strictly speaking, am not her client.

"She seemed altogether irritated that I would take up her valuable time when she had other cases that actually needed defending. I know that we can't afford a better solicitor, and I'm sure she is busy, but that's no excuse for rudeness."

"I'm sorry," Daniel said. What else could he say? He had very little experience with lawyers.

"It's fine," Ellie said, though her response was much too quick to be believed. "We'll just have to improvise."

Daniel noticed an uncharacteristic impatience in Ellie's driving. This made him nearly too nervous to ask, "And what exactly does that mean?"

"I've a mate from university," Ellie answered. "He was a year ahead of me, so he's already graduated. He's at Raigmore Hospital now, a mortuary assistant."

"Mortuary? As in the morgue? Where they keep dead bodies?" Daniel wished he hadn't asked. As a minister, he knew that officiating funerals came as part of the job description. He had even taken a course on grief counseling at seminary. He hadn't, however, seen an actual dead body since he was a child at the funeral of his great grandmother. He knew that death was a part of life. Yet, something about being in the presence of a dead body, the husk of a person hollowed out, unnerved him.

"Mortuaries are also where they store complete postmortem reports," Ellie said.

"So, we're going there to look at Tom Shaw's original report?"

"That's the plan."

"Ok." Reports Daniel could handle. "And the hospital, they're just going to let us have a look at their files? Don't we need some kind of authorization or special permission?"

"That's where the improvising comes in."

They drove on in silence, Ellie absorbed in overtaking less aggressive drivers, Daniel contemplating this unexpected progression of events. He'd nearly lost his congregation over Elspeth Gray's imprisonment; he did not want to further lose his immigration card or face jail time himself over Ellie's *improvising*. Yet, he could not help reminding himself that if not for his own meddling, his own obsession with the Broonburn House fire, that Ellie and her mother might not be in this desperate situation. Whatever it might cost him, he could not abandon them now.

"Who's this friend you have at the hospital?" Daniel asked.

"Cameron. We had Organic Chem together. We went out a few times, but nothing really came of it. He specialized in pathology, me in veterinary medicine, but we've kept in touch," Ellie said, focused more on the road than the conversation.

"You used to date?" Daniel wished immediately that he had said something different. His question felt petty given their current situation.

"Are you jealous?" Ellie asked. If her question was in jest, her voice did not give evidence.

"No, um, I meant, you're sure he'll help us?"

"Aye, Cameron'll come through," she said and then added with a playful smirk, "I think he still fancies me."

They arrived at Raigmore Hospital in record time. Raigmore's eight boxy stories of stone and glass dominated the immediate scenery. It was, Ellie had informed him, the largest hospital in the area, absorbing smaller clinics whenever they closed. Daniel followed her across the vast car park, through the hospital's main entrance, and then into its visitors' café. She looked around the room. Disappointed, she took a table near the door.

"Cameron said he would meet me here. I'll send him a quick text."

Daniel took the chair opposite Ellie as she messaged her friend. A few minutes later, a man appeared at the café's entrance and walked over to their table. Ellie stood and gave him an embrace – an embrace that was, in Daniel's opinion, unnecessarily long. Further, the man himself was, in Daniel estimation, unnecessarily handsome. His hair could have sufficed with less product, his shoulders and arms required far less bulk to function properly. Clearly, they made shopping for loose fitting shirts a struggle. And his height had to interfere with his hospital duties – having to stoop so to converse with normal sized patients.

"Cameron, it's so good to see you," Ellie said once their protracted embrace concluded.

"You too. Sorry to keep you waiting. I hadn't expected you so soon."

"I may have pushed the speed limit a bit," Ellie said with a shrug.

"You never did like to take things slow."

"Cameron!" Ellie said, slapping him on the arm, her hand bouncing off like a ping-pong ball.

"I don't think we've met," Daniel interjected. He thrust his hand in between them. "Ellie said you could help us with Tom Shaw's file."

"Sorry, Cameron, this is Daniel Darrow. He's the new reverend at Church Street and," she said with an eyebrow raised at Daniel, "he's being unusually direct just now. Daniel, this is Cameron, my old mate from university," Ellie said. The two men shared a stiff handshake.

"*Still* mates," Cameron insisted. "Rev, I think I've seen your name in the papers. You've developed a rather infamous reputation in our wee city." Cameron pulled up a chair in between Ellie and Daniel. "Right, about our, em, mutual interest. Let's get to it," he said. With an eye toward Daniel he added, "But perhaps at a quieter volume."

Ellie leaned in and asked, "What can you tell us about the postmortem?"

"Well, I didn't assist. Dr. Paxton didn't think I was ready for such a high-profile case. If you ask me, he simply didn't want to share," Cameron said, dismissively. "But I did overhear him talking with some other doctors. He didn't say much other than going on about how badly the body was burned. It's a wonder it was ever positively identified."

"And cause of death?" Ellie asked.

"The fire of course. No one could have survived long in such an inferno."

Ellie turned away. Her eyes glistened and she reached for a napkin, but stopped herself.

"I'm sorry. Your mum. I forgot," Cameron said with a slight grimace.

"You're sure nothing else could have caused his death? Anything at all odd with the autopsy?" Daniel asked.

"A few fractures and broken bones, I think. But what can you expect when a burning house is collapsing round you?"

"Still, I'd like to have a look at the report myself," Ellie said.

Cameron glanced at his mobile phone. "Dr. Paxton and a few others take a smoking break every day at the same time – half three. The mortuary and records room should be quite empty then. You'll have to be quick about it. They wont be long – perhaps fifteen minutes, twenty if you're lucky. Smoking isn't exactly encouraged amongst hospital administration."

"Hopefully that'll be long enough," Ellie said.

"It'll have to be," Cameron said. "We're mates, but I could get in rather a lot of trouble for this." He looked at both Ellie and Daniel. "We all could."

"I know," Ellie said, her confidence regained. "I'm grateful for your help."

"What do you expect to find?" Cameron asked.

"I don't know. A reason. Something that says my mother is telling the truth."

"I can't talk you out of it then?" Cameron asked. Ellie shook her head. "And you?" he asked.

"All in," Daniel said.

Chapter Twenty-Three

Cameron looked at the time and nodded. "Dr. Paxton and the others will be having their smoking break soon." He stood and led Ellie and Daniel out of the Raigmore Hospital café and down several long hallways. Once they arrived at the entrance to the mortuary, they paused. Cameron checked the time on his phone. "Five minutes," he said. "Wait here. I'll check if it's clear."

Daniel and Ellie stood in silence. Daniel was unsure what to say. Given their surreptitious mission he was unsure if he should say anything. He certainly had not expected to be sneaking into a hospital morgue when he had first met Ellie only a couple hours earlier in Rev. Calder's study. He did not want to imagine what Rev. Calder would think of his present predicament. Though she had encouraged him to work toward healing the pain that Elspeth's arrest had caused for both the Gray family and the larger Church Street community, he could not imagine that this was what his boss had in mind. Ellie, though, was not to be deterred. And he was not about to abandon her.

Ellie checked the time once every minute. When five minutes passed, she increased this to thirty-second intervals. When seven minutes passed, she paced to the door and back. "Where is he?" she whispered. Daniel shrugged. He wanted to help her, but he secretly hoped Cameron would not return, or that he would return and say that the doctors had forgone their smoke break that day.

Putting an end to their respective anxieties, the mortuary doors opened and Cameron appeared. He motioned for them to follow. They passed through a reception room for family members. It was sparsely decorated in warm, floral tones – an attempt to welcome those who would never want to be there. They passed by a door marked *Viewing* and continued down an empty hallway. No orderlies or nurses were needed here. The place had an eerie silence to it. A graveyard. When they reached a door marked *Records*, Cameron pulled a key from his pocket to unlock it. Inside were two computer consoles, a couple of small desks, and filing cabinets that lined two walls.

"Original records and reports are kept here for several months before being stored offsite. Tom Shaw's should still be here," Cameron said. "There's digital copies as well. But those are actually harder to access and we'd leave an electronic trail." He directed them to a cabinet at one end of the room. "S." He ran his finger down the shelf. "Sh – Sm. Here we are."

Space did not allow three heads to search through the files at once so Daniel extricated himself. He paced from the cabinet to the door and back, unsure of what to do. Then Ellie said in a loud whisper, "Got it!" She pulled out a thick file and brought it over to a table. She and Cameron poured over its contents. They pointed out aspects of the report to one another and used technical terms that Daniel did not understand. He felt useless – the classic third wheel.

"Shouldn't someone keep watch or something?" he suggested.

"Great idea, Rev," Cameron said. "You should stick by the door."

Not the someone I was thinking of, Daniel thought as he walked to the door. He cracked it open and peered outside. The hallway remained empty. Minutes passed by and Ellie and Cameron hovered over the postmortem. Daniel overheard bits of what they said to each other: "See, the tibia here is cracked." "That's expected." "How? How is any of this expected?" "Go back to the crime scene report." "See?" "Let me have a look at that x-ray again."

Daniel wished he hadn't inadvertently given himself the job of lookout. He tried to imagine what they were seeing: police reports, photographs of a body burned beyond recognition, x-rays of charred and broken bones. He was also keenly aware that every minute Ellie and Cameron argued over the contents of the file, was a minute closer to the end of the senior doctors' smoke break. He pictured them in their white coats with cigarettes burning down, ever shorter with each breath. He imagined them talking, laughing, smudging out the butts of their cigarettes. Entering the hallway.

Then he heard a sound. Was it a door opening? No. A mouse? Hospitals don't have mice, do they? It was definitely some kind of knock. The knock of a security guard's baton? Why would a morgue need security guards? Daniel recalled passing the *Viewing* room on their way to *Records*. Did the sound come from that direction? There had to be another room nearby where bodies were, for lack of a better word, stored. Scenes from old zombie movies flashed through his mind. Daniel felt himself sweating despite the coolness of the room. There was a reason he had yet to accept an offer to officiate at a funeral. *Calm down*, he told himself. *Your imagination is running wild. Think rationally.* A knock from the air conditioning then? The room was cold.

He turned to see if Ellie or Cameron had noticed the sound. They appeared unfazed, completely absorbed in their reading. They could have been in a university library researching a case file for all the notice they gave the world around them. Daniel looked out at the hallway again. This time he noticed a digital clock on the wall. At least fifteen minutes had passed from when they entered the room, possibly more.

"Hey," he whispered to the research table. No response. "Hey, y'all," louder this time. Ellie and Cameron looked up from their work. "Sorry to interrupt, but have you looked at the time?"

They both pulled out their mobile phones.

"Och, we should be going," Cameron said.

"Just a bit more," Ellie protested.

Cameron glanced at his phone again. "Fine, but I'm going to go check on Dr. Paxton and the others. We've only a couple minutes, if that. Keep your mobile out. If I text you, you need to leave immediately."

"Fine," Ellie said while flipping through pages in the file.

"You remember the way out?" Cameron asked Daniel. Daniel nodded. "Only a couple more minutes. If I text, get out," Cameron repeated and left the room.

"Cameron, look at this," Ellie said, holding up an x-ray image.

Daniel walked over to her. "He left to check on the other doctors."

"Right," Ellie said. "Have a look. Tell me what you see."

"Um," Daniel stared at the column of stacked bones, "the spine, I guess?"

"Exactly, and here?" Ellie pointed to a space between two vertebrae.

"I don't know."

"Look here," she pulled out another image, a photograph.

"What's th- Oh my God!" Daniel said. He turned away from the photograph of Tom Shaw's charred corpse, enlarged to show the neck region.

"Sorry, I should have warned you about that one," Ellie said. "But look here." She placed her finger above part of the neck. "This is the same place as the x-ray."

"So?" asked Daniel, trying not to look.

"So, there's a clear break here! Paxton's notes mention fractures and breaks due to falling debris, but he doesn't go into much detail. Especially here." She pointed to the spaces on the two images. Her voice held an excitement that Daniel could not match given the grim subject matter.

"What's it mean?" he asked with one eye on her mobile phone. Two long minutes had passed since Cameron left.

"Hard to tell for sure, but if I just saw this and didn't know about the fire," she said, "I might think this was the cause of death."

"Really?" Daniel said. He leaned in to get a better look at the images. Just then Ellie's phone vibrated on the table, breaking Daniel's already fragile composure, and causing him to jump. The home screen flashed: *Get out NOW- Cameron*. Ellie dropped the x-ray and photograph images. She looked at Daniel, her eyes speaking her alarm.

"We have to put this back," she said and began replacing the contents of the file.

"We don't have time," Daniel said frantically.

"We can't just leave it out here!"

"Alright," Daniel said. He stuffed the papers and photographs back into the file folder without concern for their original order or alignment.

"But-" Ellie protested.

Daniel ignored her. He snatched up the disorganized folder and returned it to the open file cabinet drawer.

"That's not where-"

Daniel closed the drawer, grabbed her hand, and rushed out of the room. They fled down the hall and past the *Viewing* room. They were about to enter the reception area when they heard laughter and footsteps. Frozen, they stared at one another. The voices grew louder. Ellie, still holding Daniel's hand, pulled him back to the previous door. She tried the handle. It turned. With a quick breath of relief, they entered, shutting the door quietly behind them. The room was dim and barren except for a single table draped in white cloth at the room's far end. The definite form of whatever was hidden under the cloth remained obscured in shadow, but its length seemed roughly that of an adult human body. Between the door and the table stood a wall, waist high, stretching half the length of the room.

Daniel and Ellie stood with their backs against the door listening. Footsteps and muffled conversation approached from the hallway. From inside her pocket, Ellie's phone buzzed again. The voices paused. Only an unlocked door separated them. Daniel held his breath. After a moment, the crowd continued on down the hall. Daniel exhaled and smiled anxiously. Ellie took off her glasses and wiped moisture from the nosepiece. She pulled out her phone. *Drs back. No Paxton – Cameron.* She showed the message to Daniel and shrugged, asking "What now?"

Daniel held a finger to his lips and gently twisted the doorknob. He peeked out the narrow opening. "It's clear," he whispered. As quickly as they could manage without making too much noise, they made their way to the reception area and out the mortuary's main entrance. Before the doors could fully close behind them, a figure dressed in a long white coat appeared around the corner. His name badge read: Dr. Paxton, Senior Pathologist.

"Can I help you?" Dr. Paxton said. An accusation, not a question. Neither Daniel nor Ellie spoke or even moved. "What are you two doing here?"

Daniel closed his eyes and opened them in an expression that he hoped resembled less that of a deer before headlights. "Um, we, yes . . ." he stumbled through words as he strained to piece together some intelligible response.

"Yes, you can help us. I, um, we're looking for someone. A, um, a parishioner. You see I'm a reverend at a church here and we're here to see one of our members. Let him know we're praying for him and all." Daniel was surprised with the ease of his lie once it finally came.

"Which church?" Dr. Paxton asked.

"Church Street Kirk and I'm Reverend Darrow. Perhaps you could help direct us? This hospital is so large and confusing. You can tell by my accent, I'm obviously not from around here. We're looking for the, um, he had a heart attack. The nurse said to take a left and then down the hall, next right." Daniel turned to Ellie. "Or was it two rights?"

Ellie shrugged and shook her head. Her face said, "Why are you asking me?"

Dr. Paxton squinted and stuffed his hands into his coat pockets. "I'm afraid you've gone too far. At the end of this hall, there's a nurses' station. Someone there should be able to direct you to the cardiac wing."

"Thank you," Daniel said.

"Yes, thank you," Ellie chimed in timidly. Hand in hand, they quickly fled down the hallway Dr. Paxton indicated. Once out of eyesight, they stopped and, in a release of nervous energy, burst into laughter.

"Wow, that was too close," Daniel laughed.

"What was that story you told?" Ellie said. "Isn't it a sin to lie? And to implicate the whole kirk in it – I'm not sure whether to be impressed or scandalized right now."

"Let's go with impressed. Now, how about we get out of here before any more surprises."

"Sounds good to me. Just let me text Cameron back."

Once they had made it to the safety of the car park, Daniel asked her, "So was it all worth it? Did you find anything that could help your mother's story?"

"I'm still trying to decide that."

"Those two images with the break in the neck? Was that significant?"

"Perhaps," Ellie said, "when it comes to bones, human and other mammalian skeletons have a lot more in common than not. Pigs for instance. If

166

I were going to kill or paralyze a pig, breaking the cervical vertebrae right there would certainly do it."

"So, if your mother was telling the truth and no one else was at Broonburn House that night–" Daniel said.

"Then Tom Shaw could have been killed *before* she was ever there!"

Chapter Twenty-Four

Land and sky rushed past, distinguishable from one another only by slight variation in shades of blue and green. Glossed over by a low hanging fog, they muddled together at the horizon into a cold turquoise. To see out, Daniel wiped back the persistent window frost with his sweater sleeve. The train ride south from Inverness to Edinburgh took several hours. Daniel had one and a half more still to go. He had already exhausted the book he'd brought along. It was an impulse buy – a summer beach read in the discount bin of a small shop in the Inverness train station. He'd stopped reading when he found himself scanning the same page three times over. Lulled into a half sleep by the steady rhythm and sway of the train, he'd dreamed up a series of events that were far more fantastic than the ones on the page.

Having become unsure of the book's actual plot, Daniel placed it on the aisle seat beside him along with his overcoat to discourage company. When the train made a brief stop in Aberdeen, a woman hauling a large suitcase trudged up to Daniel's extra seat. She paused in front of his defenses, huffed and moved on. The train by this time had become quite crowded, forcing her to find an open seat near the back of the car. Daniel intentionally did not make eye contact. The weather and the nature of his present mission had put him in a solitary mood.

He was on his way to a meeting that he hoped would shed light on Ellie's theory that Tom Shaw had died before her mother had ever set foot inside Broonburn House. He knew this mission would demand all the conversational finesse he could muster and he did not want to waste it on small talk with fellow, fleeting travelers.

He let his mind wander, hoping that some useful recollection or insight might surface. He kept returning to the morning he had visited the rubble of Broonburn House. What had Mr. Tweed said that morning, about Broonburn's owner? – "You don't get to be as wealthy as Mr. Harrow without having a few skeletons in your closet." *What an odd phrase*, Daniel thought, especially given that a charred skeleton was all that was left of poor Tom Shaw. He hadn't seen a skeleton then amongst the blackened, half-collapsed walls and debris, not that he or Mr. Tweed had had much time to look around. Had the police already found and removed what was left of Shaw? Daniel shook his head when he thought of how he had once suspected Mr. Tweed because of the older man's knowledge of Broonburn's owner and apparent familiarity with the site. He wondered now how Mr. Tweed might view Elspeth Gray's motive. On which side of history had his family fallen?

Daniel's thoughts lingered on Elspeth Gray, now back at home. According to Ellie, her mother had become more reticent than before the arrest. He wondered, given Mrs. Gray's strong emotional reaction to the Philarguria Energy Company and their letters, why she did not speak out against them more. If she truly did see history repeating itself, the shadow of the Clearances dressed up in a modern business suit, why did she not try to warn people? Surely hers was not the only Inverness family to keep the flame of that memory alive. Perhaps she feared retaliation from the company? Perhaps she had already said all she wanted to in the flames of Broonburn House? A red, hot retribution smoldering for nearly two hundred years. Or perhaps the belief that she had killed Tom Shaw, however unintentionally, had silenced her anger, transformed it into mute contrition.

Daniel stared out the window, trying to repress a question that had dogged him since he had visited Elspeth Gray in prison. He tried to focus on something close that could distract his attention – a farmhouse, a winding stone sheep wall, a clump of pine trees— but each flashed past too quickly. Points farther out, immune to the blurring of proximity and speed, succumbed to the fog and remained indistinct ghosts. No outside distraction, though, could suppress that nagging question. Given her history, Daniel wondered, could Elspeth Gray have been justified in her action?

Even if she was somehow not responsible for the death of Tom Shaw, she had still committed a crime. No one, least of all Elspeth Gray, questioned the fact of her starting the fire that destroyed Broonburn House. The property damage alone was in the millions of pounds and there was no accounting for the historic significance of the House. It had stood on that site, in one form or another, for hundreds of years. But wasn't that also her point? She destroyed that specific House – a House with historic ties to the nobility – the same nobility that destroyed her ancestral home and now threatened her current one. A symbolic act. The reverend in Daniel reminded him that Jesus also expressed a proclivity for symbolic action: riding around town on a donkey, upturned the tables of moneychangers in the Jerusalem Temple.

Daniel felt he could understand Elspeth's motive, or if not fully understand, he could at least sympathize. Yet, however sympathetic, he had difficulty endorsing her action. He recalled the old Machiavellian dictum: the end justifies the means. What had Elspeth hoped to accomplish by setting that fire? Such a philosophy could be used to justify any manner of abhorrent acts, from torture to slavery. Torture a prisoner to obtain helpful wartime intelligence. Enslave a people to produce cheap agricultural products. Hadn't the lairds and English nobility used similar logic in the Highland Clearances: remove the native people to make room for more profitable sheep farms?

This question led in turn to another: the right use or ownership of land. Was the purpose of land to increase the wealth of the elite few landowners? If so, then any means of increasing the land's value was valid, even the forced removal of viable, though not highly profitable, tenant farmers. Daniel's own family had a farming past, though he did not trace it back as far as Mrs. Gray. His grandfather had been a small tobacco farmer. Daniel had grown up with stories of the difficulties of such a lifestyle, always beholden to changes in the weather and the even more fickle markets. He knew the life of a small farmer was not one of extravagance or wealth. But he also knew the pride and satisfaction that came with self-sufficiency and producing. As a child, he had witnessed the grace of community members that sustained one another in hard times when individual self-reliance failed them. In fact, summers at his grandfather's farm had been his first real experience of the term *grace*. Could the value of such a life, or community, be summed up solely by monetary profit?

No, Daniel could not condone Elspeth Gray's action, but neither could he excuse the historical grievance that prompted it. Where justice was needed, she had settled for retribution. So, Daniel was left with his original question, or some new formulation of it: What might justice look like in Elspeth Gray's case? Surely, she should be punished for her crime of arson, if not manslaughter. Yet, was Philarguria Energy blameless in all this? By the simple act of buying up land, should they be allowed, as Elspeth Gray feared, to repeat the sins of the past? Should the livelihood of the land's inhabitants not take precedence over the short-term profits of some faraway company? Was profit even the best or only use of land?

Before Daniel could labor any longer on these questions that seemed to multiply like the mythical Hydra's heads with each attempted answer, he was spared by a sudden shift in velocity. The train slowed into Edinburgh. He rummaged through his bag for a strip of paper on which he had scribbled his hotel information. This precaution caused him to miss his exit opportunity. Passengers in the seats behind him took advantage of his hesitation and filed past in a crowded buzz. As the woman from Aberdeen with the large suitcase passed, she glared at the still empty seat beside him and grumbled a few words in a thick accent that Daniel was glad he could not understand. Once the aisle had cleared, Daniel took up his coat and bag and exited into Edinburgh's cavernous Waverley Station.

Built partly underground in a kind of crevasse between Edinburgh's ancient Old Town and still quite old New Town, entering Waverley Station required an adjustment of one's eyes. Despite a recently completed roof renovation in which many glass panels had been installed, the sun's rays still had to penetrate a thick layer of cloud, for which architects could make no improvements, before any natural light might make its way into the underground station. Daniel stumbled out of his train car, unused to steady ground. The air smelt damp and of train exhaust, grease, and densely packed human bustle. Guided as much by the hint of fresh air as by exit signs, Daniel made his way out of the belly of the beast and up an exhaustingly long incline onto Waverley Bridge.

Once aboveground, the ancient city of Edinburgh opened in a glorious panorama before him. A low-lying green space spread out immediately in front, once a loch protecting Edinburgh Castle, now the meticulously manicured Princes Street Gardens. The great gothic spindle of the Walter Scott Monument stood to the right – a lofty tribute for Daniel's own furry footed Sir Walter to live up to. Behind the monument spread the shops of Princes Street. To the left, an imposing mix of gothic and neo-classical stone edifices crowded the road leading up to the castle, which itself was just visible in the distance behind the Scottish National Gallery building. Daniel stood, dazed, an eddy in a stream of pedestrians who had grown accustomed to their city's beauty.

He wished he had been traveling to Edinburgh under happier circumstances. Ellie spoke so highly of the city: its museums, years upon years of history – new layers being unearthed every time a building underwent major redevelopment or demolition, its cosmopolitan feel that somehow retained a friendly sense of Scottish hospitality. She swore Edinburgh to be the best spot for Indian cuisine outside of London, or perhaps the subcontinent itself. Ellie still had a year left at the University of Edinburgh's veterinary school after her clinical internship in Inverness concluded. She promised that if he "popped down for a visit," she would show him all the sites. He longed simply for the chance to spend time with her away from the ever-prying eyes of Church Street. Today, though, his mind was occupied with grimmer business.

Daniel walked to Princes Street where he had been told he might have the quickest chance of catching a taxi. Though overcast, the weather was not yet cool enough for a full coat so he held his previous seat blocker in one hand along with his hotel's address. Strapped across one shoulder, he carried a small bag that held little more than a change of clothes and a notebook. The notebook contained various scribblings. It recorded musing for future homilies and an ongoing checklist of errands and visitations he needed

172

to make. On the top of a dog-eared page, he had written the address for tomorrow's dreaded visitation: 6 Whitehill Park, Dalkeith.

After he had checked into his hotel, which turned out to be quite close, Daniel took a stroll down the crowded shopping center of Princes Street. He passed the massive Jenners department store, several mobile phone shops, and clothing stores that catered to clients either younger or wealthier than himself. None of these caused him pause. He desired to stretch his legs and search for dinner. If he could not find Edinburgh's famed Indian cuisine, he would settle for anything hot and filling.

Distracted by the sight of Edinburgh Castle, Daniel made his way across the gardens to the Mound, a raised portion of land leading up to the castle. He passed the Scottish National Gallery and several partially constructed wooden structures in the courtyard outside the gallery overlooking the gardens and Waverley Station. A few workers busily hoisted up narrow walls, secured tiny roofs, and swept debris away from pedestrian paths; most had already taken off for the day. This temporary village had a rustic, European feel. Questioning one of the workers, Daniel discovered they were readying for the city's Christmas festivities, specifically, the German market. "Come back in a few days and you'll find the best beer and bratwurst this side of Bavaria!" the worker boasted.

After climbing the steep steps up the Mound and an additional inclined street to Edinburgh Castle, Daniel, in heavy labored breaths, rested in front of a sign reading: Opening Hours 9:30a.m. to 5:00p.m. Tourism would have to wait for another day. Continuing his quest for a hot meal, Daniel passed a fish and chips shop, or chippie, and a few pubs before entering an American themed restaurant. With all that he had been through in the past two months, Daniel could not resist the restaurant's promised comforts of home.

Inside, the place evoked a general feeling of the American South or what Daniel imagined the owners had attempted to emulate after watching reruns of the Andy Griffith Show. The food was decent, at least it did what food was supposed to do when eaten late and at a table by oneself; it sated his hunger and provided a focused distraction for his thoughts. The waitress's description of their version of a chicken fried steak with gravy sauce sounded too adventurous. He really wanted a brisket sandwich with vinegar-based sauce, in the Eastern North Carolina style like his grandfather used to make. But such regional fair was beyond most actual American restaurants much less American *themed* restaurants. So, he opted for the "American Classic," a cheeseburger with catsup and a thin, undercooked beef patty.

The next morning, Daniel walked from his hotel back to the train station. He enjoyed the early morning ocean air. Edinburgh, like Inverness, was open to the sea on one side. He took another southbound train, though not nearly as far this time. Before he had time to comfortably situate himself or even think about giving his bargain-bin book another try, his stop had arrived – Dalkeith. He hailed a taxi and asked the driver to take him to Whitehill Park, number six.

"That'll be far on the edge of town, nearly to Mayfield," the driver said.

"Oh, I didn't realize it was very far. Can you still take me?"

"I'll get you there, aye," the driver said and then with a wry smile he switched on his mileage counter.

After a lengthy ride and a promise to return in about an hour, the driver left Daniel at his destination. Daniel took a deep breath. The smells of the city had disappeared, replaced with the fresh, dewy scent of farm fields and open sky; though there was something else in the air, faint and intermittent, but noticeable nonetheless, something industrial. Daniel approached the house and paused before ringing the bell. He read the name on the mail slot: *Shaw*.

Chapter Twenty-Five

A middle-aged man opened the door. He wore slacks and a pressed shirt, presenting a tidy image. An astute eye, however, could see that the man was not as put together as he might have liked to appear. A patch of ruddy blond hair remained just below his left ear on the jawline of an otherwise clean-shaven face, one of the buttons on his sleeve cuff was slotted through the wrong hole, and his belt had missed, overlapping one of the loops around the waist of his slacks.

Daniel put out his hand and said, "Mr. Shaw, I'm Daniel Darrow. We spoke briefly on the phone the other day."

Mr. Shaw seemed not to notice the hand offered him. Instead, he peered out from his door past Daniel. He looked left, right, then left again before ushering Daniel inside.

"I had to make sure you didn't have a camera crew with you," he explained "Ever since Tom-" he sighed, "They've hounded us, the devils."

"Oh, no, it's just me," Daniel said.

Safely inside, Mr. Shaw offered his own hand for Daniel to shake. "You said you're a reverend up in Inverness? Is that how you knew our Tom – he visited your kirk?" he asked.

"Well, not exactly," Daniel said. He followed Mr. Shaw further inside the house, past the foyer, into a large room with a fireplace, television, and two leather couches – a typically suburban home, almost country.

Mr. Shaw sat down on a well indented cushion. "I thought you said you knew him?"

"I said we had a mutual friend," Daniel corrected. He took a seat on the other couch at a right angle to his host.

Before Daniel could explain further, Mrs. Shaw entered the room. Her appearance captured the image of composure that her husband had attempted. Her hair was curled and hair sprayed into immovable perfection; her low heeled shoes matched the blue of the flowers on her wrinkle-free dress. Two different approaches to grief, Daniel observed.

"Paul, why didn't you tell me our guest had arrived?"

"He only just sat down, Alice," Mr. Shaw said.

"And you haven't offered him anything to drink?" she chided her husband.

Daniel stood, "Hello, Mrs. Shaw. I'm Daniel Darrow. Thank you both for seeing me this morning."

"Yes," she said, "let me put the kettle on."

"You don't have to. I'm fine, really," Daniel said.

Mr. Shaw shook his head to tell Daniel that protesting was futile; he should simply return to his seat and accept the inevitable. Daniel shrugged and sat down. Mrs. Shaw proceeded to the kitchen, which was open to the living room. She grabbed the kettle from the stove and began filling it from a large plastic water jug that sat on a counter next to the sink.

"Oh, Mrs. Shaw, please don't go through so much trouble for me. Tap water's fine. I'm actually not even very thirsty," Daniel said. With such grim business to discuss he did not want to inconvenience her. Yet, he knew that he could not reject her offer of tea. He knew that grief took many forms and busying oneself with minutia and routine was one such manifestation.

"It's no trouble," Mrs. Shaw said. "You don't want the tap."

"I wish you wouldn't," Daniel said.

"No, you don't, laddie," Mr. Shaw said. Then to his wife he asked, "Should I show him, Alice?"

"Must you? It seems so dangerous."

"Come along Reverend, you'll want to see this," Mr. Shaw said and directed Daniel to the kitchen. "Where is it?" he said, rummaging through drawers.

"Where's what dear?" Mrs. Shaw asked him. "Mr. Darrow didn't travel all the way here to see your parlor trick."

"Here, I've found it," Mr. Shaw said, grasping something in his hand. Daniel could not make out what it was. A piece of blue plastic? "And the glove." Mr. Shaw slipped an oven mitt over one hand.

"I'm going to the other room," Mrs. Shaw said.

Daniel glanced at her and then at Mr. Shaw, unsure of what to do.

"Oh, don't worry. Come closer," Mr. Shaw instructed. Daniel met him at the sink. "Not that close." Mr. Shaw turned the knob to produce a stream of water from the faucet. With the mitt covered hand, he wafted the air around the stream. "Can you smell that?"

Daniel inhaled and then shook his hand. It smelled of dampness and the earthy scent of a faucet that hasn't been used in a while. Mr. Shaw waved the air toward Daniel again. "Wait," Daniel said. "There is something there. It's very faint. What is it?" The water had a chemical odor to it, almost like a run over skunk on the side of the road.

Mr. Shaw raised his eyebrows in a knowing smile. He uncovered the blue object from his other hand, a cigarette lighter, and flicked the metal mechanism to create a spark. He transferred the flame to his mitted hand and held it, arm outstretched, to the stream of water. Nothing happened. Daniel gave him a quizzical look. Mr. Shaw blew the flame gently, closer to the flow. It flickered before rapidly expanding to envelope the entire stream. Daniel jumped back.

In a flash Daniel was transported back to his first Sunday at Church Street Kirk. He had just finished washing up in the kirk hall and the lights were dim. He was alone in the room except for the small, but surprisingly strong hand that held him. Eliza MacGillivray, with rabbit in tow, impressed upon him, "You left me so quickly. I have messages for you." Daniel could see her free hand holding the strange, donut shaped stone from her necklace. She rubbed it between her fingers and stared directly at him, though she appeared to no longer be present behind her glassy eyes. Then she spoke:

The day will come when
Fire and water shall run in streams
Through all the streets and lanes of Inverness."

* * *

"You all right there Reverend?" Mr. Shaw had just reached over to turn the water off. "Looks like you left us there for a minute."

"Sorry, I-" Daniel blinked hard to regain his sense of place. "Have you ever heard of the Brahan Seer?"

Mr. Shaw shook his head no.

"Never mind," Daniel said. "That's quite a trick."

"Now you see why we use the tank there," Mr. Shaw said, indicating the large plastic water container on the counter. "We're done, Dear," he shouted to Mrs. Shaw in the other room.

"Put the kettle on while you're in there," she shouted back.

When they returned to the sitting room, Daniel asked how it was that their water could catch fire.

"Wasn't always like that," Mr. Shaw said. "When we first bought this house, the water was fine. But then they discovered the gas deposit underneath us, natural gas."

"It's miles wide," Mrs. Shaw added. "This whole area south of Edinburgh. We were thrilled at first. They promised so many jobs. Our young people wouldn't have to leave for bigger cities."

"And our property value," Mr. Shaw continued, "They offered so much. They just wanted the rights to what was underneath. We didn't even need to leave our house. But now-" He stared ahead blankly and then toward the kitchen. "Well, you've seen. We couldn't sell if we wanted to."

"I'm sorry, I still don't understand. This natural gas deposit poisoned the water?" Daniel asked.

"No, not the gas. That's been down there for ages, likely before Dalkeith was even here. No, our headaches started once they began extracting it," Mr. Shaw said.

"He's not joking about the headaches either," Mrs. Shaw jumped in. "Since the drilling started, people haven't felt well. Not everyone, mind you. It affects people differently. But for those that are more sensitive to that sort of thing. Our neighbor two houses down, for example, headaches plague her. The poor woman hardly goes outside anymore except for work."

"Wait, who's *they*," Daniel asked.

"They? Em, it begins with a P or F. Some energy company. I always forget. Paul?"

"Philarguria Energy," Mr. Shaw said.

"Philarguria Energy?" Daniel repeated, taken aback. The Shaws' story now seemed more than just a tragic accident. He wondered if Elspeth Gray had known about this connection.

"You've heard of them?" Mrs. Shaw asked.

"Yes, they've got a presence in Inverness too. Not everyone's happy about it."

"I'm not surprised," Mr. Shaw said. "The English have always felt they could just come and take whatever they wanted from Scotland. They say it's for our own good, that all of Britain will benefit." He took a breath and then continued his original line of thought. "You see it's not actually the natural gas that's the problem; it's the chemicals they use to get it out of the ground. Fracking, they call it."

"Hydraulic fracturing," Mrs. Shaw clarified.

"They pump these chemicals and water into the ground and the pressure builds and breaks up the rock that holds the gas, forcing it up. Of course, some of the chemicals leach out and the water they used for pumping is worthless – worse than worthless. It's toxic. If Tom were here he could explain it all much better. He learned all about it. He was so determined to do something – to make things right. He attended protests once things started to get bad. Tom was quite a lad. Not like my generation: Stiff upper lip and carry on; ignore the problem and hope it goes away."

"Natural gas," Daniel said. "Yes, this is starting to sound familiar." He did not tell them why. He was intrigued by the connections, but unsure how the Shaws would react to hearing Elspeth Gray's name. Her action, however sympathetic to their own domestic crisis, was also the most likely cause of their son's death.

"It should," Mrs. Shaw said. "You're from the States, right? It's very popular over there. Tom told us all about it. He showed us this video on the computer of some family in, where was it, Pennsylvania? Anyway, they were demonstrating how they could light their tap on fire. It's what gave

Paul the idea to try it here. Now, theirs was more impressive. Have you seen it?" Daniel shook his head. "Paul, where was that video?"

"I don't know, somewhere on the internet. It might be on Tom's computer."

"How did you say you knew Tom?" Mrs. Shaw asked Daniel.

"I didn't exactly. I told your husband that we had a mutual friend. That's why I wanted to have a talk with you. We were wondering if you knew why Tom was in Inverness?"

"Oh, a mutual friend," she repeated. "What's his name? Perhaps we know him."

"Her," Daniel corrected, "Ellie Gray." Before he had finished speaking her name, Daniel knew he had made a mistake. He quickly added, "They were at the university together," in hopes the Shaws wouldn't notice.

Mr. Shaw's face hardened. "Ellie Gray? She wouldn't be a relation to Elspeth Gray?"

"She's, um," Daniel stammered. He needed a lie. Where was the quick thinking that had gotten him and Ellie away from Dr. Paxton at Raigmore Hospital? He looked from Mr. to Mrs. Shaw and could sense the feeling of betrayal growing in them. He gave up. "She's Elspeth Gray's daughter."

"Get out," Mr. Shaw said softly.

"But-" Daniel protested.

Mr. Shaw rose to his feet. "Out!" His voice now a roar.

Daniel stood. He did not know what to say, but he could not leave yet.

"How dare you come here!" Mr. Shaw continued. "Pretending to be a friend. Taking advantage of our hospitality. Did you come to gloat for that... woman?"

"Paul said you're a priest. How could you?" Mrs. Shaw said.

"You've got it wrong. I'm not here to-" Daniel back peddled, verbally and physically. Mr. Shaw moved toward the door, pushing Daniel along by sheer emotional force. They reached the threshold and Mr. Shaw swung open the door.

"Someone else killed Tom!" Daniel shouted out of desperation.

Mr. Shaw froze. "What did you say?"

Chapter Twenty-Six

Daniel knew immediately he shouldn't have said that. He had no hard evidence that Elspeth Gray had not killed the Shaws' son, even accidentally. He had only an illegally viewed x-ray and the opinion of a medical student, a *veterinary* student, motivated by the desperate hope that her mother was not a killer. But Daniel was also desperate. He couldn't return to Ellie with nothing.

"What did you say?" Mr. Shaw asked, frozen at the door.

Daniel knew he was walking a razor's edge. He took a step inside. "There's a chance your son wasn't killed in the fire. Or, um, I mean that something else besides the fire caused his death."

"But the police said."

"I know what the police have said, but I also know Mrs. Gray. I can't explain or justify her actions, but I know that she would never intentionally hurt someone. That's why I came down here to talk to you – to find out why Tom was in Inverness. Why he might have been at Broonburn House that night. I should have been more upfront about that. I'm truly sorry if you feel I misled you. The last thing I want is to cause you more pain. I just really need to talk to you about Tom."

"Aye, you should have," Mr. Shaw said. He remained unmoved from his post at the door.

"I know you probably don't care, but Mrs. Gray is absolutely devastated about what happened to your son. She feels responsible and that weight has broken her, completely. But please Mr. Shaw, Mrs. Shaw, if there's a chance the police missed something, we owe it to Tom to find out."

Mr. Shaw looked to his wife. She nodded and he took a step back.

"Thank you," Daniel said. He followed them back inside. Once seated he asked tentatively, "Can you tell me why your son was in Inverness?"

"The police already asked us that. I don't know what more we could say. Holiday? Perhaps to see this mutual friend of yours?" Mr. Shaw said.

"He was always doing that, going off with his mates, usually to film some adventure. He wanted to be a filmmaker you know," Mrs. Shaw said. "We didn't even know he had been to Inverness until we received a call from his hostel. He had missed his checkout date – never picked up his things, never paid. I tried his mobile, but he didn't answer. We became worried. He's never done anything like that before, so we rang the Inverness police. They filed a missing person report. It wasn't until after the fire at Broonburn House that we heard anything."

"They asked us for any medical records, x-rays, dental," Mr. Shaw continued. "Just a normal part of their investigation, they said. They had to look into all the missing persons. Then nothing for days. Finally, we received the call. They wanted us to come up to Inverness. Because of the fire, there was no body as such to identify."

"We couldn't look at-" Tears began to fill Mrs. Shaw's eyes. They choked her words. "At what was left of him."

"But the police were certain. The medical records proved it. That was our Tom," Mr. Shaw said. His voice remained steady, but forced.

"So you have no idea what might have brought him to Inverness? He just went alone?" Daniel asked. Mr. and Mrs. Shaw shook their heads. "You said he made videos? He was studying film?"

"Aye."

"Could he have been working on a film? Did the police find a camera or anything?"

"Nothing like that in the things he left at the hostel. He did use his mobile for wee films sometimes. We bought it for him when he started classes in Edinburgh. He insisted on one with a top of the line camera. It was pricy, but Tom was a difficult boy to say 'No' to," Mrs. Shaw said. She sniffled, bringing out a tissue from a hidden pocket in her dress.

"But it was destroyed in the fire," Mr. Shaw added. "A mere puddle of plastic, the police said. We checked with the phone company; he hadn't made or received any calls that day."

The three of them sat in silence. Their dialogue seemed to have no further trails to follow. Then Daniel had a thought. "Your water faucet trick," he said. "I wonder, could that have anything to do with why Tom went to Inverness?"

Mr. and Mrs. Shaw gave him skeptical glances.

"Hear me out," Daniel said. "You told me that Tom was angry about what's happened to your community. He went to protests, studied up on fracking."

Mr. and Mrs. Shaw nodded.

"Well, if he learned much about the company that actually did the fracking, Philarguria Energy, then he must have learned that they've also found a natural gas deposit under Inverness. People all over town, several from my church, have received letters notifying them of Philarguria's intentions. All the things they promised you: jobs, energy security, generous buyouts, they've promised us the same. Add Broonburn House's remodel into a Highlands tourism hub, and people could see only blue skies ahead.

"But your son knew the darker side of Philarguria's promises. He had experienced firsthand the real cost. And, if he was as determined as you say he was, then he might have discovered a secret that very few people knew. Broonburn House was recently bought by the CEO of Philarguria Energy."

"And that's why Tom was in Inverness?" Mr. Shaw asked.

"I don't know," Daniel said. "But Philarguria is the only thread I can see that connects Tom to Broonburn House."

"Even if he knew that, why would he go there?" Mrs. Shaw asked.

"You'd be surprised what that kind of knowledge can do to a person," Daniel said. He thought of Elspeth Gray but decided to keep that particular revelation to himself. "I know I'm getting a little personal now, but did Tom keep a diary or anything? Right now I'm just speculating, but if we could learn what he was thinking before he headed to Inverness..."

Mr. and Mrs. Shaw glanced at each other. Mrs. Shaw said, "If he did, he would not have shared it with us."

"No, I don't think so," Mr. Shaw agreed. "He was always on his computer, but the police already made a copy of the hard drive. If there was anything there, surely they would have found it."

"But they might not have known what to look for," Mrs. Shaw said. She looked at Daniel. He responded with an encouraging shrug that said, "It's worth a shot."

Daniel followed Mr. and Mrs. Shaw to their late son's room. Mr. Shaw hesitated before he opened the door. "We haven't been in since the police had a look round." His wife entwined her arm with his and they entered. The room appeared tidy. It had clearly been some time since a university aged boy had occupied it. The bed was made. The floor vacuumed and cleared of clothing and other debris. Primary school trophies lined a shelf. They stood silent in the room, taking in the terrain of their lost son. Mr. Shaw moved to the computer desk. While they waited for it to turn on, Daniel hovered over his shoulder and Mrs. Shaw pulled up a chair. The screen glowed, displaying an image of Tom and two other boys on top of a hill overlooking a city.

Mrs. Shaw's eyes welled up again. "That would be Tom and his mates atop Arthur's Seat in Edinburgh. He must've just taken it at the beginning of the term."

"Right, where do we start?" Mr. Shaw asked.

"The documents folder?" Daniel suggested. Mr. Shaw opened the folder. A scroll through the files revealed school papers, job applications, film scripts, but nothing remotely diary related. Mr. Shaw tried another folder entitled "Film." This folder was further divided into two subfolders: "Shorts" and "In Process." He scrolled through the titles in each, but found none that matched what they were looking for.

"Can you just search for 'Inverness' or 'Philarguria'?" Mrs. Shaw asked. The computer took a minute to compile the results: a few downloaded news articles. Calendar alerts for past protests and community talks in Dalkeith. Reservations for a hostel and train to Inverness. "We already knew all this. There's nothing new here," Mrs. Shaw said, defeated. "Can we stop looking through his things? Please, it's too soon. I, I simply cannot bear any more right now."

"She right," Mr. Shaw said to Daniel. "You had a clever theory but there's nothing to support it. We must face the facts. The woman you're trying to defend, she killed our son when she set that fire, for whatever reason he was there."

Daniel rubbed the back of his neck and sighed. He couldn't think of a way forward. He had to admit that they made sense. His theory had no legs. It was simply his mind desperately trying to see a pattern where there was none. Even Ellie's observation about the x-ray was nothing more than speculation. The break in Tom's spine could be explained by falling debris, as Dr. Paxton had said. Daniel had desperately wanted Ellie to be right. He needed her to be right.

"Ok," Daniel said, "I'm sorry I- Hold on." He noticed a familiar icon in the computer's application menu. "Can you open that one?"

Mr. Shaw clicked open the icon of a cloud with an arrow coming down from it like lightening. A pinwheel spun as the computer connected to the internet. Then a menu appeared containing several files with the title *auto.upload* followed by a date. "What's all this?" Mr. Shaw asked.

"This is a CloudFile account. It's all online, so it might have been overlooked when the police searched the hard drive. I use the same system for hosting my church's website. It's great, I can upload from anywhere and we don't have to worry about computer crashes or storing anything. Tom's looks a little different though, he must have the upgraded paid version. Open one," Daniel said. Mr. Shaw clicked on the middle of the list. A video file appeared. They saw a frozen image of Tom's face. Mr. Shaw pushed *play*.

"Right, Benji here has challenged Reuben to a European Union. What is a European Union you may ask? We have here six beers from across Europe. The rules? Well that should be obvious. It *is* a drinking game." Tom shifted the camera's lens from his own face to show two rows of full pint glasses. "We begin with Belgium on the left – a refreshing Stella, and of course a Heineken from the Netherlands, then France's 1664, on to Germany's Paulander, and what's that one?" Loud pub noise made Tom's commentary difficult to understand. "No, the one near the end." He seemed to be arguing with someone off camera. "We'll begin in a moment. I'm providing exposition. No..." Shouting and laughing followed. "For posterity, Benji. Your future children will want to know how continental you are!" The camera returned to Tom's face. "Finishing out the Union, we have a Budweiser – Czech, not American, and finally a hardy Irish Guinness." The camera returned to the pub scene with two young men standing proudly at the start of their representative beer lines. Mr. Shaw paused the video.

"Are these more of Tom's wee films?" Mrs. Shaw asked

"It just looks like goofing about to me," Mr. Shaw said.

"No, you see the file names?" Daniel said. "They're auto uploads – that's only available for paid accounts. I always thought it was a cool feature, but I couldn't justify the expense for a little church website. When the app is enabled, it simultaneously uploads whatever images or video you take to your CloudFile account. Look at this one," Daniel pointed to a file at the top of the list. "That little green arrow means it's a recent upload. These others are grayed out. They've all already been viewed, but this one. Highlight the file name, I want to see the upload date."

When Mr. Shaw clicked the file, its full name appeared. They all stared at the screen in stunned silence. "That's–"

"I know," Daniel said. "That's the day before the Broonburn House fire."

Mr. Shaw opened the file. Another video appeared. *Play.*

A close-up of Tom Shaw's face showed that he had turned his mobile phone's camera toward himself. He appeared to be outside. The light was bright and greenery showed in the distance, possibly trees, though little could be seen other than his narrator's head.

"I am standing in front of the famous, the infamous, Broonburn House in Inverness, Scotland," Tom said, speaking into a wireless mic. His tone in this video was markedly different from the previous one they had seen. He was calm and informative – the documentarian. His words were deliberate, prepared, as if spoken from a memorized script. "I have traveled all this distance to talk with, no to confront, the owner of this House, a certain Mr. Alec Harrow." Tom paused. "End scene. Production note: insert popup text reading 'Alec Harrow, Owner Broonburn House, CEO Philarguria Energy,' End text." He swiveled the camera to face the opposite direction to show Broonburn House with its manicured front garden, high towers, and decorative slotted parapet, all still standing. After another brief pause Tom continued. "There she is, Broonburn House, home to nobility, playground to the rich and famous. Status symbol for those who want to make all of Scotland their playground." Turning the camera back to himself, Tom held it out at arm's length and began walking toward the House.

"I've obtained a letter stating Philarguria Energy's plans to extract natural gas from a recently discovered deposit here. We'll see if he admits to that. I've also brought along independent tests of air and water quality since his company began fracking in Dalkeith. I've got three written testimonies, from two neighbors as well as myself, that I plan to read. I'll shout them from the doorstop if he won't answer. And here," he touched his bag, "I've got a jar of water from the tap at my house. If his company claims it's so safe, then Mr. Harrow shouldn't have a problem drinking it himself!" Tom said with a self-satisfied smile.

He climbed the front steps, showed his hand ringing the bell, and then panned back to his face, smiling. The knob turned and the camera spun back around. A man in coveralls opened the door.

"I'm here to speak to Mr. Alec Harrow," Tom said, enthusiastically.

"Eh? You'll have to speak up lad," the man said. Hammering and power tools could be heard in the background.

"Alec Harrow, I'm here to speak to Alec Harrow. He owns this place," Tom shouted.

"Calm down, I'll see if he's available," the man said. Then, "Who are you? What is this regarding?"

"My name is Tom Shaw, regarding his other company, Philarguria Energy."

The man left, shutting the door behind him. "It's so loud," Tom mumbled to himself. "Doing a little remodeling are we?" He looked at his mic and tapped it against his chest to make sure it was working. The camera panned around the front of the House to show various building equipment strewn about the lawn. When the doorknob turned, Tom jumped to attention and focused the camera on the opening. A man in dark gray slacks and a white pressed shirt appeared and shut the door behind him. He had a stern look about him: short cropped hair of matching color palate, sharp eyebrows, and a long angular face.

"What's this?" the man asked, abruptly.

Tom to a step back, "Alec Harrow?"

"Yes."

"Your company is responsible for fracking operations in Dalkeith and you've repeatedly ignored our grievances, so I've come here so you'll have to listen. Are you aware of the effect your drilling has had on our water and air? You've run away so far you can't feel the earth tremors. And yet Philarguria says it's all perfectly safe. What have you got to say?" Tom's arm thrust forward holding the mic in front of Mr. Harrow's face.

The man did not flinch, quite the opposite. Instead of anxiety at being put so unexpectedly on the spot, Alec Harrow's mood transformed into an unassailably offensive stance. His face became stone – an angry tiki mask. "Who are you, son? Damn environmentalists, coming to my house like this? All of my business dealings are perfectly legal, I assure you. Now you need to leave." He swatted away the mic along with the hand holding it.

"I've brought testimonials I would like to read you."

"I'm not playing around. Leave now or I'll call the police."

"When was the last time you were even in Dalkeith? If you're so sure everything is fine, I've also brought along a wee *refreshment* I'm sure you'd be happy to try."

"What's that?" Mr. Harrow said pointing to the camera phone. "Are you recording? Turn that off! Get out!"

Tom held his ground and repeated his original question, "What have you got to say about Philarguria Energy and the communities you've poisoned, Mr. Harrow?"

"That's it!" Mr. Harrow shouted. He reached for the camera, but Tom deflected. The video was a blur of light and motion. The audio, however, recorded clear signs of struggle: labored breaths, a scuffle, then Tom's voice: "Get off!" The video went dark – the unfocused palm of someone's hand.

A scream.

"Oh my God!" Mr. Harrow's voice was short. "Are you-"

"Help!" A faint, almost inhuman cry was heard. "Can't move... It hurts...

CHAPTER TWENTY-SIX

HELP."

In a flash the camera fell to the ground and landed at a slight incline. Cloud and sky filled the screen except for the far bottom corner. There, a bit of grass gave background for an image that caused Daniel Darrow and Mr. and Mrs. Shaw to turn in horror. Mrs. Shaw immediately burst into tears and backed away from the computer screen. "Turn it off!" she shouted. Frozen in shock, Mr. Shaw and Daniel allowed the video to continue.

An arm lay limp in the foreground. Behind that were Tom's head and part of his shoulders. The rest of his body remained off camera. His neck was twisted at an abnormal angle, embedded with a masonry trowel, red and wet. His eyes stared out widely, unfocused. His lips twitched, mumbling.

A new voice could be heard shouting, "Mr. Harrow, are you ok, I heard screaming. What happened? Oh God!"

"It wasn't my fault, I..." Mr. Harrow's voice said, faintly. "He just fell and landed on that pile there."

"I'll call the police."

"No," Mr. Harrow said. "NO," now with confidence, "help me get this tarp over him and into that wheelbarrow."

"What?"

"Did anyone else hear?"

"I don't know. I don't think so."

"Good. I can't afford any more bad press. This Inverness project is already such a mess."

"Press? What? Mr. Harrow, you have to-"

"Shut up and help! We'll wheel him round through the back."

The sound of footsteps plodding down stairs grew louder, then muted from grass. The towering image of Mr. Harrow appeared on the screen. The view was a steep vertical, like peering up from the base of a skyscraper. His eyes, at first distracted by Tom, focused on the camera. His foot raised and the sole of his boot filled the screen, then the heel. A rush of black and the video file cut out.

Chapter Twenty-Seven

A conglomeration of choir robes shuffled around in a corner of Church Street Kirk's sanctuary. Like some giant fabric sea urchin, legs and a few arms sprouted out, along with a couple heads – insufficient to match the number of appendages. Fisher, the choir's director, wearing an expression of exasperation as part of his own uniform, attempted to hurry the group's dressing in order to have time for a warm-up chorus. Standing a head taller than most of the choir, Fisher first noticed the Revs. Calder and Darrow enter the room. He called out a greeting and added, "We're just about ready here. No need to panic," as a subtle hint to his disorderly assemblage.

"Is that Reverend Darrow back?" a head popped out from a newly found neck hole. "Aye, it is. The prodigal son hath returned!"

"Rupert, it's good to see you too," Daniel said, approaching the choir. "Wait, prodigal son?"

"Reverend, you of all people should know the story of the prodigal son," Rupert said. "A man's son leaves home because no one likes him. He goes out into the world and redeems himself – makes a fortune gambling or something. I always thought that bit odd. Anyway, when he returns home, everyone loves him again."

"Um, that's not quite it. But thanks...I think," Daniel said, hesitantly. "We should talk more about that story sometime." Daniel gave a "Bless your soul" look to Fisher and then joined Rev. Calder at the altar.

She was making a last check of the Eucharistic elements, ensuring the wine and wafers were securely tucked away in a hidden shelf under the table.

"Rupert has always preferred songs to sermons, but I can understand his sentiment," Rev. Calder said. "You've come a long way, Daniel, in redeeming yourself to this congregation. You've helped Elspeth Gray more than anyone could have believed possible. She'll still be tried for arson, but murder or manslaughter – you've saved her. And the Shaws. Finding Tom's true killer the way you did, giving him a voice."

"We'll see. I'm not quite done yet," Daniel said. He pulled a paper out of his pocket and unfolded it anxiously.

"Aye, we'll see. Don't be disheartened if you receive some initial skepticism. I took a bit of convincing myself, but I kin we're on the same page now."

"Yes, you did."

"Elspeth is saved, mostly. The bad guy is locked away. Can't we be satisfied with that? I'll grant you the kirk has a long history of championing the causes of social justice: feeding the poor, the abolition of slavery, suffrage. But I might wonder if what you're proposing truly falls in that line. Is it not more proper for industry or government to decide?"

"You sound like you need more convincing," Daniel said. "The Church has also had a long history of jumping on the bandwagon belatedly, after a cause has already become economically or socially viable. Believe me, I know it's scary stepping into unfamiliar territory, but we can't let fear hold us back. Not now. Through whatever stumbles may come, we must press on and do what we know to be right."

"Right, right," she reached up and put an arm on Daniel's shoulder. "But you must remember that this sort of thing is easier for the young. The world is still all possibilities for you. We oldies, we get settled and comfortable in the way the world is, or was. We often require an extra bit of stirring up."

"You give yourself too little credit," Daniel said with a grin. "You're the one who started me down this road. After Elspeth's arrest, you gave that big speech about me making things right and Scots having long memories."

"All rhetoric," Rev. Calder laughed. She looked up at the ceiling. The water stain that had begun in the kirk hall had made inroads into the sanctuary. She sighed. "I was so looking forward to having a new roof. But I can't see how we can accept the donation from Philarguria Energy. Now it simply feels like hush money."

"I know. We'll just have to have more fundraising dances."

Rev. Calder nodded assertively, "That we will!" She took Daniel's hand and, with the hand already on his shoulder, she guided him into a few quick dance steps. He stumbled, surprised, and nearly took them both down before catching on. They laughed and danced around the alter table.

One of the choir noticed the sudden gaiety on stage and shouted, "Ready the pipes!" Then the whole choir, in semi-unison, began clapping a spirited beat for the two dancers. Daniel spun his partner and they took one more round about the alter before halting and giving a bow. Fisher alone was unamused. Parishioners now began to trickle in, and his choir would have no time to practice before the service started.

* * *

After the hymns and scripture readings, Daniel stepped up to the pulpit. He told himself this would be easy. He told himself he had already done the hard part. He had uncovered Elspeth Gray's motive, cleared her name, and found the real killer. Yet, as he looked out upon row after row of expectant faces, he doubted himself. News of Alec Harrow's arrest had spread quickly like a fire through Inverness and these people had come to hear from the one who had sparked it, the gumshoe reverend, the conquering hero. Daniel took a breath. He knew his real work was just beginning.

"I'm glad to see so many friendly faces here today. I'm sure it's got nothing to do with the recent arrest of Alec Harrow and subsequent dropping of some very serious charges for our own Mrs. Gray." A few laughs came from the pews – not as many as Daniel had hoped for. He gazed out and suddenly wondered whose lap Sir Walter Scott, the kirk cat, would settle on in Elspeth Gray's absence.

"I've been thinking a great deal about justice lately," Daniel continued. "I am grateful that Mrs. Gray will not be punished for a crime she did not commit. I am grateful that Tom Shaw's true killer will now be held accountable. Justice, it seems, has been done. And yet," he paused. His relationship with the kirk, their trust in him, had been unstable at best since he started a few months ago. It had fallen through at times. Still, he had managed to redeem himself in the eyes of Rev. Calder. He hoped now that his recent efforts were enough to entrust the rest of the congregation to take this next step with him as well.

"And yet," he continued, "I find myself strangely dissatisfied. There's an itch deep in my soul or conscience that keeps nagging at me – a little question that won't stay quiet. *Has* justice been done? Or, perhaps, *What* does justice in this situation look like, for Elspeth Gray, for Tom Shaw, for all of us?

"Yes, on an individual level, right seems to have won out. Alec Harrow is behind bars. Our justice system is satisfied. I can't help but wonder, though, is justice simply a matter of individuals? Is putting one bad man away sufficient when the institution or the ideology that he represents still runs free? What I'm trying to get at here is that our focus on one man, Alec Harrow, has distracted us from a larger crime – a crime that is corporate and historic in nature.

"Please don't think I am trying to belittle the death of Tom Shaw. That was a cruel, greedy act and the perpetrator should be held accountable. We'll never know if Tom's life could have been saved had Alec Harrow acted with compassion. Instead, he let Tom die and tried to hide Tom's body in the disarray of his house's renovation. If there were no record of Tom's having been to Broonburn House, Harrow believed, there would be no investigation into Tom's death. An investigation that would have delayed his company's plans, costing him a great deal of money. I'm sure you've all heard the story by now, so I won't go into it anymore. The point is that he chose to put profit above a life – a life of infinite value to God and to those that knew Tom.

"What's been troubling me, though, is not the fate of Alec Harrow, but that of Elspeth Gray. We cannot condone what she did. Setting fire to Broonburn House was not a wise or right thing to do. But the more I've talked with her about that night, specifically why she did what she did, I can't help wondering if going to jail for arson truly constitutes justice in her case. Of course, part of that is up to a jury to decide. What I'm talking about is that larger crime that I mentioned earlier. Justice for Elspeth Gray will not be complete until that crime is addressed.

"To see this, we must first look at what led her to set the fire. Someone once asked me, 'Can a good person do a bad thing for a good reason?' Mrs. Gray's motivation, however misguided in execution, was, I think, understandable – good even. She wanted to redress the sins of the past. She's kept alive in her memory the greed and injustice her family and countless others were subjected to during the Highland Clearances of the 19th century. This led her to be more suspicious than most of the news that Broonburn House had been sold. As she once told me: 'When I hear that a piece of the Highlands has been sold off, I take notice.'

"She eventually uncovered the connection between the House's new owner, Alec Harrow, and Philarguria Energy, a company wanting to *invest* in the Highlands - I think that's the term they use in the letters many of you have received. It did not take long for Mrs. Gray to learn what such *investment* could mean for Inverness.

"If you do not know much about hydraulic fracturing or natural gas extraction, Church Street Kirk will host an informational community meeting next week. I hope I will see many of you there. Suffice it to say, Philarguria's plans involve retaining the majority of the profits and externalizing most of the costs. In other words, they get to keep the money, and we get to deal with the polluted air, water, and minor earthquakes. As you may have heard by now, Tom Shaw experienced all of this firsthand when Philarguria moved into his hometown of Dalkeith. That is why he went to Broonburn House. To confront the man behind Philarguria.

"Broonburn House, then, became more than just some old, fancy mansion. It became for Tom Shaw, and certainly for Elspeth Gray, the symbol of centuries of greed and manipulation. I'll mention a conversation I had with Elspeth once more: 'The characters may have changed,' she said, 'but it's the same old story. They want sheep farms.'"

At this, Daniel received the warm audience response he had hoped for at the beginning of his sermon. *Mmmms* and whispered *Ayes* broke the congregation's silence.

"I think we can all sympathize with the frustration she felt," Daniel continued. "Setting fire to Broonburn House was, for her, a kind of symbolic retribution for all those lives burned up in the Clearances. It was also a warning for us to not let history repeat itself. Yet, there was a flaw in her reasoning and I think it is the same flaw that implicated Alec Harrow in Tom's tragic death. That flaw is the false belief, or really beliefs (plural), that wealth equals value and its twin: that violence is necessary to retain that value. Mr. Harrow valued this land for the wealth he could extract from it and he used violence when he felt that wealth threatened. Mrs. Gray, because of her family's history, knew the falsehood of the first lie, but she still succumbed to the second.

"So where does that leave us? What can we now say about justice? I think as a kirk we cannot speak of justice without also speaking of forgiveness. And here I am going to cheat a little and draw from a passage not in today's lectionary readings. In the gospel of Luke, chapter 23, verse 34, just before he breathed his last on the cross, Jesus prayed, 'Father, forgive them, for they know not what they do.' Jesus asked for forgiveness for those that crucified him, for those that had truly sinned. In Jesus' life and death, they, we, who have sinned and are estranged from God are restored. Forgiveness, then, is the completion of justice because forgiveness moves us past sin and punishment into new life.

"And here's the hard part of this long and rambling sermon - we must forgive as Jesus forgave. Yet, forgiveness does not mean simply rolling over and allowing Philarguria Energy or anyone else to continue to manipulate and exploit us. We cannot allow another Clearances. Turning the other cheek does not mean allowing corruption to continue. Rather, it means working together to restore broken relationships and unmask false beliefs.

"The value of a place and its people cannot be equated solely with money or economic productivity. Short-term wealth is a poor, insufficient measure of real economy. If the land is destroyed or poisoned and the people cleared out, there is no more economy. So, even though Alec Harrow is in custody, we must continue Elspeth Gray's fight. We cannot, though, fight Philarguria's short-term greed in a spirit of revenge or violence. Rather, we will fight by forgiving. We will heal broken relationships. We will show that wealth can be sought in ways that do not demean the value of this place or its people.

True wealth, true economy, must be sustainable and benefit us all. Only then will justice be fulfilled.

"Because we are a community, one body, we must decide together what exactly this vision of justice looks like. It will not be an easy or a quick process. But I believe that together, and with God's help, all things are possible. I pray that we are up to the challenge."

Daniel stepped back and took his seat next to Rev. Calder. While Fisher roused the choir for a hymn, unexpected applause followed by low intonations of approval sounded from the pews.

"My, I feel as though we're in one of your American tent revivals," Rev. Calder whispered to him.

The endorsement was so polite it would barely alarm a decibel meter – what one might expect after a poetry reading. "Hardly, but, I'll take it," Daniel said with a grateful smile.

Chapter Twenty-Eight

A line quickly formed in front of the refreshments tables. The first speaker had had more to say than time to say it in and thus encroached on the evening's intermission. He had also used a degree of scientific language and charts as to make the last twenty minutes, which should have only been five, seem like thirty. When the last infographic faded out, everyone in the room stood to stretch their legs. The speaker was the sole exception, seeming to relish the opportunity to relieve his own legs from their portly burden into the nearest folding chair. Coffee, tea, and assorted biscuits promptly appeared on serving tables near where they had been waiting in the kitchen. General socializing and milling about then transformed, without any explicit signaling, into an orderly line that snaked a tidy curve around the back corner of the Church Street Kirk hall.

"It's in our blood," Philip Morrison said to Daniel. "We'll queue up for anything. Two or three people form up and before long, like moths to flame, we canna help it."

"Looks like," Daniel said. "I wish I'd realized what was going on sooner. We might not be way back near the end."

"The most orderly bunch of sheep I've ever seen," said William MacCrivag. He crossed his arms and squinted up toward the front of the line. A woman at the front obtained her refreshments, freed to return to her seat or visit with friends. They all took a step forward.

"Baaa," Philip Morrison snickered.

Daniel glanced at his watch. "We're going to have to speed this up if we're to stick to schedule. That talk was interesting, but a wee long. Did I say that right?"

William MacCrivag and Philip Morrison laughed. "I hope you know how to brew a strong cup down here," Philip Morrison said.

"I came prepared if it's not up to your specifications," Mr. MacCrivag said. He patted his jacket's chest pocket to the sound of a muffled metallic cling.

"Good man," said Philip Morrison.

Just then, Mr. Tweed passed by with a plate stacked full of biscuits and a slice of cake. He doubled back upon noticing them. "Reverend Darrow, William, I nearly didn't see you there," he said. "And who's this with you? William's infamous Hebridean mate?"

"How do you know Philly?" Mr. MacCrivag asked, sharply.

"The kirk webpage. There's a photo of the three of you at Calanais. I like to be in the know, you know," Mr. Tweed said with a smile. Then to Daniel he said, "I'm happy to report that my golf game has improved splendidly, or more like my partner's has declined."

"So it was the gloves then?" Daniel said.

"Aye. Rigid plates were hidden in the wrists to keep them straight. Rather cheeky. Now that he's been found out, he hooks right every swing!"

"Well, I'm glad I could help, I think," Daniel said, feeling a touch of sorrow for the grief Mr. Tweed's partner must now be enduring. "How did you like our first speaker?" he asked to change the subject.

"Oh, fascinating, if a bit dull. Still, I have a friend in the Environmental Health Service and this kind of thing is right up her street. I'm looking forward to Mr. MacCallum's talk. I still remember that fight. Should be quite inspiring," Mr. Tweed said and nodded his goodbye.

When Daniel and the others finally reached the food table, they filled their small plates with the picked over remains of sweet biscuits and filled their cups half full from a shallow coffee carafe.

"I was going to bring a cup over to our guest expert, but I don't think I can get through to him," Daniel said as they left the table. A small, though densely packed crowd had formed around the first speaker. He looked as if he were ready to bring back out his charts and graphs.

"People are interested in this fracking business," said Mr. MacCrivag. "And rightly so if it's going to be happening in our own community. I have a few questions for him myself."

"Nothing's set to stone, Willie," Philip Morrison said. "That's why you've brought us down, isn't it."

"Yes," agreed Daniel, "This meeting is about becoming more informed to hopefully come up with an alternative to fracking in Inverness, not just learn how to deal with the consequences. Speaking of which," Daniel scanned the room, "Philip, I was hoping to meet your friend Mr. MacCallum in person before he speaks. We've only talked over the phone."

"Call him Robbie, all his mates do. I think I saw Robbie and his daughter, Bridget, just there." He indicated a corner at the front of the room near the podium. Daniel saw a man of stocky build with short cropped, gray hair talking with several parishioners. The man wore a fitted tweed jacket of a color and pattern similar to that of the scarf Daniel had around his own shoulders. One member of the group around Robbie MacCallum, Daniel noticed, wore a black, lace dress with a high collar. She cradled a large purse against her chest. Two long, furry ears poked out from the purse's opening.

"Oh, I see Ms. MacGillivray's found him," Daniel said. "We really should rescue him."

Eliza MacGillivray placed the smooth stone of her necklace between her fingers and began rubbing it, just as they arrived.

Daniel greeted the nearby parishioners. "Ms. MacGillivray, I saw you earlier but didn't get a chance to say 'Hello' yet." Daniel reached out his hand. She gave him a suspicious look and then, letting go of her stone, gripped his hand.

"And you must be Robert MacCallum. I'm Daniel Darrow," he said, turning to the man.

The man shook his head. "We've talked on the phone, aye. Call me Robbie. I'm happy to finally meet." They shook hands. Then to Philip Morrison, Robbie MacCallum said, "Philly, there you are. I feared you'd abandoned me." Philip Morrison introduced Mr. MacCrivag and more hands were shaken.

Eliza MacGillivray touched Robbie MacCallum on the arm. "I'm off to my seat, but don't sneak off after your talk. I've still got a message for you."

She along with two other women left. A man and woman who were talking to their right quickly joined the three that had left. A young girl with dark brown hair appeared from behind them.

"Bridget," Robbie MacCallum called to his daughter. "You've met Reverend Darrow and Willie, was it – friends of Philly here."

She greeted them. "I see you've still got the scarf I sold you," she said.

"Yes, it's come in handy this winter. Worth every penny."

Robbie MacCallum reached for the end of the scarf that Daniel had draped around his coat collar. He felt the material between his fingers. "I thought that looked like one of mine. You'll not find a better weave in all of Scotland. If you find any imperfection in it, you let me know."

"No complaints here," Daniel said. "Mr. MacCallum, Robbie, I'm so glad you were able to come and speak with us this evening. From what you've told me about your work with the campaign to save Mount Rone–, your mountain, I'm sorry I still cannot pronounce it."

"Roineabhal," Robbie MacCallum said.

"Yes. Well, I think you're just the man we need right now to help us save our own land."

* * *

Snow began to fall. The crowd that had gathered along Glenurquhart Road in front of the Highland Council offices huddled tightly together. In their thick coats and earmuffed hats, they had to get in close to discern a familiar face. Close enough to smell the coffee or hot chocolate on one another's breath. The snow might have been a pleasant distraction from the blood cooling temperature, a cheerful reminder of the upcoming Christmas and Hogmanay, or New Year, festivities. Instead, a wind coming in off the North Sea blew snow stinging onto their rosy, unprotected cheeks and swept away any collective heat the crowd might have hoped to conjure.

"We should probably go ahead and get started. We've got a pretty good size crowd already and I don't know how long they'll last in this weather," Daniel said to Fisher. "How does one *start* something like this?"

"Do you think the council members are in yet?" Fisher asked.

Daniel looked at his watch. "I would assume so. Anyway, Mr. Tw- uh, Mr. Fraser's friend in the Environmental Health Service is set to speak at ten. I think a reporter from the *Courier* is supposed to stop by around then. Maybe even someone from the *BBC*. We should probably look like we know what we're doing before they get here."

Fisher nodded and clapped his gloved hands together, rubbing them for warmth. "Where are the lads with the signs? If you'll distribute them, I'll start the crowd on some songs."

"I think I saw them over there," Daniel looked to his right. He tightened the scarf around his neck and headed in that direction. He searched for the familiar blue and white Scotland rugby hoodie, the *X* that marked the spot. It stood with several others of its kind at the edge of the mostly adult assembly.

"Hello, boys. Oh, and girls," Daniel tried to sound as cheerful as the weather permitted. "I'm thrilled to see so many of you here this morning. Those signs you made look really great! I think we're going to get started now. Do you want to help me pass them around?" He was met with grumbling and teenage indifference.

"Oi, mates, come on," one of the boys said - Finn, if Daniel remembered correctly. Finn slapped two of his friends on the back. "This is our chance to stand up and be heard. Let's make those officials listen to *us* for a change!"

"There's that youthful rebellion I was hoping for," Daniel said. He reached for a few signs. "You heard the man. Let's go!"

They distributed the signs, poster board and cardboard stapled to wooden stake handles. Fisher warmed up the crowd with a slightly sharp, a capella version of Joni Mitchell's *Big Yellow Taxi*. By the second chorus, placards of hand painted slogans had sprouted up like wildflowers: "Keep Calm and Frack Off," "Say 'NO' to Environmental Clearances," "Clean Energy Before We're All Kilt."

Daniel shook Finn's hand and thanked him before the boy rejoined his friends at the edge of the crowd. Daniel found his own spot next to a group of other familiar Church Street faces. Rev. Calder stood next to Eliza MacGillivray who wore a long, high collared, black overcoat and held tightly to her large handbag as if it were an infant. Beside them, in matching woolen plaids, were Hugh and Marjory Macpherson. He waved across the crowd to William MacCrivag and his Hebridean cohort of Philip Morrison, Robbie MacCallum and his daughter Bridget, and a few others Daniel did not recognize.

A spontaneous chorus of *We Shall Overcome* began from somewhere to their left. From the front of the crown, nearest the entrance to the Highland Council building, Fisher's eyes narrowed as he searched out the source of this deviation from his planned program. The refrain spread quickly. Fisher, unwilling to admit full defeat, quickly moved his directing arms to the beat as if this had been his plan all along.

"I can't believe this many people showed up for our little rally," Daniel said.

"You're welcome," said Eliza MacGillivray.

"Huh?"

"You don't think the kirk is the only place I am known?" She patted the lower neck of her coat. "You are not the only recipient of my prophecies. I go where the Seer's stone tells me."

"Eliza," Rev. Calder interjected, "I didn't realize we had such a local celebrity in our midst."

"Fine, they may not all be mine, but I've brought along a fair share."

"I know, I'm only joking. You've helped tremendously," Rev. Calder said.

"I got *you* here," Eliza said, returning to Daniel. Daniel gave her a quizzical look.

"The day will come when
Fire and water shall run in streams
Through all the streets and lanes of Inverness," she said knowingly.

"But that was before any of this started. Before we even knew about Tom Shaw or Philarguria's plans," Daniel protested.

"Was it?"

"Um," Daniel was not sure how to respond. "Well, either way, I'm glad you're on our side."

"I'm on Scotland's side."

"Yes," Daniel said, unsure once again of the correct response. The large handbag she held gave an unexpected shudder. Daniel jumped. Eliza laughed and unzipped the bag. Two long, furry ears popped out. Glad for the distraction, Daniel offered the rabbit his hand and then scratched its head between the ears.

"Have you seen George Fraser? It's nearly ten," Daniel asked Rev. Calder.

She nodded in the direction of the Council building. "He's just there by Fisher, who seems reluctant to give up his post."

At the front of the crowd, Daniel saw a man dressed in a thick olive colored tweed overcoat with matching slacks and hat. Mr. Tweed's hand was on Fisher's shoulder as a not so subtle indication that his time was up. Fisher indulged himself one final chorus before abdicating. Mr. Tweed switched on the microphone and portable speaker that had been set up for the occasion.

"That was some quite spirited singing," Mr. Tweed said. "I think they must have heard us all the way down in Edinburgh!" The crowd cheered, their clapping muffled by thick outerwear. "My name is George Fraser and I must say how splendid it is to see so many of my fine countrymen here this morning. We stand here in front of the Highland Council headquarters, on this the last session before the festive break, to make our voices heard." He stomped his cane firmly on the ground. "We will not sit meekly by while a foreign company invades our land and poisons our children. This is our land, our home, and we will protect her. This land is a part of us and we a part of her. We are the Highlands!"

The crowd roared in approval. Mr. Tweed held up a folder. "I hold here a petition to ban hydraulic fracturing in and around our great city of Inverness – over one thousand signatures. And this is only the beginning!" Another roar of applause followed. He raised his hands to silence them. "Now, it is my great pleasure to introduce my personal friend and your council woman, Helen Buchanan." Mr. Tweed stepped aside and handed the folder to a woman wearing a long, fashionable coat. She stepped up to the microphone. She scanned the crowd and smiled before focusing her gaze on the television news camera crew that had arrived moments earlier.

"My, thank you George, cheers. That was rather inspiring. Quite an introduction. I must commend all of you for coming together on such a lovely

Inverness morning as this." The crowd laughed accordingly. "I look forward to delivering this petition to my fellow council members, particularly my colleagues in the Environmental Health Service."

Daniel quietly stepped away from his companions as the council woman continued her speech. He made his way to the back of the crowd. She had said she might be in attendance, but he hadn't see her. He couldn't see much besides the anonymous backs of coats and hats. The microphone setup, on a raised curb, looking out over all of their faces was the best vantage point. It was also the most conspicuous. Perhaps she had arrived late and remained on the fringe of the crowd? Daniel decided to embark on a discreet reconnoiter toward the front. If she was here, surely she would seek him out as well.

* * *

The taxi let Daniel off at Auld Angus Rd. When he reached the black, iron gate, he squeezed the pack he had been carrying through two bars. No one had ever bothered to remove the gate's lock. He then walked a little further to the break in the stone fence and climbed over. Once he regained his pack, he emptied its contents, spreading out a weatherproof picnic blanket, covered on one side with thick vinyl fabric. Two deli sandwiches sat beside him, kept fresh by the outside temperature. With the stone fence protecting him from wind, he opened the morning's paper and waited. His eyes scanned again the front-page article that he had read in the taxi.

He stood when he heard an engine and tires rolling slowly up the gravel drive. He waved from behind the gate. "There's an opening over there." Ellie exited her car and followed him to the collapsed section of the wall.

"Are you sure we can be here?" she asked as Daniel helped her over.

"If anyone asks, we were out for a walk and got turned around in the woods."

"And that line is supposed to be believable?"

"My American accent helps," Daniel said with a chuckle. "Come on, I've got lunch ready. How is your mother?" he asked.

"She's...coping," Ellie said, nodding as if to convince herself. "Prison is, well, prison. It's certainly not how she was planning on spending her retirement. It's good of you to visit her like you have."

"She's still a part of the kirk."

"No, it's more than that. This campaign you've started against Philarguria, it's all helped keep her spirits up."

"I like to think it's been a community effort, but in any case, it's become much more than anything I could have done," Daniel said.

"Oh, have you seen this?" Ellie pulled a tightly folded newspaper from her purse.

Daniel laughed as she unfolded it. "I actually bought one earlier on my way here."

"Then I'll save this one for Mum." Ellie read aloud the headline and first few lines: *Moratorium on Highland Fracking. Councilwoman, Helen Buchanan, announces a moratorium on granting new unconventional gas extraction permits. A surge of grassroots pressure from environmental campaigners, farmers, local business and community groups, and religious organizations have put a stop to planned schemes in Inverness and across the Highlands. The moratorium will remain in place pending the results of an independent environment and public health assessment.*

Daniel paused. He took a long breath and smiled. Hearing someone else read the story made it seem less like a dream. "Not bad," he said.

"That's an understatement. You've come quite a long way from calling the police on some kirk kids."

"And yet I still can't live that down." They both laughed and continued along the fence toward the gate. "Well, here we are."

Daniel had left his pack in the middle of the blanket as an anchor in case of a capricious wind. They sat down on either side of it.

"Bottled water and plastic wrapped sandwiches, quite the five-star treatment," Ellie said.

"Only the best." Daniel handed her a water bottle. They tapped lids together. "Cheers," he said and reclined back on one arm. He reached for a sandwich with the other.

Ellie pushed the pack aside and moved closer to him. "The ground's rather rocky over there," she said. Daniel smiled. She touched his hand. "You know, this is the first time I've seen this place since I was a wee girl."

"Has it changed much?" Daniel asked. Ellie rolled her eyes. Daniel put his sandwich down and they sat, hand in hand, gazing at the scene in front of them.

The ground was still frozen. It needed another month to begin to thaw. Even then, a late snow could set it back several weeks. The Craigphadrig Wood stood, a mottled wintery scene in the background. Unchanged by season, firs and Scots pines displayed their usual greenery, through their cones had long fallen, while their deciduous neighbors remained bare and brittle. The ruin of Broonburn House lay peaceful under a thin veil of melting, morning frost. Only two walls remained standing, broken hunchbacked sentries. A small memorial of various trinkets, deflated balloons, and handwritten letters to Tom Shaw sat against the west-facing wall. Police tape had long ago blown away or been taken down. In another month, grass would grow here once again, quickened by the fire and hard, wet winter.

Acknowledgement

In the 17th century, the Brahan Seer, or Coinneach Odhar, lived and prophesied in the Highlands of Scotland. His visions were too specific to the Inverness region to have such wide appeal as those of his vaguer French predecessor, Nostradamus. In this novel, Eliza MacGillivray channels Odhar's prophetic tradition in citing his actual prophecy concerning fire and water running together in streams through the streets of Inverness.

While Broonburn House itself is a fictional creation, it is based upon similar structures in the region. Without going to the trouble of setting fire to an actual grand house, Broonburn House provides a symbolic connection to the Highland Clearances and to the modern threat of hydraulic fracturing for natural gas. In January 2015, the Scottish Government implemented a moratorium on unconventional oil and gas extraction, or fracking, pending a full public health impact assessment and public consultation ("Moratorium Called on Fracking," https://news.gov.scot/news/moratorium-called-on-fr acking, 01/28/2015). The results of these environmental and public health studies, along with continued grassroots pressure, resulted in the Scottish Parliament concluding the monetary benefits of fracking could not offset its risks: earthquakes, polluted waterways, lower air quality, and worsening climate change. In 2016 they voted for a total ban on fracking in Scotland. Three years later the Scottish government voted to extend the ban, though it has yet to pass legislation making the ban permanent ("Scottish Government Extends Ban on Fracking," https://www.theguardian.com/uk-news/20 19/oct/03/scottish-government-extends-ban-on-fracking, 03/10/2019). Pressure and court challenges from large oil and gas companies still hold considerable sway.

For a detailed historical account of the causes and immediate consequences of the Highland Clearances, Eric Richards' *The Highland Clearances: People, Landlords and Rural Turmoil* (Birlinn, 2013) is a great place to begin. Inspiration for the character of the Harris weaver, Robbie MacCallum, and his island's fight to save their mountain from quarrying came from Alastair McIntosh's *Soil and Soul: People Versus Corporate Power* (Aurum Press, 2004).

About the Author

Daniel K. Miller holds advanced degrees from the University of Edinburgh and Duke University. He is the author of Animal Ethics and Theology (Routledge, 2012) as well as several short fiction and nonfiction pieces. He lives in Texas with his wife and a motley assortment of horses, cats, and wildlife. Fire on the Firth is his first novel. Visit him at www. danielkmillerauthor.com

CPSIA information can be obtained
at www.ICGtesting.com
Printed in the USA
FSHW011628161221
86984FS